SEKRET

AN EMPTY

SEKRET

MIND IS A

LINDSAY SMITH

SAFE MIND

ROARING BROOK PRESS · NEW YORK

For Gwen,
Who put the Russian enigma in my heart

A NOTE ON RUSSIAN NAMES

Russians have three names—a first name, a patronymic (like a middle name, but derived from their father's name), and a last name. The endings for the middle and last names differ for men and women, so a brother and sister, like Yevgenni and Yulia, would have different middle names derived from their father's name, Andrei: Yevgenni *Andree*vich Chernin and Yulia *Andree*-vna Chernin*a*.

In formal settings, Russians will address others by their first name and patronymic. In more familiar settings, Russians often address their friends, family members, and equals by a standard nickname of their given first name. The list below provides the nicknames encountered in this book.

FEMALE NICKNAMES

Anastasia – Anya

Larissa – Lara

Maria – Masha

MALE NICKNAMES

Mikhail – Misha

Sergei – Seryozha

Valentin – Valya

Yevgenni – Zhenya

CHAPTER 1

MY RULES FOR THE BLACK MARKET are simple. Don't make eye contact—especially with men. Their faces are sharp, but their eyes sharper, and you never want to draw that blade. Always act as though you could walk away from a trade at any moment. Desperation only leaves you exposed. Both hands on the neck of your bag, but don't be obvious about it. Never reveal your sources. And always, always trust the heat on your spine that haunts you when someone is watching.

I pass through the iron gates to the alley off New Arbat Street. A mosaic of Josef Stalin smiles down on the ramshackle market he never would have permitted. If he were still our leader, the man wearing strings of glass beads, snipping them off for customers, would vanish overnight. The little girl with jars of bacon fat would emerge years later in a shallow ditch, her skull half-eaten by lye.

Comrade Premier Nikita Khruschev, the USSR's current leader, is content to ignore us. The Soviet Union provides everything you need, as long as you don't mind the wait: a day in line for butter and bread rations, another day for meat, seven years for automobiles, fifteen for a concrete-walled apartment where you can rest between factory shifts. Khruschev understands the stale-cracker taste of envy in every worker's mouth when a well-dressed, well-lived Communist Party official, more equal than the rest of us, strolls to the front of the ration line. If we quench our own thirst for excess in the black market, then that's less burden on the State. His KGB thugs only disrupt the market when we do something he cannot ignore—such as trading with known political dissidents and fugitives.

And I happen to be one.

A tooth-bare man lunges at me with an armful of fur coats. I don't want to know what creatures wore that patchwork bristly fur. "Not today, comrade," I tell him, straightening out my skirt. Today I must restock Mama's clinic supplies. (Average wait for a doctor's visit: four months. Average wait for a visit with Mama: three minutes, as she wrestles my brother Zhenya into another room.) The sour, metallic tang of fish just pulled from the Moskva River hits me, and my stomach churns covetously, but I can only buy food with whatever's left over. We've lived off of two food rations split five ways for some time now. We can live with it for some time more.

I spot the older woman I came for. Raisa, everyone calls her—we never use real names here. In this pedestrian alley, wedged between two disintegrating mansions from the Imperial days, we are all dissidents and defiants. We do not inform on each other for illegal bartering—not out of loyalty, but out of having to explain our own illegal deeds.

Raisa's whorled face lifts when she sees me. "More Party goods for Raisa?" She beckons me into her "stall," a bend in the concrete wall, shielded by a tattered curtain. "You always bring quality goods."

My chest tightens—I shouldn't be so predictable, but it's all I have to trade. The finer goods reserved for high-ranking Party members are worth their weight in depleted uranium here. I glance over my shoulder, hoping no one heard her. A boy and a girl—they look one and the same, with only a mirage-shimmer of gender to distinguish them—turn our way, but the rest of the market continues its haggling, lying, squawking. I let their faces roll around in my thoughts in case I need to remember them later.

"Maybe you brought a nice filtered vodka? My boy, he wants a pair of blue jeans." Raisa ferrets through her trash bags. She still reeks of sweat from the summer months—not that I can criticize. I have to boil water on Aunt Nadia's stove to wash myself. "I have ointment for you, peroxide, gauze," she says. "You need aspirin? You always want aspirin. You get a lot of headaches?"

I don't like her making these connections, though for clinic supplies, I have little choice. If she knows about Mama's headaches, that's a weakness exposed. If she suspects we were Party members before we fled our home and became ghosts—

No. This is paranoia, gnawing at my thoughts like a starved rat. The KGB—the country's secret police and spying force—can only dream of training drills as thorough as my daily life, with all the ridiculous precautions I take. My fears are outweighed by one simple truth: I need something and Raisa needs something, and that will keep us safe.

Capitalism is alive and well in our communist paradise.

"Pocket watch." I hold Papa's watch by its twisted silver chain. "Painted face commemorates the forty-year anniversary of the Union of Soviet Socialist Republics." My voice falters as memories of Papa ripple through me: He clicks it open, checks it, exhales a plume of smoke, tucks it in his coat, and turns back to the snow-slashed streets. "Wind it once a month and it'll run forever." I drop the watch in Raisa's palm, happy to bid those memories farewell.

"Not bad. Expensive . . ." She bounces it in her hand, as if checking its weight. "But is it so practical? It will be forty-six years since the revolution this November. Outdated, yes?"

I wince. Has Papa been gone for five years? I turned seventeen last month, but there was no extravagant celebration like when we were favored in the Party. I've forgotten the taste of sugar frosting, the sound of wrapping paper tearing apart. I passed it as I had the last four, keeping Mama and Zhenya hidden while I pawned away our history.

"Then it's a collector's item." I must be careful when defending an item's value. I've seen too many others expose their past or reveal their emotions when justifying a high price, but that's giving valuable information away. I must tell her only what she needs to hear. An empty mind is a safe mind, Papa always said.

Raisa nods, but looks unconvinced. Now we play the games of the market that can't be written into rules. Gauging your trading partner, assessing their offer, luring out what they really want and need. Knowing when to reveal what more you have to trade, and when to keep it hidden.

And I am better at this than most.

I move for the watch as if to take it back, but my fingertips linger against her skin. *Concentrate, Yulia.* In the moment when our skin touches, time shatters apart, like the world is run by a loose watch spring. I plunge into the emptiness, the silence around me, and when I surface from it I'm inside Raisa's thoughts.

She can turn a huge profit on the ointment—castoffs from the factory, because the formula was off. The peroxide cost her too much—a kilo of pork, and it was fresh, too. Raisa wants compensation. And me, always turning up with rich Party goods that raise too many questions when Raisa tries to sell them off—

I fall back into the void and thrash toward myself, and time winds itself once more. I finish snatching the watch back and narrow my eyes.

"I don't want your ointment. I heard about the factory mishap. You thought I didn't know the formula was off?"

Raisa's jaw droops, the wart on her chin wobbling.

"You're not the right person for these goods," I say. "I'll look for someone who knows the value of Party items. Someone unafraid." I sling the bag over my shoulder and turn to leave.

"No—please, wait—" Her Baba Yaga witch-nails catch my sweater. The brief contact isn't enough for me to slip into her thoughts, but I sense her emotions in that touch: panic, fear, and . . . loyalty. She will not turn me in.

How do I explain this ability I have? It must be something everyone does, unknowingly. Mama's textbooks say our sight and hearing are not such dominant senses as we believe. We smell others' emotions and taste their weaknesses. Me, I've found how to focus thoughts and memories through touch, like steadying a radio antenna with your fingertips, the static sloughing off until a clear melody remains.

Or maybe, like my paranoia, I'm only imagining.

"Then let's talk seriously." I yank open my bag. "Keep your ointment. I want double the aspirin, and the gauze . . ."

Warmth spreads along my back. The discomfort we feel when being watched—another intangible sense. Through a tear in Raisa's curtain, I get a better look at the twin boy and girl, russet halos of hair catching the afternoon sun, with matching disgusted expressions for their matching clothes. Their matching, *expensive* clothes. My nails split the bag's burlap fibers. Only junior members of the Communist Party—Komsomol, the youth wing—could dress so well.

"What's the matter, girl?" Raisa leans toward the curtain. "If you've brought the KGB to me . . ."

The twins' gazes flit around the market like flies but keep returning to me. They duck under a cage of rabbits hung from the rafters, and glide toward us like Siberian tigers on the hunt. My blood is molten in my veins. The gnawing paranoia urges me to run, run, escape their doubled stare, run where their stiff new shoes can't follow. But what if I'm wrong? What if they aren't here for me, or only recognize me from my old life?

"Yulia Andreevna." The girl twin speaks my real name from lips that have never felt the rasp of winter. "Too easy. You don't even make it fun."

Raisa's curtain tears down easily in my grip. I swing its rod into the girl's face. She's caught off guard, but the boy twin's hand is there to catch it, like he already knew what I would do. I'm running, leaping over a stack of fabrics from the southern republics, shoving a bucketful of handmade brooms behind me to block the path.

"You can't run from what you are!" the boy shouts.

I chance a look over my shoulder. Yakov slows the twins, jabbing his box of rusty nails in their faces, but they disentangle from his sales pitch and knock over a little boy with bundled twigs. Who are they? Old schoolmates eager to turn in our family? I've cut all ties to our old life—we had to shed those snakeskin memories.

Vlad, the unofficial market guard, stands between me and the wrought iron gate. I duck around him, but Aunt Nadia's shoes are a little too big on me and I skid to the side, losing my balance. He seizes the collar of my sweater in his fist. "You bring trouble, comrade?"

I wriggle out of the sweater and launch myself through the gates. My arms immediately prick with gooseflesh; it's too cold for just a blouse. But I have to ignore it. I have to reach Mama and make sure she's safe.

"You'll be sorry!" the girl twin screeches at me as I run past afternoon workers, shuffling out of the Metro stop. If I duck my head and keep my eyes to myself, they'll provide the perfect camouflage. "Don't you want to know what you are?"

What I am? I climb down the escalator slowly enough that I don't raise suspicion. My ratty clothes are lost in the sea of gray-brown-blue. Just another half-starved waif with empty eyes and empty hands. I know just what I am.

I am Yulia Andreevna Chernina, seventeen years old, daughter of former high-ranking Communist Party members. I am a fugitive in my own country. And sometimes I see things that can't be seen.

CHAPTER 2

OUR SHELL-SHOCKED TANK of a neighbor lumbers toward me on the walkway, stinking of potato vodka and sleeplessness. I don't like the way his eyes pull from mine, like a magnetic repulsion. It's a guilty act, one I can't afford to ignore right now. Like the market, I need every advantage. As he brushes past me, I tighten up my mind—tuning that imaginary radio—and am thrown into his skin.

We are no longer standing in front of 22 Novaya Rodina, where the all-new apartment towers already look beaten and cowed. We are outside Lubyanka Square this morning, standing in the bronze-cast shadow of Felix Dzerzhinsky, the father of the KGB, the secret police who tell us how to act, who to be. I peer out of the neighbor's eyes at a KGB officer in a mud-green coat who is smiling just enough to show the edge of his teeth. The officer scribbles in his notebook and says *How long have the Chernins been hiding there?*

This is the traitor, this neighbor who has reported us to the secret police sentencing what's left of my family to death—for what? A bit of spending money? The twins at the market were no accident, though they didn't look like the usual KaGeBeznik thugs.

The officer lowers his notepad and jams his fist into a pocketful of worn-out rubles. *We have been looking for them for some time, you know.* The wad of notes dangles below my neighbor's nose. *The Chernins are dangerous people. You were right to come to us.*

I should have known, but there's no time to berate myself—or even this scum—so I fall back into the present and rush past him on the walk, thoughts of Mama pulling me toward the building.

Our building hangs over me as I rush up the too-long walk. It's made of giant concrete slabs cantilevered into place as if by magic—a Stonehenge for the people, the worker, the State. When Khruschev first built them, the workers were thrilled to leave the old roach-rotted, subdivided mansions that housed three families to a room. But to me, the building is our prison—I only leave it for the market or for a breath without four other bodies pressed against me. The rest of the time, my caged-animal stare could peel the lead paint from the walls. That girl dared to ask me what I am? I am the weed growing through the sidewalk's cracks, resilient, but knowing I'll someday be ripped out by the root.

I have to warn Mama. I don't know how long I've lost the twins for, if I've lost them at all. I don't know how many are with them. As I fumble with my key, I strain for the soft fall of boots on cement of a team sneaking around me, guns trained.

But there is only me, with every instinct coiled in my genes screaming to save my family.

The elevator button clicks; an electrical current travels lazily down its wire, gears whirl, and the car yawns as it descends, as if it can't believe it must haul yet another person to the tenth floor. My nerves play a scale up and down my spine as the car jerks upward, rattling my teeth, the light of each floor drifting too slowly past the door's crack.

Can I trust this strange sight of mine, or is hunger and a five-year weariness in my bones confusing me? Maybe my head is just finding images it likes and stitching them together into patchwork paranoia. My parents are scientists—I don't believe anything that can't be proved. But it's been right too many times for me to doubt.

I reach the door to Aunt Nadia's apartment. Like the others in the antiseptic hall, it is black and densely padded, like we're in an asylum and can't be trusted with sharp, bright things. Unlike them, however, ours stands ajar. That little crack of air that should not be. My heart hides in my throat.

Sunlight dapples the front room, but it looks false, like someone's shaken an old, stale bottle of springtime and let it loose. No one sits on the bench, reading Gogol or trying to quiet the hunger that follows us as surely as our shadows. Only my gaunt reflection fills the foyer mirror, frazzled black hair escaping from its braids. Mama's coat hangs from the high hook with Zhenya's miniature one beside it; Aunt Nadia's and Cousin Denis's are gone.

It's four in the afternoon, the time I always walk Zhenya through the neighborhood, though I hate how predictable it makes us. It's hard to avoid routine with a brother who requires order the way some plants require a wall to anchor them. He'd have a fit if we didn't go, or worse, crumple up inside of himself and refuse to unfurl for the rest of the night. I open my mouth to call for him but can't force the words out into the open.

I turn to the kitchen on my left, just past the washroom and the water closet. A cup of tea steams, abandoned, on the table. An issue of *Pravda* lies open beside it: "Khruschev Promises Moon Landing by 1965." Vladimir Vysotsky croons one of his safe, tepid folk ballads through the AM radio, Aunt Nadia's prized possession that cost her more rations than she'll ever admit. She can't be so impulsive with us around. Each ration must stretch until it snaps to feed Mama and Zhenya and me.

Maybe, I think desperately, Mama went to lie down with another of her headaches. Perhaps a patient showed up, and they're all crammed into Nadia's old bedroom that we share. Perhaps she stepped across the hall to chat with neighbors, safe neighbors, neighbors who would never surrender us to the KGB—

I stop with my hand resting on the bedroom door knob, my extra sense wiping memories from it like a layer of dust. The scream that I cannot unleash burns back into my lungs, ripping through me in search of escape.

In my mind, I see the other side of the door. Two men hold Mama and Zhenya as if they are dolls. Hands clamped over their mouths, they are motionless, waiting. A third man flattens against the wall beside the door, wedged in that narrow pass between our fold-out bed and the cabinet full of molding Tolstoy and medical journals. He will grab me as soon as I walk in.

I nudge the door with my shoe and jump back.

Silence, dusty and dense. I barge into the room, but it's empty and still. I'm too late. The memory is just that—come and gone, and with it, my family. Tears burn in the corners of my eyes. I trusted my sense, and it failed them. I've failed.

Something flutters against the smoke-stained curtains.

A woman—she wears the same mud-green uniform as the KGB officer on Lubyanka Square—steps down from the balcony. Her hair is dyed the riot-red that every Russian woman over forty sports these days; it's styled in an overgrown bob that does no favors to her sagging shape.

"Yulia Andreevna Chernina."

My name hangs between us as we study each other. She might have been beautiful ten years ago, she might have had the endless lashes and silver screen lips of Tatiana Samoilova for all I know, but the weight of her deep frown appears to have recast her face. She folds her hands behind her back. She's physically unimposing, but the spark in her eye betrays a mind that never stops churning. I've seen that spark before. The superior spark of informers, spies, politicians—anyone smart enough to use you for all you're worth.

"Daughter of Andrei and Antonina Chernin." Her eyes narrow. "Sister to Yevgenni—"

Yevgenni—Zhenya. My brother, whose own thoughts turn against him if his supper's five minutes late. "Where is he?" I ask. "And Mama? What have you done with them?"

She smiles, though her face fights to hold the frown in place. An old gypsy song floats through the room like a breeze. Something about lost love, crying-in-your-vodka folk music; it must be Nadia's radio still, but the music sounds watery, like it's soaking into my skin.

"Your mother and brother will be safe, but I require your cooperation, Yulia." She smiles—the confident smile the twins in the market wore. The smile of someone who holds all the cards, when their opponent doesn't even know the game's rules. She takes a step toward me, lamplight slithering off the edges of her brass military emblem. "It's time to show you what you really are."

I step back, but two men have appeared behind me. Their leather gloves are cold on my skin. I buck against them as they wrangle my arms behind my back. "Mama!" I scream. "What have you done with them?"

They yank me from the doorway. If I were stronger, perhaps I could scream and break free, but I'm weak from too few rations and too many years of unfocused fear. They press a rag against my mouth, and the last thing I see is our old family photo with Mama and Papa smiling right at me before I'm lost in endless black.

CHAPTER 3

WHEN I WAS EIGHT YEARS OLD, I read about an experiment where biologists took silver foxes and bred the friendliest, most docile specimens to determine if domestication could be genetically inherited. In just a few generations, they'd produced playful, calm foxes that wanted to cuddle up to human beings and looked to them for happiness, like pet dogs.

The experiment was written up in one of Mama's professional journals, back when she practiced medicine, before we went into hiding. I'd always been enamored of genetics, which had been Mama's specialty before joining Papa in developmental psychology research, and something in this experiment strummed the right chord in me. I'd ramble about it to anyone unlucky enough to let me corner them. I dreamed of attending the Mendeleev Genetics Institute at Moscow State University, where Mama and Papa met, and researching a cure for the storm of thoughts inside my brother's head.

I read every book about genetics and biology that I could find, forever lugging around books that unbalanced my eight-year-old frame. But I was not satisfied; I was desperate to fix my brother and his growing fits of fear. And so, in the meadow behind our dacha, our summer cabin in Kazan, I tried to catch and breed some foxes of my own.

The only thing I ever caught was a raccoon, and when I lifted up the quivering, seething, chattering cardboard box, he flew from it and latched onto me, a ball of claws and desperation. Mama snuck me into the laboratory where she and Papa worked—past the patrolling soldiers with AK-47s—to get a rabies shot immediately, instead of waiting at the state hospital. I didn't understand why their clinic had armed guards, but I realized, then, that my parents' work was perhaps not as straightforward as I thought.

But I kept dreaming of the Mendeleev Institute. I spent months formulating my strategy—everything in the Soviet Union is a system, a game, and you must learn the system's rules. I devoted myself to earning perfect marks in biology. Papa only offered his constant platitudes; "An empty mind is a safe mind," he'd say, though I wanted to fill my head with knowledge until it overflowed. After he left, and we went into hiding, Mama swore she'd help me find a way to attend. We would craft another identity for me to slip into, like I was learning to slip into others' skin.

There was a second part to the fox experiment that I didn't like to think about. In addition to breeding the friendliest creatures for domestication, the scientists bred the aggressive foxes as well. For years those raging monsters, similar to the raccoon I'd caught, invaded my nightmares, striking at the cage wire, ready to attack the moment a person came near. When I joined the program, I told myself, I would do away with that part of the experiment.

CHAPTER 4

THE TILED INTERROGATION ROOM could double as a grade school sports equipment closet, or a changing room for the community pool—there's that lingering musk of sweat and bleach, and the rusty drain in front of the wooden chair that I've been bound to. But I know the real reason for the smell, the drain, the walls so easy to hose down. These are the sorts of closets dissenters get lost in, never to be found again. In my cotton-mouthed, sluggish waking, I fight to keep from touching the chair's wood. I'm not in control of myself enough to keep from slipping into past prisoners' battered skin.

When the door opens, it's the red-haired KGB officer, clicking along the floor in black pumps with only a sly wink of a heel. The door shuts behind her and I catch a whiff of her weary body odor. I hope it's been days since she slept; I hope her daring mission to capture me, a fearsome unarmed, half-starved teenager, has kept her from showering and eating. I don't want to be the only prisoner here.

"You know why you are here." She steps toward me, close enough that I could punch her if my hands weren't tied.

I hold her gaze and don't answer. Anything I might say could be used as an admission of guilt. I'm better off saying nothing and thinking even less. Whatever happens, I must play this like the market games: carefully, controlled.

"Your parents are Andrei and Antonina Chernin." Air whistles through her front teeth, which I notice are bent inward, when she says our last name. "Both are wanted for political subversion and theft of state property."

The theft part is news to me, but I don't let it show. She lifts one eyebrow. Icy fingers of panic worm into my lungs. Why is she looking at me that way? A wisp of weepy gypsy music runs through my mind. In my foggy logic, I suppose she wears that music like others wear perfume.

"You are not troubled by these crimes? Perhaps you do not understand their seriousness."

"I understand what you do to people who commit them," I say.

She tightens her lips and *hmm*s. "Your family is already in my custody. It would be so easy, very easy, for you to help them out of this unfortunate situation. I only need for you to cooperate."

"You don't have *all* my family."

I clamp my teeth down on my tongue. I shouldn't have revealed that. But Papa is safe, Mama swears it; she just won't tell me where. *An empty mind is a safe mind*, he would say. I can't help thinking of the last time I saw him. Scarf wrapped tight at his throat; steel-rimmed glasses fogging as he steps into the cold.

20

"Do you know this for a fact?" she asks, pacing away from me.

We're both fighting to keep our faces blank. Like the market, it's a game of getting what you want without paying a price that can't be counted in rubles. But she's had her whole career to master this art. Think, Yulia. Everything is a system, and systems can be learned. Figure out the rules for her game. She's not asking any questions. Isn't that the whole point of interrogation? She mentioned cooperation—

"I'm not asking questions because I know everything I need to know from you. You are not here for what you know, but what you can do." Her hands curl into fists, making her leather gloves creak.

I stare at her, shock momentarily numbing my resolve to keep quiet. "Did you just—"

"—Read your mind?" she asks, and her smug smile is like a liter of vinegar in my gut. "Did I? You tell me."

"I'm not telling you anything until I see my family." I try to sound confident, casual. But I can't erase the memory of the empty apartment, their coats still hanging up.

"I will offer you the next best thing." She reaches into her pocket and pulls out a necklace, dangling it before me by its chain. The clasp is broken and bits of black hair are snarled in the links, as if it was ripped from someone's neck. I recognize the medallion spinning at the end of the chain: an emblem of Saint George slaying the dragon.

My mother's necklace.

"It could be anyone's." I tilt my head away. "Lots of Russians pray to Saint George."

She holds the necklace in front of my bound left hand. "But you can prove that it is hers. Go on—touch it."

Does she mean what I think she does? The medallion spins back and forth, the image on one side flickering like a zoetrope. She can't possibly mean my little trick, my market strategy. My funny extra sense that shows what I shouldn't see. I stretch my fingers toward the pendant.

No, no, this is my secret. I can't possibly share it with the KGB.

"What do you want from me?" I ask, my fear making the words soupy.

"You want to keep her safe, yes?" Her eyes narrow. "Your brother Yevgenni. I know he has some . . . mental concerns. His condition requires extra attention, I am told. I will need to justify such care to my superiors."

"You can't hold him in a cell. I need to be with him." I strain at the bindings. "He needs to follow his routine—"

"Why do you think they are in prison cells?" She waves her hand before her face as if waving away the very words. Or her bad breath. "They are cared for. But you want this care to continue, do you not? And so I require something in return. Come now, Yulia." She sighs. "You barter all the time. You know how this works."

I grind my teeth together because they're the only thing between her face and a wad of spit right now. This isn't an interrogation—it's a sales pitch. "What could you possibly want from me? I'm not a political criminal or—or any of those things you say my parents are. I'm just a girl."

Her chapped lips pull back into something like a smile. "Yulia, but we both know that isn't true. You aren't *just* anything."

I squirm away from that awful smile. My wrist brushes the chair arm, and there's a candle-flicker memory of terrifying pain—but it is quickly, mercifully gone. "No. I'm just another person you've chosen to harass. You want to arrest me over things my parents have done? Careless things they might have said?" I roll my shoulders. A Russian shrug, a dismissal, a shifting of blame—*What do you want from me, this is just how things are.* "You'd have to imprison the whole country if that's such a crime."

Her gaze drifts away from me, and she stands perfectly still, like she's watching a memory. "You see things sometimes," she says, suddenly somber. "Things that can't be seen."

I stop squirming around.

"You think it's your imagination, or a phantom déjà vu. Sometimes it appears to come true, but not enough to make you believe. Coincidence. Anything more would be searching for patterns where there are none," she says.

I realize that my mouth is hanging open, and I hurriedly shut it. She can't possibly know about that. I barely believe it myself.

"Do you ever think about these occurrences? Do you ever wonder if there is a power behind them?"

I shake my head. A word comes to me to describe my trick sometimes, but it seems like a castoff of our superstitious past. The realms of magic, religion, mysticism—things beyond the laws of science—died in a dank basement with the last emperor. Bullet to the brainpan—flatten these outdated beliefs with tank treads.

"Psychic. That's the word you're looking for," she says.

I don't like the way she's looking at me: her smile is too

23

genuine, too familiar. I jerk my head away and stare at the tile wall. I can see my reflection in it, but it's blunted, all shadow and light.

"Touch the necklace—see for yourself that it's your mother's. I know you can do this." She holds it out to me again, Saint George dancing on the end of the chain. "See through it to the past it contains."

I curl my hands into fists; my nails burrow into my palms. She is guessing wildly, or making things up. "Who are you?" I ask.

"I represent the First Chief Directorate for the Committee of State Security—"

"Committee of State Security—" *Komitet Gosudarstvennoy Bezopasnosti*— "KGB, I know that much," I say.

She sighs—delicate, measured—and stuffs the necklace back into her pocket. "My name? Why don't you try to see it for yourself?"

I look back at her with my eyebrows furrowed.

"It's very simple. You look at me, and then you imagine stepping inside."

"You—you want me to read your thoughts." I squeeze my eyes shut before she can nod. "No. It's not possible—"

"Yulia. I know all about your ability." She chuckles. "You're quite easy to read, yourself."

That slams my heart into my throat. I suspected it earlier, but to have my every thought laid bare? My eyes fly open like she's thrown cold water on me. "You can't really mean—"

"You have a skill. Others, like me, have similar skills—but none quite like yours. So you will work for me, and I will help you refine it." This time when she smiles, the patient motherly look is completely gone, and all that's left are her cold, animal teeth bared at me in dominance. "Otherwise, as you know—we have ways of dealing with people who commit crimes against the State."

CHAPTER 5

THE COVERED TRUCK BED SMELLS like rotted cabbage and wilted lettuce. The soldier on the bench across from me holds an AK-47 across his lap, casually, like it is no more threatening than a walking cane; but his eyes are unlit matches, and his arms, his steady fingers, are full of energy waiting to be unleashed. He is potential; he is a threat. But when our knees bang together, I get a whiff of his thoughts—the kielbasa sandwich awaiting him for lunch and the nightclub dancer awaiting him for dinner. He isn't plotting my execution just yet, and I mean to keep it that way.

My red-haired interrogator, Comrade Major Lyubov Grigorievna Kruzenko, says I'll be living with six other teenaged children who are, she claims, like me. (I tried plucking her name from her mind, as she asked, but she was sitting across the room from me. I heard nothing save the anguished cries muffled through concrete.) She is our instructor, helping us develop our skills to eventually work for the KGB as psychic spies. Classes, field trips, meals—she makes it sound like the Komsomol summer camps I attended as a little girl, but I think of the Siberian gulags instead—the life-sentence permafrost prisons. For there is a steep price to pay if I disobey; I must play along to keep Mama and Zhenya safe.

But no one can bend the rules quite like me.

The truck takes a sharp turn and slows to a stop. Someone unlatches the back for us. The soldier stands, hunched over, and prods me with the butt of his rifle. I shoot him a frosty look. We hop down into a bland, pathetic courtyard overrun with weeds and surrounded by high concrete walls. Razor wire frosts the top of the walls, softened by a fine dusting of snow. I try to gauge their height. The razor wire doesn't scare me, not if I'm bundled up for winter already. A few cuts and scrapes. The blood trail I'd leave behind could be a problem. I scan the courtyard, but it's thick with armed guards.

Careful, Yulia. Your mind isn't a safe hiding place anymore. I push down thoughts of escape as Major Kruzenko marches our way.

"Come, come," she calls to me, holding out her hand like I'm a schoolgirl who needs to be herded everywhere. I wrap my arms around my chest—the scratchy white blouse, sweater, and wool skirt she gave me aren't nearly warm enough for late September—and stomp past her. We round the truck and I stare up. And up.

The building is an old Georgian-style mansion—the sort that once housed princes and countesses, those long-extinct fairytale creatures. The walls are robin's egg blue, though the plaster has chipped in places to show its gray flesh. White stones

27

scale the corners and windows; the slate roof billows and peaks over three stories. Rusty water stains trail from window corners like tears, and cracks spider up the façade. Someone has taken a chisel and hammer to the frontispiece above the entryway, marring the old Romanov seal of a two-headed eagle—the symbol of the imperial family before the Communist Party took over.

"The house is yours to roam." Major Kruzenko opens the front door. No lock, no electronic callbox, just a heavy wooden door, its carved face worn smooth. It creaks when it opens—not a good escape route. "Your room is on the third floor, with the other girls. Take some time to get acquainted with everyone. We'll start our lessons for the day soon."

The stench of mold overwhelms me as we enter the dark foyer. A chandelier hangs overhead, but it's been stripped of its crystals; only half of the fake candles screwed into its sockets are lit, and all are capped in dust. Wood planks squeal and shift beneath us. The grand staircase ascends into darkness, its marble steps sagging in the center, worn down by decades of feet.

"Yeah, it's a shithole."

I whirl to my right. A blond boy leans against a nearby doorway, watching me like he might watch a pigeon at the park: bored indifference. Then he hoists his head high, showing off his chiseled everyman face. I know it from countless Stalin-era murals, the kinds slathered across Moscow as tribute to the Communist state: muscle-bound factory workers with a perfect curl of hair in the center of their foreheads and chins that could hammer rivets into place. My gut does a quick gymnast tumble, and I don't even *like* blonds.

"Never hurts to try." He laughs to himself.

I stare at him. "Try what?"

Major Kruzenko cuts him off before he can answer. "Sergei, since you are here, would you please show Yulia Andreevna around before class?"

"Sure." He shoves off the doorway with his foot and stretches to his full height. He's a beast. Hulking shoulders, thighs like tree trunks—and it's all muscle, over two meters of it. "Hockey," he says, casting a glance at me over his shoulder. "I was going to play for Spartak before . . ." His gaze slides toward Major Kruzenko, and he trails off.

"Sergei Antonovich!" Major Kruzenko's voice is piercing as icicles. "Stop reading the poor girl's mind."

My cheeks instantly flush. I can't let my thoughts stray for a moment here. But the more I look at Sergei, the more I'm compelled to think everything about him that I wouldn't want him to hear me think. Horrible things that I *wouldn't* think otherwise, if I weren't worried about him overhearing—

"It's all right." He smiles at me, and it feels like the sun's rays slipping around dense clouds. The sun? I'm comparing some smug boy's grin to the sun? *Bozhe moi*, Yulia. "The less you want to think of something, the harder it becomes to think of anything else."

"Wonderful," I mutter.

"It'll get better." He leads me through the archway. "First stop: our extensive library."

Near-empty bookshelves grin back at us like a toothless old babushka. "I thought we're taking classes here?" I glance at a few of the titles—all Leninist-Marxist political theory, economic dissertations proving the perfectness of the Communist system, historical accounts of the Great Patriotic War against fascist Germany (Uncle Stalin did not believe "World War II" adequately described our quest for revenge). The bookshelves are hairy with dust.

Sergei shrugs. "It's not that sort of school."

"Then what sort of school is it?" I try to match his lazy half-smile, but it feels wrong, like a too-tight boot.

"Spycraft, mostly." He looks away from me. "We're training to join the psychic operations wing of the KGB. We use our skills to monitor the Americans and hunt down traitors."

Like me, I think.

"I'm a remote viewer, myself. I can see inside places without going to them. I've never met someone with your particular power. Reading thoughts and memories through touch?"

"A lot of good it did me," I say. But maybe I can turn it to my advantage still. If I can find out where Mama and Zhenya are being kept . . .

"I suggest you take it easy," Sergei says, though I'm not sure if he's answering my thoughts or not. *Bozhe moi*. It hurts my head to contemplate it. "Hey, Boris," he adds, to the lanky uniformed man in the corner of the room. I hadn't even noticed him. Boris makes no acknowledgment, but his eyes follow Sergei, and as we approach another doorway, Boris glides along behind us. "He's my pet spider," Sergei explains. "Anytime I think I'm alone, he comes spinning down on his web."

"Do we all have—er, pet spiders?" And can they read minds as well? Have they heard me thinking about escape? My chest tightens.

Sergei chuckles. "You'll have one you know by name. It's the ones they change around you have to watch out for. Right, Boris?"

Boris grimaces and positions himself in the doorway.

We enter a cavernous, window- and mirror-lined room that must have hosted balls in the Imperial days. Velvet ropes dangle from the ceiling, bereft of their chandeliers like leashes missing their dogs; channels on the walls that once housed gold leaf have been stripped bare. The bank of windows looks onto a desolate stone terrace along the house's side, full of weedy flowerbeds and dry, leaf-smeared fountains. The same high concrete walls from the front yard block the rest of the view. I curse under my breath as a pair of guards patrol through the yard. Missile silos have less security than this.

At the far end of the ballroom, someone plays a soft Tchaikovsky waltz on a battered baby grand. The piano isn't as out of tune as I'd expected. Two teens waltz around the piano: a boy and girl, slender without looking starved, with soft brown hair and matching French noses. I suck in my breath—the twins from the market. They're dressed in far nicer wool and cashmere than the scratchy tweed and cotton on Sergei and me. Little crescents of perspiration lurk under their arms as they twirl, carefree, smug.

"Misha? Masha?" Sergei calls. "Our twins," he tells me. Of course their names match—I can't help but grin at their parents' cruelty. "Though I believe you've already met."

My jaw tenses and I manage a curt nod. I can't think about anything around them. Nothing is safe.

Misha—or Mikhail, I assume—saunters toward us. "The little trapped rat. Not worth the effort, if you ask me."

"If you were dumb enough to get caught, you have no place here," Masha says.

"Then what's your excuse?" I ask.

Masha eyes me with sudden wolfish dominance. "How long have you known you were a psychic? You're not a very good one. I mean, you didn't even see us coming."

I shrink back from her, which I realize a second too late is about the worst thing I could have done. "It took you five years to find me. What's that say about you?"

Masha scrutinizes me for a minute more. The piano music has stopped. She breaks the gaze first; relieved, I lower my head and stare at the decades of scuffmarks gouged into the floor. It doesn't matter, these people don't matter. As soon as I find out where Mama and Zhenya are, I can leave this all behind, and—

Shit.

Masha's face lights up, triumphant. "You can scheme all you want. You won't get far." She wrinkles her perfect nose, glancing toward the piano. "No one ever does."

Sergei nudges my shoulder with his own, though he has to stoop down to do it. "Just ignore them. I do."

Misha jabs his thumb toward Sergei, eyes still on me. "You think this hockey hooligan will protect you? I used to think I couldn't read Sergei's thoughts until I realized he didn't *have* any." He shares a smirk with Masha and they strut out of the ballroom.

"Can you believe they actually want to do this work? I figure that's punishment enough." Sergei's face is flushed, but he keeps his half-grin lacquered to his face. "Come on, tour isn't over."

We circle the piano, revealing a dark-featured boy seated at it, hands steady as a surgeon's above the keys, as if stopping the music has frozen him, too. Sergei sighs and leans against the splintering piano. "And this is Valentin."

Valentin's deep cherry-pit eyes watch me from behind thick-framed glasses; he nods once at me and scrubs his black hair. He has a large frame like Sergei's, but his muscles are lean and withdrawn. Something about him reminds me of the brooding photographs of Russian composers and poets in Aunt Nadia's encyclopedias.

"You play very well," I tell him. "Was that Tchaikovsky?"

He looks down like the compliment was too much to bear. "It was supposed to be *Swan Lake*, but . . . it's out of tune."

I shouldn't act like I care. I don't need any friends here; I'll be gone at the first sign of gaps in the security. But something in his musical phrasing reminded me of the old Kondrashin piano recordings Papa and Zhenya and I listened to, Zhenya dutifully transcribing the notes in his private notation. "Have you been playing for long?"

His dark eyes meet mine again. I know that tightness around them well—the look I gave to anyone who noticed me, the slip of a girl darting along Moscow's streets. I don't blame him for not trusting me; I'll use whatever and whoever I can to escape.

"All my life." He eases his posture; I uncoil in turn. "My mother taught me so I could accompany her when she played violin."

"She must be very proud of you," I tell him. But it was the wrong thing to say. He drops his head and the tension returns.

"Valentin here wants to be the next . . . What's his name,

Valya?" Sergei nudges him in the ribs—none too gently, I suspect. "Dave Barback?"

"Brubeck," Valentin says to the piano keys.

"Yes! Great American jazz composer, Valya tells me. But no one in the Soviet Union cares about jazz. Colored people music," Sergei says. I bristle, though I'm not surprised. Most Russians think like Sergei—Africans, Asians, even olive-skinned people from Georgia and the other southern republics like myself are treated suspiciously.

Valentin eyes me with a slight tilt to his head. "My family is Georgian, too."

"Did I give you permission to read my mind?" I snap. He winces and tucks his hands into his lap.

"Come on, let me show you the view out back," Sergei says. "Valya won't follow us out there. He hates the river."

Sergei pulls me onto the rear balcony of cracked concrete. A long shadow in my periphery marks Boris, moving closer, but Sergei closes the door before he reaches us. My blood races when I realize that this side of the mansion is not hemmed in by the cold concrete wall. But my hope instantly deflates. It's a sheer drop—the mansion perches on a cliff overlooking the Moskva River. We're somewhere in the hills of southeastern Moscow. Barges chug through the oily gray water beneath us; the Metro trains clatter across the river bridge. To the north, at the heart of the city, I can make out the peaks of the Seven Sisters—Stalin's skyscrapers capped in gold and red stars—and the pink turrets of the Novodevichy Monastery jutting defiantly above the river.

"There's Luzhniki Stadium." Sergei stands behind me and

points around me to the low white pod just opposite the river from us. It looks like an alien craft that could take flight at any moment—sail into the stars like the cosmonaut Yuri Gagarin or the *Sputnik* satellite. "I'm going to play for Spartak there someday. I'll be the greatest hockey player in the world."

I don't mean to, but I can feel the sadness sheening his bare arms. They've taken something from all of us. For me, it was Mama and Zhenya, and my dreams of studying at Moscow State so I could fix Zhenya someday. What else have they taken from Sergei, besides his hockey career? But when I glance back at him, his face is blank, a frieze of the Worker as He Advances the Motherland, unmoving.

"You want to go to Moscow State?" He swings me around to my left by my shoulders. "Look."

I stumble back into his dense chest. I can only see the top of the tower over the mansion's roof, but I know it instantly. It's the greatest of Stalin's Seven Sisters; the bright red star and the golden sickle and hammer upon it are perfectly clear. The education I crave is just out of reach.

I scrub at my eyes—they're moist from the wind, I tell myself—and look away.

"I didn't mean to upset you," he says. "I just thought you'd like . . ."

"It doesn't matter." When I find Mama and Zhenya and run away from this place, I'll have to leave it behind. I'll keep teaching myself, like I've been doing. We'll keep running; we'll watch Moscow shrink to a speck over our shoulders. Always running, forever—

Sergei's hand touches my shoulder. It burns with conflicting emotions: sadness? Anger? "Yulia, you have to stop thinking about escape. It's too dangerous."

"What do you care?" A barge sounds its horn; I peer over the balcony ledge. If it were straight down, I could survive it, but the embankment slopes just enough . . .

"Maybe I don't. You wouldn't be the first to try." He shrugs. "But believe me, if there's one thing I've learned here . . . There are worse things than a bullet in the back, a broken neck. What they can do to your brain, or your family's . . ."

Sergei flinches; his gaze roves anxiously, unsettled. I step away from him, not liking the sudden darkness I sense on his skin.

"Death would be a mercy," he says. "For you and your family both."

CHAPTER 6

MAJOR KRUZENKO TEARS open the balcony door, and as she squeezes between Sergei and me, her arm touching mine, I glimpse what Sergei's talking about. Her head is full of bees. She buzzes with panic—with the sound of a shadow peering over her shoulder.

And then, just as abruptly, the panic dissolves into a soft melody.

"I said a quick tour, Seryozha." She waggles her finger at Sergei, who rolls his eyes. "I just spoke with Comrade Rostov. They are ready for you to resume your training exercise." That buzzing sound around her again when she leans in close—and then it's gone.

"Then I'd better not disappoint." Sergei sets his mouth in a grim line and slips out the door.

I start to follow him, but Kruzenko catches my shoulder. "A minute, Yulia, if I may."

I squeeze my escape plans to the back of my mind, with no

clue whether it will do me any good. Pay attention, Yulia. You must first learn the rules.

"Masha tells me you are planning to escape," Kruzenko says.

My heart thuds into my chest. Adrenaline burns through me; I need a quick excuse. "She has it out for me. She thinks I—"

Kruzenko holds up one finger. "No, no, it is all right. I know this is all new to you; it is very difficult to accept. So I will make you an offer." Her voice is softer than in the interrogation room, maternal even: It's too easy to trust her when she's unintimidating this way. "Follow your studies diligently and work hard for a few months, and I will let you see your family."

My effort to focus my thoughts is lost in a deluge of rage. Who is she, to act so damned generous when offering me what I should already have? I want to reach out and slap her. She flinches, either because she read it in my thoughts, or in the way my shoulders draw tight and my fists cock. I step back. My skin is boiling in the crisp winter air. I take a deep breath, but nothing fills the ache in my lungs.

"I'm only doing this for them as it is. Don't turn my family into a reward. A treat for obedience."

"I am permitted to do whatever the State authorizes me to do, if it means your cooperation. Don't forget this." She matches the chill in my voice, but she's perfectly motionless, eyes as unflinching as a photograph. No rage prickles through her like it does in me. I'm sure it's standard KGB training. I'll have to sever emotions if I'm going to outsmart her.

"Now, then. I am not angry at you for having such thoughts, though I am sure I don't have to tell you how foolish an escape attempt would be, for you and your family both."

I say nothing and watch the treetops below us ripple in the wind. She won't make the same offer to see my family again; it will be chiseled away and forgotten like the imperial sigil over the front door.

"But your classmates cannot be blamed for believing you might try. So let me teach you a little technique. It's how we shield our thoughts from intruders."

I stand up straighter. "Intruders like you?" I ask.

"Don't flatter yourself. You aren't *that* strong." She smiles, patronizing, and clears her throat. "I am speaking of enemy agents. Your fellow classmates—at least in casual passing. Your thoughts and feelings flow far too freely. You fling them at me when I'm not even trying to peer inside."

I look away, trying not to think how much I hate her, so of course it's foremost in my mind.

"Yes, always troublesome, that. Someone tells you not to think about elephants, and you can do nothing but." She bares her ragged teeth in a grin. They remind me of the metal tank traps along the Moskva River that held back the fascists. "But there's a simple way to guard them. It's easy enough to understand, but takes a lot of effort to master. Try peering into my thoughts." Major Kruzenko steps closer to me and reaches for my wrists. I instinctively yank my hand back. "Come now, I know it's easiest for you when you're making physical contact. Tell me what you hear," she says.

I rest two fingers on her arm, close my eyes, and listen. The river flowing beneath us—fluid, glassy, not raging today. The wind whispering through the birch trees and rustling the occasional sparrow from its roost. Cars sputtering on a faraway road.

Then I hear that melody: catgut balalaika strings and a mournful, keening voice. Notes with hooks in them to yank out your heart and make you bawl. A gypsy song, one that sprouted from the dark Russian earth long before the Communist Party took root.

Not so far away from here, the River Volga flows
Among the ripe and golden wheat, among the pure
white snow
The River Volga flows past me, when I am but a child

"I hear an old folk song," I say. "Is there a radio somewhere?"

"No, no." She shakes her head with a smile and drops her arm. The music dissipates like steam. "It's how we guard our thoughts, you see. We can't redirect them, so we must shield them instead. Straighten up." She taps my hip. I scowl and stand upright, but fold my arms protectively across my chest. "Now choose a song—one you won't get sick of."

I mull over the possibilities. Tchaikovsky's oeuvre is bursting with loud, ponderous music, perfect for concealing thoughts, and I pause on the dark, heavy opening to his piano concerto. No, it's too much. What have I heard on the radio? A few snatches of American pop songs—wonderful sunny songs, about girls in California and California dreams—but I'd only caught a few bars before the static curtain of the radio jammers closed on the frequency.

The radio triggers another memory—huddled in Aunt Nadia's kitchen with Mama, Cousin Denis, and Zhenya just a few months back. The new voice of Russia, the poet Yevgenni Yevtushenko, was reading his poem that decried the Nazi slaughter of Jews in the Ukraine. But there was more than just words. Dmitri Shostakovich conducted his Thirteenth Symphony live, set to the reading, in a delirious and dangerous waterfall of violent strings, blunt elbows of brass, slow bleeding drums.

The melody rises in my mind, and Yevtushenko's words guide it along. *No monument stands over Babi Yar. A steep cliff only, like the crudest of headstones.* My gaze drifts down the cliffs to the Moskva River below us.

"Interesting choice," Kruzenko says.

I lurch forward, startled by her voice, and the melody falters, slipping through my thoughts as if it's turned to sand. I try to catch it, but the farther away it goes, the more thoughts pop up in my head. Everything I wouldn't want Kruzenko—or anyone— to know. How long until my next period. Where Mama hid our rubles. The more I reach for the melody, the more absurd my thoughts turn. Sergei's luscious muscles. Cleaning up after Zhenya when he's been too lost in his own world to visit the toilet. Valentin skewering me like a reindeer kabob with that gaze of his. How I'm already memorizing the patrol routes of all our guards. The time I walked in on Cousin Denis kissing his best friend Timofei—

"I am not judging you for your thoughts," Kruzenko says. "Empty your mind, and let only the music in."

The horns sound in the distance, mournful; the drums hint at soldiers on the march. A banal thought trickles through the trees—hunger. Yes, the buckwheat porridge at the KGB holding cell was not enough to last me through the day. But Yevtushenko's voice booms over the stray thought, bouncing off the shadowy snow. When will we be eating? As the violins slide in to have their say, I suspect I will be stuck here for far too long. No, I must focus: the sawing cello matches my pounding heart, until there is nothing more.

"And just like that, I cannot hear your thoughts." Kruzenko smirks. "Well—you are no longer broadcasting them to the whole world, at least. You must keep practicing. Any time you feel it falter, call up the melody again."

I open my mouth to speak, but the music stutters. Two tries, three—around the seventh try I think I can manage it. "I—I think I understand."

She nods. "Eventually, it will be as natural to you as breathing."

I take a deep breath and gust it out. Shostakovich's melody plays at the back of my mind, but I can fit other thoughts in my head now, too; they don't have to drown him out. It's a comfort to have him there, like an extra blanket in winter.

Major Kruzenko reaches into her pocket. "Now let us tame your gift—enough for you to participate in today's class."

Mama's necklace spins before me. My heart lurches, but I smother it in my new music. I can't panic.

"Admittedly, you are the first I have encountered whose powers work primarily through touch. But I understand some of it. Memories and thoughts can cling to objects like a film, and the psychic—you—must sift through the layers to find the correct memory."

I reach for the medallion, but she pulls it out of my reach. "Gently, child. Try the lightest brush of skin, so only the most recent memory flakes away."

I extend my index finger until it barely bumps against the medallion. Kruzenko nods at me, and I close my eyes.

Thrashing—water rushing up my nose. I suck in air but darkness floods my lungs instead. Images drift past me like bubbles: Kruzenko holding the necklace out to me in the interrogation room; Kruzenko in an office, one I've never seen, discussing the pendant with a uniformed man. I can't see his face, but there's that buzzing sound again, overwriting her gypsy song.

"Deeper now." A bubble with Kruzenko's voice inside punctures as it hits me. "Deeper, into the past." I swim on.

Mama, slumped in a chair, blood trailing down her nose. I thrash again and surface in the sight. She does not look afraid— she does not *feel* afraid, a fact I am certain of, though I can't explain how. Zhenya sits beside her, making a high-pitched whine that I might have mistaken for a fan belt had I not heard him make this noise before. I don't need my "power" to know this sound for the very essence of his fear.

"Give her this," Mama says, and tears the necklace free. She is not bound to the chair—not in any way that I can see. "She won't listen to you. She'll have to hear that I'm alive—see it— through me."

"I hope she listens, then, for your sake," a man's voice says, but when I try to look at him, I fall through a white fog. No more memories lie beyond it. The balcony reforms around me, blurry with the vision's residue.

"A respectable first attempt," Kruzenko says. I surface back into reality, but Mama's expression, her blood clings to my skin. My music is gone. Shostakovich, I need Shostakovich, I don't want Kruzenko in my head. I pull the melody around me like a towel, and scrub away the thoughts of Mama, of her tired acceptance.

Surely she has not already given up. Surely she is only waiting for the right opportunity to fight.

Kruzenko pockets the medallion before I can reach for it again, and ushers me through the doors. I keep a safe distance from her as she leads me toward class. I think Shostakovich is working, but I don't want to take any chances.

I didn't recognize where they're keeping Mama, so finding that out will be my next goal. It's good that she's with Zhenya—good that he isn't locked up alone. But why was she so resigned? As if she—wanted it this way.

No. Focus. If Kruzenko can reach through my musical shield with some effort, then eventually, I can reach through hers and learn where Mama's being kept. I've already got a lead.

Because whenever Kruzenko carries that buzzing noise, her music shield stops.

CHAPTER 7

OUR "CLASSROOM" IS an old sitting room on the second floor of the mansion. The others huddle around a marble fireplace that spits smoke into the room, while the pet spiders lurk in the back—I count three, though they tend to blur into the shadowed alcoves. Sergei, the twins, and Valentin are there, listening to an old wooden radio that's as tall as a child, as well as a girl and boy I haven't met, probably a few years younger than me, who sit practically on top of each other on the groaning floor. "Ivan and Larissa," Sergei says to me, tilting his head toward them.

Vladimir Vysotsky's melodramatic folk song ends, and the Soviet national anthem blares through the radio. ". . . morning news. Our most esteemed Comrade Yuri Gagarin, the first man ever in space, may soon beat the Americans to yet another space exploration milestone—"

"I see you all have been hard at work." Major Kruzenko smiles as she clicks the radio off. "If we can complete our current exercise today, the Colonel has some exciting news for you."

Sergei slumps back, propped on his palms; only Misha and Masha look remotely enthused. Masha's hand jets into the air. "Comrade Major? I'd be honored to conduct today's exercise."

"In a moment. We must get Yulia Andreevna properly acclimated." Kruzenko scans us with shrewd falcon eyes, and I suspect this is how a mouse must feel as it scampers through open grass. "Though every psychic can be trained to read the unguarded thoughts of people around them, we each have our different strengths." Her gaze settles on me before she addresses the others. "Yulia's power works best when in contact with the person of her focus, or an object through which she can 'see' events."

"Something like that." I look away to the far side of the room. There are no windows in this part of the house; nothing to distract me. No paintings on the walls, and the floral wallpaper has faded to a mushy salmon hue.

"Larissa is best at seeing what may come to be. Predicting future events, weighing possible outcomes." She looks at Larissa, who reddens under a tangle of dingy blond hair.

"Maria and Sergei are what the American CIA calls 'remote viewers.'" She nods to the girl twin—Masha, or Maria—who sits up straighter. "Have you ever known a street so well that you can close your eyes and see it as vividly as if you were standing there? They can actually see such places—watch what is happening like it's a television show."

I have known such a street. An oak-shaded path beside our old home outside of Moscow, where Zhenya and I strolled every afternoon, even in blizzards and baking heat. In winter, we could hear deer crunching through the icy top layer of snow, just out of sight, and Zhenya would count their footsteps to guess how many there were.

I wonder if I will ever walk this path, or any other, with Zhenya again.

She strides past me, low heels slapping on the wood, and ruffles the hair of the rat-faced blond boy, Ivan, beside Larissa. "Ivan and Misha are strongest at hearing others' thoughts and getting them to focus on thinking about the information we want so we can pry it from their heads."

I look at Valentin. A black curl obscures his forehead, and his knees bounce up and down with restless rhythm. "What about you?" I ask him.

Major Kruzenko smiles in a way that twists into my gut. "Valentin . . . he is best at changing the very stream of someone's thoughts—altering their memories, or creating a new reality around them."

I draw my knees up under my chin. Valentin keeps fidgeting like he doesn't hear us, but I hear him: a frantic saxophone bouncing up and down a scale and drums goading it along. I must be extra careful around Valentin. I pull Shostakovich tight around me like a shroud.

"So!" Kruzenko clasps her hands together. "We are a well-rounded team. Just as in hockey, we cannot all play the same position—we need goalies, defenders, scorers. We must practice as a team and learn to trust one another's movements. If Sergei has the puck to pass, then he has to trust that Mikhail will be there to pick it up. Are we understood?"

Subdued heads bob all around me. I nod, eager to get her gaze off of me.

"Excellent. Sergei, Maria, let us proceed with the training exercise."

Masha bounces to her feet; Sergei stands slower, looking at me as if in apology, like this is his crazy family and I'm just an observer, a guest. Major Kruzenko shepherds them into two nicked wooden chairs. Masha's glossy hair moves as one solid curtain along her shoulders as she perches on the chair. She looks like a porcelain doll, too pretty to play with, that must sit on the shelf and stare out with superior eyes. Her knees press perfectly together and she smoothes the hem of her skirt. Sergei slumps beside her, knees wide, arms crossed; his blond hair scatters across his brow.

"In this exercise, we are hunting an escaped spy who has stolen important documents from the Ministry of Finance. In today's session, we have tracked him to the Ukraina Hotel. We must recover the documents and find him before he meets with a British agent." Kruzenko's lips curl into a thin smile. "And with our remote viewers, we can find him without even leaving the mansion. Children, place yourselves on the street. You should have it memorized from out last field trip."

"Should," Sergei says, with his naughty boy smirk. Kruzenko raps him on the hand; there's something familiar and playful in the way she does it, as though this is a well-trod routine between them. "Yeah, yeah, I remember it. Big boulevard, trees, one of the Seven Sisters towers."

Kruzenko strides to the desk at the far end of the room and snatches the telephone. "Begin," she says. The Russian word is harsh, three-syllabled; it sounds like sandpaper rubbing back and forth.

Sergei takes a deep breath, like he's going to plunge underwater, and screws his eyes shut. Kruzenko paces behind them. They're both deep in thought, eyes closed, and Masha's head is slumping toward her chest. Drool glimmers on her lower lip.

"Latch onto the details you remember. Let them guide you to the places you haven't been."

"Marble floors," Masha cries sharply. Her slim figure contorts as if she's possessed. "I've stepped through the doorway. I can see the chandelier—"

"There's no chandelier," Sergei says. "Just a mural on the ceiling."

"No—I'm already way past that, inside the restaurant. There's a chandelier there."

"Whatever you say." Sergei sighs.

Masha wrinkles her nose in his direction. "Stop distracting me. There's a table by the window . . ."

Valentin's fidgeting brings his knee to rest against mine. I start to pull away—but his frantic jazz music ebbs and two words slip off of him onto me, like a drop of sweat.

Let's talk.

Our eyes meet. His are a burned shade of brown, smoldering like the last winter log. I'm thankful he wears glasses because I feel like I need shielding from his intense stare. I drop my gaze and slowly peel the thrumming bass of Shostakovich away from my thoughts. *What do you want to talk about?* We aren't making physical contact now, but if he's capable of what Kruzenko claims . . .

I know you're scared—hurting, perhaps. You have good reason for it. I can't blame you for wanting to run.

Great. Does everyone know about my plan? I bury my head between my knees. Major Kruzenko is still talking through the restaurant's description with Sergei and Masha. "The drapes!" Masha cries. Her hand clamps onto Sergei's. "They're *blue*!" Like she wants to impress Kruzenko so badly it's hurting her.

Yeah, I hear Valentin say, *she likes this too much.*

Anger percolates in my mind like the onset of timpani drums. *I wasn't thinking that* at *you.*

His head hangs; he looks like a beaten dog. Outwardly, I roll my eyes, but I do feel bad. The feeling only lasts until I remember what he can do. *You were saying?*

Please don't try to run just yet. You aren't ready. I promise, I'll help you find a way, but you're not strong enough yet to keep them from catching you—

I dare to let the light of optimism flicker through my thoughts. *What do you mean, you'll help? Do you know a way out of here?*

There's a lot you need to know, but we can't discuss it right now. The low bass line creeps up on his words. *We'll talk later.*

"Yulia?"

I jerk my attention back to the front of the room. Major Kruzenko watches me with one eyebrow curved. "I asked you to come up here."

"No, thank you," I say, pulling the strains of Shostakovich back around me. I am present and accounted for—isn't that cooperation enough?

Misha snickers; Ivan and Larissa lean apart from each other

enough that they can stare at me. Kruzenko folds her hands behind her back. "You will join us now, Yulia Andreevna."

"Please—not today." I will endure their demonstrations, but it's all too much. Valentin's words are a storm within my skull. What more does he know? Why shouldn't I run?

Her low heels click on the wood as she marches toward me. She rears back. Strikes me across the cheek with a hot, fearsome crack. The sound of the slap scares me more than the slap itself; I hear it ringing in my skull. "You will join us at the front."

Pain burns on my cheek, as though I've been scalded, but I won't give her the satisfaction of seeing me rub the wound. "No," I say.

Kruzenko lifts her head to catch the attention of a guard in the back. "Vasily. Place a call to the Colonel." Larissa whimpers at the mention of a colonel. "Tell him that the Chernins are to be transferred."

Death would be a mercy, Sergei's voice echoes in my head. It is not a whispery psychic thought, but a physical presence, echoing against my thoughts over and over, demanding to be heard.

I spring to my feet. "No! Leave them alone." I'm shaking; my mouth tastes like ash. Mama's tired face flashes in front of my eyes. The spider called Vasily looks from Kruzenko to me. "I'll do it," I say. "But please—"

"The telephone call will not be necessary." Kruzenko walks back to Sergei and Masha, and Vasily retreats into his shadows. My heart is still racing; I'm too terrified to move. Is that all it takes to lose my grip on Mama and Zhenya? Only a few words of disobedience? "Quickly, quickly, Maria and Sergei are already growing tired."

Valentin is watching me as I move to the front of the room, but I can't look back at him. My stinging cheek is punishment enough without his skewering gaze. Kruzenko drags a third chair next to Sergei and motions for me to sit. "Take Sergei's hand. I want you to practice watching the scene through someone else's eyes. You won't have to call on your own abilities for this part."

Sergei grins at me—crookedly, but he's too clever not to know he's got such an endearing crooked grin. He's even missing a front tooth. How hockey of him. I tremble as we join hands.

It's like a jolt of electricity. A new room unfolds before me with wooden floors, elegant lighting sconces, high-backed dining booths. But there are gaps in the room—foggy, blurred segments where there are sometimes chairs or windows, but sometimes not.

"There will always be uncertainties in a viewing, especially with inexperienced viewers like Masha and Sergei," Kruzenko says. "Just do the best you can."

A table has been abandoned by the window, a wadded-up napkin dumped into a bowl of soup. Someone has fled here in a hurry. Tucked into Masha's famous blue drapes is a leather attaché case.

"Once you are stronger, you will be able to use your powers inside their vision to remotely gather information from the attaché," Kruzenko says. "For now, though, I have a prop for you to work with."

She places the case in my lap. I run my fingers over the stiff, shiny leather. It still smells of the tannery.

"Trace the spy's footsteps. Show us where he's been."

I plunge into the case's memories.

A man in oversized sunglasses with a ridiculous, false curlicue mustache sets down the attaché by his table. This is the KGB's impression of an American secret agent? No matter. I need to go further back. My fingers press deeper into the leather. He runs backward out of the Ukraina Hotel, backward down the street, on the Metro, to the train station, the ticket counter—there. He is buying a ticket. What did the ticket girl say?

"Prague—he's bought a one-way ticket to Prague."

But I keep going. I follow him back to the KGB station where he prepares for our training exercise. I see the KGB's costumers dressing him up like a movie star, smoking their cigarettes, whispering under their breath about how stupid the whole program is. The mighty state swears there is no god, no superstition, no supernatural world, they murmur, this conceit of special powers is pure foolishness.

"Prague is correct. Well done, Yulia Andreevna."

I open my eyes; find myself under the needle of Valentin's gaze. "See what memories you can find on the documents," he says, his voice thick. I narrow my eyes at him, trying to read his expression. What's his game here?

Kruzenko lifts an eyebrow. "Yes, excellent idea, Valentin. Give it a try."

I reach into the attaché case and yank the documents out. Big red Russian letters stamped on the front declare them SEKRET. The cover has been stamped three times, and each subsequent page twice—just in case I missed it before. I leaf through the pages. There's text here, something about currency regulation, manufacturing output, Soviet economic supremacy, but every paragraph bears the noose of classification and, much smaller than the stamp, "for training purposes only." I run my fingers across the ink, smudging it, so I can see what the paper sees.

A tiny gasp escapes me, completely unbidden, as the document overwhelms me with a sense of hate.

"Focus," Kruzenko barks, but her voice comes from outside, from down the street, from a *Sputnik* satellite in space. "You don't have to dig so deep."

But I can't control it. The memories are a hand reaching from the water, pulling me back down. I'm screaming, I'm pulling away, but their dead eyes are locked onto mine and they won't let go until I'm drowning with them.

Hatred. A man stands over the documents—gaunt to a degree that only Russian men can be, as though his whole face hangs on the two pegs of his cheekbones. His jawline is sharp as a scar, and his eyes are guarded deep within his skull. His lips, chapped and thin, curl back as he puts together this false little case of documents, this pathetic training exercise, this farcical project. What do little children know of spy games, of the real power of the mind? They are too undisciplined. They are too free. Obedient minds, not rebellious teens, are needed to run the program, the Soviet Union. I will make the necessary changes when I'm in charge, when Antonina breaks, when their minds belong to me—

Antonina. The memory falls into the background, leaving this one too-sharp word in my trembling grasp.

"Well?" Major Kruzenko rests her hand on my shoulder, and

cool gypsy music drifts between us. My mind snaps out of the false document, the false training exercise, the false little window into the KGB's idea of perfectly controlling the populace through psychic spies. "What did you see?"

"It's—it's nothing. A secretary preparing the documents." I shake her off and stand, staring right at Valentin.

Why did you want me to see this man? I ask him, though I don't know if he can hear. *Why does he want our minds for his own? Why does he need to break Antonina for his plans to succeed?*

And because I can't bear to let anyone else know, I swallow the next thought: Antonina is my mother's name.

CHAPTER 8

MASHA THROWS OPEN THE DOOR to our dormitory and glowers at me. "Pick a bed," she says. "Away from mine."

"Excuse me?" I ask.

"I saw you eyeing the silverware at tea. You're like all the other ration rats—always scouting for trinkets you can trade or hoard." She tosses her hair over her shoulder. "I don't want you near my things."

I narrow my eyes. I'd pocketed a knife for prying open the door to Major Kruzenko's office, in hopes I might find a clue as to where my family is being kept. Not that it's any of Masha's business—or the two spider-guards hovering in the doorway, watching our every move. The *Babi Yar* music, my chosen shield, bellows in my head to cover up my anger.

The girls' dormitory was once two rooms—a sitting room and a bedroom, maybe, for a single countess—whose dividing wall was torn out long ago. Its extraction point stands bare, a gouge in the wall, exposing wooden bones. The walls may have once been painted pale green, but are now a dingy gray. Beyond the windows, I can see only treetops; the sound of the branches shushing in the wind fills the held-breath silence of the room.

There are ten beds in two rows, metal-framed and barely more than cots, like the hospital pictures we see from the Great Patriotic War. What must be Masha's and Larissa's cots are claimed at opposite corners of the room, but everything else is empty, with sheets piled at the foot of the skimpy mattresses. The whole mansion seems designed for a much larger group.

I march down the aisle to the middle bed on Larissa's row, my footsteps echoing. I barely know her at all, but she doesn't offend me nearly as much as Masha. *It's only for a few nights,* I tell myself, *until I can find out where Mama is.* I reach for the folded sheets, coated with a thin film of dust.

"Wait!" they both shout in unison, but I'm already leaning against the bed frame.

Fever runs up one leg and down the other; needles pin my thoughts in place like captured butterflies. It's like an electrical current arcing across my skin, full of anger, razor blades, panic, dark eyes, pain—

I jump back from the frame and fight to fill my lungs with air that won't come.

"That was . . . Anastasia's bed," Larissa says, speaking to the floor.

Masha nods, face drained of her usual smugness. "You'd better take another one."

I grit my teeth. Maybe if I clench them hard enough, it'll kill the images of blood and electricity. "And what happened to An-astasia?" I ask, but Larissa fiddles with a strand of blond hair while Masha locks up all her belongings in the trunk at the foot of her bed.

"Fine. Forget I asked." I unfold the sheets on the opposite bed, in Masha's row. My eyes are on the mattress, but in my peripheral vision, Masha and Larissa exchange a look. Even I can hear their dueling musical barriers swelling to fend me off: a schmaltzy Vladimir Vysotsky fool-the-censor ballad for Larissa and the blurty, chest-puffing national anthem for Masha.

"She was here until a few months ago," Masha finally says. "She . . . wasn't cut out for our work."

"You mean she went crazy," Larissa says. "What?" she hisses at Masha, who gives her a dirty look. "It's *true*."

I tuck in the sheets, hospital corner style, learned from years of helping Mama. "Does that happen a lot?"

"Not as often as you'd think," Larissa says. Then she moves up my ladder of regard when she looks sideways at Masha and adds, "Only to the ones who try too hard."

"Girls." One of the guards steps forward. "It is better not to worry our new friend this way." His words take on an edge. "You should talk of other things."

"Shut up, Lev." Masha says it so casually that even Lev doesn't know how to react. His puffy lips hang open for a moment before he falls back to the doorway. If her parents are the high-ranking Party officials I suspect they are, maybe Masha can get away with such insolence, but I'll need to be far more subtle. "It depends on your genetic constitution," Masha continues, strutting down the aisle in time with the national anthem shield billowing around her. "If you're strong enough, come from good stock, you'll have nothing to fear."

"Good stock?" I laugh. "What are we, cattle?"

They exchange another look over my head.

"Come on. It's obvious there are supposed to be a lot more of us here." I flop onto my bed and sneeze as the cloud of dust hits me. "Did they all go crazy?"

"Of course not!" Masha's anthem swells. "Most of the KGB's psychics are like my parents—highly decorated psychological spies who served the Motherland during the Great Patriotic War. They stopped Hitler's fascist forces from taking Leningrad by guiding our supply trucks into the city when it was under siege." She runs her hand along the metal frame of my cot, and I'm sure the humming her touch leaves behind is intentional. "Their children, like Misha and I, have been monitored from birth."

"Sounds like fun," I say. My father never fought in the Great Patriotic War—one of the many privileges we enjoyed in our former life. He stayed shielded in his antiseptic lab, flirting with Mama, enjoying the Party life.

"So most of us are the children of these spies, or other documented psychics' children. Their powers show up at around eight or nine, and they're carefully monitored until they're our age—old enough to be trained. Then there are wildlings, like Larissa, whose powers show up later," Masha says. "Someone got suspicious about her predictions that always turned out true. They reported her to the KGB, and they brought her in once they discovered what she was."

Larissa lets her blond curls fall over her face to hide her crimson cheeks, as if she's still ashamed at being found out. I grimace. I hadn't discovered my own powers until the day we moved in with Aunt Nadia. She'd hugged me tight and told me out loud that she would do whatever it took to protect us, but I heard doubt and disgust running through her mind. "So I guess I'm a wildling," I say.

Masha pauses as the national anthem builds back up around her thoughts. Then she forces her sweetest spun-sugar grin to her lips and tilts her head just so, a poster girl for the Komsomol youth. "I guess you are," she says.

But Masha's made a mistake. She may have elite KGB spy training in her blood, but she has not learned how to survive—not like a "ration rat" like me. I don't need to read her mind to see the signs that she's lying. Shostakovich hammers around me. Liar. Liar. The word screams through my thoughts, screeches across the violins.

But what is she lying about—and why?

"Girls?" Major Kruzenko's voice floats upstairs. "Come downstairs, it's time for dinner!"

A cold fist grips my heart as I follow Masha and Larissa down the staircase, two guards sauntering along behind us. What does Masha know about me that I don't? I never told Mama or anyone else about my ability—the KGB can't possibly have been monitoring us for years, or they would have arrested us before now. But I never noticed any sort of ability when I was eight or nine, when Masha said the "legacy" psychics discovered theirs. My parents were doctors—glorified teachers, really—not psychic spies. They spent their days at the clinic training children with mental disorders to become just another cog in the Soviet machine. Surely they never noticed that I—

I crash into someone at the base of the stairs. Valentin looks down at me, his burning eyes wrenched open wide. But I barely see them—I'm tangled in the sight I saw when we collided, vivid even through his musical shield.

I saw myself.

Larissa seizes my wrist, her hand oozing with her Vysotsky song, and yanks me away from him. "Let's get a good seat." Valentin stands motionless at the base of the stairs, staring at us and adjusting his glasses like I've stunned him. The folk ballad circles lazily around Larissa. "Be careful with Valentin," she whispers. "He's powerful, but sometimes, he has trouble controlling it. He's a freak."

"And the rest of us aren't?" I ask.

She grunts; a dizzying blur of images drifts off her skin to mine, too fast for me to sort through. "Not like him. He's going to end up just like the Colonel someday."

"Who is the Colonel—" But I stop short as we round the corner to the dining room, painted in caustic baby blue. Staring us down from the opposite end of the banquet table is the gaunt, too-tall, furious man I saw through the documents. The man who knows my mother's name.

I hear Kruzenko's voice behind him. "You must be cautious with her. We aren't used to guarding against touch," she says, the angled double doors sheltering her from view. "There is far worse she could have learned."

"Colonel Rostov," Larissa squeaks. He turns away from Kruzenko. Larissa drops my hand and stands straight as a piston, snapping gearlike into a salute. The Colonel stands and strides down the length of the dining table.

Something about him makes it hurt to look at him—it's like

looking at the sun, too bright to stare at directly, searing my eyes, making me itch all over. The closer he draws, the more the feeling swells. My stomach churns and there's this sharp, twisting pain in my head.

It's the buzzing I heard in Kruzenko's thoughts this morning, cutting through her mental shield like a bone saw. Is this his power, this way of splitting straight through someone's mind, so they're exposed even after they're away from him? No mental barrier could possibly repel that. I'm trying to focus on Shostakovich but this pain, this noise—it's like someone's scrubbing the inside of my skull with steel wool. Those onyx eyes flash at me from the deep recesses of his face. He walks like a tiger—sinuous, confident, crisp.

"Comrade Chernina. I am pleased to have you join us." He stops half a meter from me. I try not to double over as my stomach protests. "A shame your mother is not seeing reason, like you have."

"What are you doing to my mother?" It's all I can manage to say. That awful steel scritch-scritch-scratch consumes all sound. His words are trimmed in razor wire.

"It's very sad." He examines his fingernails, though they're perfectly clean. "She does not want to resume her old research. Who knows why? It was good, fulfilling work, helping the mentally ill. She was a Party member, she received extra rations, all the medical access she required for your brother. He really needs special attention, doesn't he? A bit of a borscht-for-brains." His gaze rakes over me. "Maybe you can convince her."

He smells like hot tar, burning rubber. It's the stink of the fresh Leninskoye Highway as they built it past Aunt Nadia's block. And still, that abrasiveness, scouring my brains . . . He reaches out and grips my chin, tilting my head from side to side. Admiring the welt Kruzenko gave me with her slap? Or inspecting me like a cow brought to the butcher? He lets go, and my skin feels raw where he touched it, like he splashed it with bleach.

"Anyway." He makes a little laughing noise with his mouth closed. "I know you'll serve us well. She'd want you to, eh? Her skills are still valuable to the State, and they won't do us much good at the bottom of a ditch. But, if she refuses to cooperate . . ."

If I didn't feel like someone was scooping me hollow like a melon, I'd be taking a swing at him right now.

"I trust she'll come around. She'll realize how good life was when they played by our rules." Rostov grins like a toad. "And so will you." He turns to Larissa. "Larissa Maksimovna. I hear a rumor that your brother might be released soon for good behavior."

Larissa flashes him a venomous smile. "Don't worry, I know exactly how to make that come true." She puts her arm around my shoulder and turns me gently toward the table.

Rostov and Kruzenko sit at the head of the table, but Larissa steers me to the far end, thankfully, since my nerves are shot from being near him. I wonder if it's his way of shielding his thoughts, if he's too much of a machine to use music, or if it's like what Kruzenko said this morning about Valentin—he slips into your head and shreds it apart.

I'm hoping to talk to Larissa during dinner, as I'm starting to think she's the only decent one of the bunch. Despite her ballad's best intentions, despite Ivan at her other side leaning against her, her shield is slipping. I see her first encounter with Rostov:

tearing her down, mocking her powers, sending her brother away to work far beyond the Urals . . . How selfish I am, to worry about my family so much. I'm hardly alone in my suffering. I prop my elbows on the laminated tablecloth and stare down at my cabbage soup.

"Cheer up, tough girl. It's only the first course." Sergei, on my other side, grins at me over his steaming spoonful.

"Of how many?" I scan the table—baskets full of bread, trays of sliced kielbasa and cheeses; sardines, cucumbers, tomatoes, jams and jellies, and sugar and cream for our coffee and tea, all in tarnished silver platters and chipped chinaware . . . It's probably more food than I've seen in the past three months combined. I don't care if Masha calls me a ration rat—I'm going to stuff my pockets tonight.

Sergei adds a dollop of sour cream to his soup and stirs it in. "Not the best food, of course, or the freshest, but they take care of us here." He jabs his spoon at me. "Beats splitting one ration three ways, huh?"

I imagine Aunt Nadia and Cousin Denis back at their apartment. As worried as they might be, they must be relieved to eat a whole ration for dinner tonight. Sleep in separate beds, separate rooms once more. No longer fear the KGB's head popping out from every cupboard . . .

I lift a spoonful of stew, then let it dribble down into the bowl. Sure, I'm starving, but I've been starving for months, years even. I'm afraid of eating too quickly, filling my shriveled stomach with more than it can bear. I need this food to last. I grit my teeth and slurp up a bite, but the psychic noise from Rostov nearly makes me choke.

"How can you stand to eat around him?" I ask Sergei, glancing toward Rostov.

"Oh, you learn to tune it out." His brow furrows. "You can't let him get to you. He's just like Valentin—he can scrub away thoughts, memories, whatever he needs to change, but Rostov's not permitted to do it to us."

"And that actually stops him?" I ask.

Sergei shrugs. "Sometimes I can tell when he's been around. That static noise he gives off—it lingers, you know? On the people he's been manipulating. So it's obvious where he's been."

Like Mama's necklace—that wall of noise that kept me from looking deeper into the past. *Bozhe moi.* "How do you do it?" I ask Sergei quietly. "Put up with this. You don't want this life, either."

He pushes away his empty bowl. "I'm in no hurry—Spartak will still be there next season." He half-smiles at me, revealing a dimple in his right cheek.

"But if you're working for the KGB, how will you have time to play hockey, too?"

"We can buy our freedom in bits and pieces. I finished a major exercise, and now they let me practice at the Luzhniki Stadium rink three mornings a week. Eventually, I can live the life I want most of the time, working for them only when they need my particular skills."

But I'm not so easily convinced. The Party only dangles enough freedom in front of us to keep us moving forward. What might they offer me, to convince me to stay? More time with my family? A chance to study at Moscow State, learning about genetics to decipher my brother's sickness?

I'd rather free Mama and Zhenya for myself.

I steal a glance at Rostov, sitting like a tsar in his high-backed chair, the disheveled chandelier illuminating every last medal pinned to his officer's uniform. His painful power seems well suited to torture. Is that what awaits Mama and Zhenya if I disobey? I need patience—I'll need to play their games until I have all the information I need.

I take careful, small slurps of soup as Sergei works a tower of toast into his mouth. My stolen knife presses into my calf, tucked into my woolen sock, but I'm afraid to break into Kruzenko's office now that Rostov's around. I uncross my legs under the table, trying to get comfortable, and accidentally kick Valentin across from me, but he keeps his laser sight trained on his plate.

"All right, children," Rostov says, "I believe Major Kruzenko promised you all a surprise this evening." He throws her a tight, mirthless smile. "Though we were given a splendid opportunity in Cuba to halt America's aggression once and for all, Comrade Premier Khruschev chose not to take it, and of course I respect his decision."

That smile never wavers, but I recognize his tone. Saying one thing when you mean another. I suppose even KaGeBezniks deviate from the Party line now and then, but what sort of man regrets that we didn't start a nuclear war? Just a year ago, the United States and Russia were staring each other down in Cuba, fingers hovering over the nuclear triggers, waiting for the other to flinch. A "missile crisis," they called it in the news. My stomach turns to think Rostov craved something more severe.

"But we are asserting our supremacy in other ways. Comrade

Yuri Gagarin has already dealt another blow to America's space program by becoming the first man in space, but Khruschev wants us to aim higher. We have been asked to investigate the secret *Veter* program, which is designed to circle the moon. Unfortunately, despite the secrecy, there is some concern that members of the spacecraft's design team have been compromised by foreign agents who want to steal our superior Soviet technology. Which is where you come in."

Masha squeals. "Our first real assignment?"

Rostov nods. "I believe you have proved yourselves ready for field work, though you will continue with training missions, as well. Once I am satisfied everyone is prepared for this task—" He glances toward me. "Then we will begin the operation in earnest."

Sergei lifts one eyebrow, like he's excited despite himself. Valentin's face is sharp as ever, but his foot brushes against my shin under the table. I can't tell if he did it on purpose—there's no message in the jazz music he leaves on my skin. Larissa and Ivan's faces are blank, but they lace their fingers together on top of the table. "Whatever the Motherland requires of us," Ivan says. Larissa nods once, decisively, at his words.

Rostov spends the rest of the meal deflecting questions from Misha and Masha, assuring them that he'll tell us more about the operation once we're ready. "But *we're* ready now," Masha insists, gesturing to her brother and herself.

Sergei nudges me when Major Kruzenko excuses us for the night. "Want to listen to the radio? Spartak's playing Dinamo tonight," he says.

I hesitate. Ivan and Larissa are already slinking off, and I know better than to follow. Misha and Masha are latched onto Major Kruzenko like thistles on a sock. If Rostov leaves, it might be my perfect opportunity to break into Kruzenko's office, if I can ditch my spider entourage. Or I could approach Valentin, who's watching me from the doorway— this morning he hinted at knowing something and information is the most valuable currency.

But then Colonel Rostov approaches us. "Come, boys. We must work on our special task, yes?" He laughs, but Sergei and Valentin both abruptly hang their heads, as if he's just scolded them, and—even I am not paranoid enough to imagine this, I swear it's true—both their gazes dart toward mine for one guilty, piercing second before they follow Rostov into Kruzenko's office.

In this moment, I decide to trust no one. I can't count on Larissa and Masha, who won't tell me the truth of who, what I am. Not on Ivan and Misha, too absorbed in their own success to consider breaking free. Not on Sergei who gives up his life for a morning on the ice. And especially not Valentin, with his heavy, lovely, intrusive eyes.

I will have to find freedom for myself, though I fear it will take longer than I'd first hoped. I can bide my time until I find out where Mama and Zhenya are being held—I can smile and mimic Masha's enthusiasm until I have everything I need to make my escape. But as Rostov's psychic noise echoes through my skull, I'm not certain I can even trust myself.

CHAPTER 9

IT TAKES ME SOME TIME to fall asleep. I listen to the silky sighs of Masha and Larissa, but fear Rostov's steel wool scrubbing my shield raw. When exhaustion finally claims me, I find myself in a strange dream: I am sitting around the table in our summer dacha with Mama and Papa. Mama with her hair still long like when I was little, and Papa—almost unrecognizable in his old glasses and ill-fated attempt at a beard. Zhenya sits with them, so tiny and frail—he doesn't look more than five or six. He is whistling three notes to himself over and over like a sniper calling his comrades out of hiding. His lips are glossy with spittle but he doesn't quit. Mama keeps pinching the bridge of her nose—she is getting a headache from the whistling—and Papa pours himself a glass of vodka—he refuses to look Zhenya in the eye.

"No," Papa says after too many minutes staring into his drink. "I don't care what Anton offers. We can't go back to that, Antonina. We can't."

"They'll find out one way or another. At least then, we'd be close—we could keep an eye on her . . ."

Wee-oo-toot. Zhenya giggles to himself. My heart aches just watching my little brother. His high cheekbones, dusted with a fine powder of freckles just like Mama and me; same straight black hair and wispy frame we inherited from Papa. His face is one of pure bliss. He finds perfection in those three notes.

Papa looks at him, skin too tight around his eyes. "He needs us more, Anya. All the children like him at the clinic do."

"It's glorified brainwashing," Mama said, lip curled. "They'll never be cured of their illnesses."

"Then let me try it my way," Papa said, and reaches straight for me.

I scream, but my voice is a shadow, and the darkness is filling in like a fresh grave.

Wee-oo-toot.

I wake up tangled in thin bed sheets, the harsh floodlights in the courtyard spraying blue across the dark room. I reach for Mama and Zhenya, expecting to find them by my side, but there's emptiness, just too many unclaimed cots. Floorboards creak in the distance as a guard makes his rounds.

The dream has the fuzzy shape of a memory, although I can't remember it actually occurring. What were my parents afraid of and what were they doing to me? And where did this strange vision come from? Cold sweat presses like a hand on my forehead.

I burrow back into the sheets, shivering, and squeeze my eyes closed again.

CHAPTER 10

WITHIN A WEEK, our days at the mansion become routine as we prepare for our first real mission: in the mornings we hone our psychic abilities, learning to apply them to different scenarios, and in the afternoon we study spycraft—conducting surveillance, or luring out information from someone on their guard. I reintroduce food to my system carefully, like I'm building up a tolerance to poison; my socks still slink down my ankles, but at least my cheekbones no longer look like lethal weapons. Larissa keeps me sane in the evenings. Without her distracting me, chatting about her favorite radio show, my frustration would have swallowed me up already. Major Kruzenko plays our mother, our headmistress, and our warden, a softer presence to counter Colonel Rostov who makes thankfully rare appearances to check on our progress.

Only when Kruzenko departs one day with Ivan and Sergei do I have my chance. Everyone is gathered in the ballroom, reading or chatting or listening to Valentin practice his scales;

even the pet spiders let their shoulders droop and bow their heads toward one another to gossip. I'm among them one moment, on the periphery of their conversation, and gone the next, wedging the knife between the door to Kruzenko's office and the rotted wood frame. It pops open easily. I'm inside with the door latched again behind me before I hear the ostinato of heavy boots resume their well-trod patrol route.

The office is tinier than I expected, and disappointingly bare. The room is little more than an oversized closet, stuffed with a heavy oak desk that must've been a nightmare to fit through the doorway and a tiny window, grimy and fogged, that overlooks the shedding autumn trees. I was hoping for at least a file cabinet, but I settle into the creaky chair behind the desk and test the first drawer: empty. The second holds pencils rubber banded together and a hand-cranked sharpener. My nerves crackle, bracing for disappointment as I tug open the final drawer—

My heart slams against my ribs. Lying at the bottom of the drawer is a single folder stamped SEKRET.

I pry the folder out. Something rattles underneath it—a framed photo. It's old—a harsh image of stark blacks and crisp, pleated whites, too sharply contrasted to show the image's subtleties. A crowd of people are wedged into a narrow metal room, like the hold of a ship, all of them wearing soldier uniforms. I immediately recognize the gaunt, blazing stare of Colonel Rostov, though he's almost smiling and has a flop of pale hair covering his forehead. The woman beside him, raising a glass toward the camera in salute—could that be Kruzenko? All her fat's been trimmed away, revealing a strong, sturdy gymnast's body.

Her shoulder presses seamlessly against Rostov's, as if they're cut from the same block of stone. Another man, on Rostov's other side, must be the twins' father. I'd know that smug grin anywhere. A few others glance toward the camera, annoyed to have their card game disrupted, but I don't recognize the rest. These must be the original psychic spies, the ones who fought in the Patriotic War like Sergei said.

I set the picture aside and reach for the folder. It's too thin. My hope ebbs even before I open it. Sure enough, it's only a few pages of handwritten notes with today's date across the top.

MIKHAIL: attempts to increase distance of mind reading progressing slowly. No improvements from last week's test at a 20-m range.

LARISSA: still lacking clarity on Veter 1 test results. Too far in future? Too uncertain? Reminded her there are lives at stake, but she remains frustratingly blasé. I quote: "Even if I saw someone's death, the events that led to it would be so knotted together, who knows what one factor you'd need to change? You people have set these events into motion knowing what could happen. I'm just the wind vane." Will consult with Rostov on re-education options to correct attitude.

YULIA: works best with objects that have no emotional attachment. Still too easily *overwhelmed with emotionally charged memories. I see no problem in keeping her in that state—if she cannot control the emotions entering her, then she remains easier to subdue.*

Easier to subdue? I start to crumple the paper, then stop myself. So much for controlling my emotions. I shove the framed picture and the notes back in the desk drawer and slam it shut.

There has to be more here. Some clue, something that will lead me to Mama and Zhenya, some hint that'll allow me to escape. I run my fingers along the walls, the desk, searching for hidden compartments and begging for memories to jump out at me. Nothing. There's nothing. Like a criminal wiping away his fingerprints, Rostov must have scrubbed it clean, just like he did to Mama's necklace, destroying the memories beyond anything he'd want me to see.

I sink my palms into the desktop. I *have* to break past the barrier. I have to know where they are! White light prickles against my skin, pins and needles, the onset of numbness, but I keep pushing. "Where are they?" I sob. "Where is my family?"

The static wave bursts through me, knocking me back into the chair. My hands ache as if from a flash burn. His echo stings like an atom bomb under the wood grain. Embarrassment scalds my cheeks as the room around me slowly rights itself, the white flare of hatred receding. There's nothing here for me.

I lean against the door, watching the other side through the wood. I'm still not good at this—I can only catch a murky glimpse of what lies on the other side—but it's enough for me to tell when one of the guards strolls by. The door opens silently and I slip out.

I follow the strains of Valentin's piano playing back to the ballroom. There's a melody in my head, three notes buoying me from utter despair at making no progress in Kruzenko's office. The notes that Zhenya whistled in my dream. I need to hear them again.

I hover beside the piano bench. Each note ebbs away a bit of my anger, erodes my barrier just a little more. Valentin glances up, his eyes holding mine for a few bars while the notes flutter on, then he tapers the melody into a graceful set of closing chords.

I study the black and white bars, then plink out the three-note melody in the high register of keys. Artlessly, I admit, but at least I summon up an ancient music lesson to hit the right ones. The notes are the heart of one of Zhenya's convoluted, unending symphonies that sprawl across multiple folios of sheet music. I can almost see him whistling the tune, but the image distorts in my mind when I look at it straight on. After all, it was just my dream, not a real memory that I can cling to.

Valentin flexes his fingers over the lower register, hesitating for a moment, then plays a shimmery, chorded version of the three notes. His chin tilts toward me in a tiny, questioning lift.

I plink out the notes again. Each one drains a little bit more of my frustration away, leaving a blissful emptiness behind. Space for me to breathe.

Valentin improvises with the three notes, turning them into a phrase, then variations on that phrase, hands dancing along the keys. He drums them out along the lower register, then reaches around me to twinkle in the high octaves with a red-cheeked smile. He pulls his hands back together and, diminuendo, the notes trip over each other, rising and falling, punctuated by a sharp chord here and there, growing and growing until I can almost hear the brass section exploding behind us in a Rachmaninov-style riot of luxurious noise.

Finally he reins it in, taming the chaos of Zhenya-inspired noise until it's just a fragile, dimming light, and it subsides into the final chords that are so perfect that I can't imagine anything happening in that moment except this ending, even though I desperately want the song to go on and on. Valentin is shaking. A droplet of sweat creeps down his temple toward his jaw, sneaking under the thick black earpiece of his glasses. His eyes are clamped shut like the piano itself scares him. His fingers slip off the keys of the final chord and drift down into his lap.

I squeeze my eyes shut for a moment. *Thank you.* I mean to say it, but the words lodge in my throat; I can't break the silence of the song's memory. Valentin watches, stoic, as I back away from the piano—from Zhenya's music. From the exposed wiring of my brother's knotted-up brain. I have to see him again. I have to get to Moscow State or some sort of school, to the life I left behind, here or somewhere else, and break the Zhenya code.

Someone claps politely; Larissa is tucked onto a dining chair behind me, legs crossed beneath her and bare toes wiggling. A notebook lies open in her lap, covered in squiggles and swirls. "You were smiling for a minute there," she says. "You should smile more often."

Of course my reaction is to scowl.

She shrugs. "Or not. But it wouldn't kill you to be happy every now and then." She pats the chair beside her. "You'll be here longer than you like, you know. But not so long that you'll lose yourself. I'm confident you'll find your way."

My heart beats faster, but there's no malice in her smile like I'd expect from someone like Masha. "I don't know what you mean." I sink into the chair beside her.

"It's funny," she says, her eyes becoming unfocused from mine as if she's looking at something beyond me. "You can see backward, and I can see forward."

I don't find it very funny at all, not after my failure in Kruzenko's office. "Doesn't it overwhelm you? Seeing everything before it comes."

"I don't see everything," she says. "I see all the *possible* everythings."

"That sounds even worse." I muster a weak laugh.

"You should ask Kruzenko to help you with your power sometime. I think you'd be surprised how much she can help."

I shudder before I can stop myself. "I don't think that's a good idea—"

"Trust me," Larissa says, with a tap to her temple. "I think you'll feel better if you do."

I find Kruzenko in the parlor the next day after lessons, writing out more of her notes. The fireplace is dark, and the radio off; the only light comes from a brassy sconce on the wall. It edges Kruzenko in a sinister glow.

Her eyes dart toward me for a moment, acknowledging my

presence, but she keeps writing until I speak. "I want to control it," I say, my voice too frail. I clear my throat and try again. "The emotions and memories. You're not challenging me, but I want to be stronger."

She sets aside her notes with a satisfied grin. "Very well. I think I know just the thing." She throws open grungy cabinets, rummaging through them as she talks. "Tell me more about how you used your powers before you came to us."

Before my abduction, she means. I will not call it anything else, lest I grow too comfortable. But I do want to control my powers: I will need every last tool at my disposal to find Mama and Zhenya and escape. If we are rewarded for good behavior, like Sergei claims, then I will swallow the KGB's propaganda and lay golden eggs of psychic brilliance until Kruzenko has no choice but to lead me to them.

"This children's toy. How might a person use it, if it was their dearest possession?" She holds up a stuffed teddy bear with dingy, matted fur and awkward lumps where the stuffing has shifted from years of use. "A happy child might play with it, walk around with it tucked loosely in his arms, yes?"

"Sure," I say. The black glass eyes staring at me are scratched and worn down. A lighter-colored band of fur around its neck marks where a ribbon might once have been tied.

"But what would a sad child do, when burdened with sad thoughts? She might curl up in bed and squeeze it fiercely while she cries." She smiles, though it's fake—her muscles have forgotten how to handle a real grin. I can't reconcile her with the radiant woman frozen in that photograph. "We have all done this, have we not?"

I shrug. I never had stuffed animals. I had a little brother who needed my love and care, and two parents whose words salved whatever wounds couldn't be cleaned with soap and ointment. But Kruzenko and Rostov have taken that from me.

"Please, sit." She beckons me to the couch. "I must warn you there are strong memories attached to this toy. Push too hard, and it will punish you. You must learn control if you don't wish to be overwhelmed."

"I can handle it." I hold out my hand, but she drops the bear into my lap. One of its black glass eyes looks up at me, while the other gazes off into the middle distance somewhere past my shoulder. I can do this. I won't let it overwhelm me like the desk in her office. I snatch the bear by his cylindrical arm.

skeletal girl screaming

there are gravestones in her hair, her blond hair, and fingernails

eyes watching from behind glass

wood between her teeth as she slices their souls away

I drop the bear like I've been scalded, and my knees jerk up under my chin. The guard chuckles until Kruzenko shoots him a nasty look.

"A pity, Yulia. You hear me, but you do not listen." She nudges the bear toward me with her shoe. "Start delicately before you plunge in."

I'm shaking with cast-off memories. This terror, this unfocused panic—I've sensed it before. The bed in our dormitory. "Anastasia," I say. "What did you do to her?"

"Me? I can't be blamed for what happened. But why not see for yourself?"

I lower my legs and pick up the bear between my thumb and index finger, gingerly, like the diseased, disgusting rag it is. Surface memories skitter off its fur and onto my skin—childhood tea parties and make-believe ballet recitals in a cramped communal home.

"Much better. See if you can press a little further while holding the deepest memories at bay."

Whispers stir around my feet like fog as I wade into the frosty lake of thoughts. The fog thickens, and the water chills; memories fly past me, swarming now, on insect's wings. Nasty thoughts, happy ones, thoughts that no one would dare to speak. Anastasia hears them all. They soak into her skin. She can't get rid of them; she can't shake them away. I try to dispel the fog and swat the insects, but more keep coming. They are full of secrets; she's drowning in their pain and selfishness. A man—a boy?—tries to wipe them clean, but it's a sponge trying to soak up the sea. An ocean of the other voices' inner worlds, smothering, crushing, heavy. Her skin's too tight with their secrets. She needs to slice it open, pour them out. I see it, and like her, I just long to *forget* . . .

"Easier when you show some restraint, isn't it?" Kruzenko says.

I set the bear in my lap, so it's not in contact with my skin. "She was overwhelmed by all the thoughts she heard."

Kruzenko nods. "Now go deeper."

Anastasia's memories hum through the air. I know how she

feels when she's going mad with the voices, when the psychic electricity turns her inside out. I see the razor glinting under dank bathroom lights. I don't need to watch it slice her veins open. "I can't." I'm already bracing for Kruzenko's slap.

But none comes. She collects the bear and places it back inside a desk drawer.

"You will have to accept all aspects of your power someday," she says, leaning against the desk. "You can't be afraid. You must strengthen your shield, too. You take emotions in without pushing them out. Do not try to be an empath—one who shares the feelings of others. You'll torment yourself that way."

I work one thumbnail beneath the other. I can't watch that razor. I can't listen to Anastasia's head full of whispers or see the dark eyes that track her every move. "How did she get this way?" I ask. Surely our powers alone can't do this to a person. Is this the exception, the abnormality? Or is madness the usual path—our inevitable fate?

"She thought she could cultivate her powers on her own, without our assistance. She hungered for more and more, when she wasn't ready. This is the fate of all of those who do not learn control. She did not listen to our rules." Kruzenko holds her hand out to usher me out the door. "She fought against our teachings, and it drove her mad."

CHAPTER 11

WE START OUR first real operation with one of Larissa's visions: Red Square, a specific date, a member of the *Veter 1* engineering team. Too many possibilities, she claims, to pinpoint the exact member. Then Misha and Ivan confirm her vision on a trip to the Academy of Interplanetary Sciences. There's a traitor in the team's ranks. He or she is plotting to smuggle secret rocket designs for the *Veter 1* out of the academy and deliver them to a waiting American spy in Red Square. But Misha and Ivan can't get close enough to identify the traitor. Under their cover as a school tour, they have to keep their distance, the thoughts of the *Veter 1* team members blurring through the heavy secure doors like snowflakes melting into a single drift.

Now it is my turn to put my skills to use. My first time out of the mansion in the month that I've been there, and I can't be more relieved. While the others edged us closer to the *Veter* conspiracy, Kruzenko's been choking me with KGB training manuals. Leave it to the KGB to make even spycraft read as dull as economic dissertations, and anyway, the manuals are ill-suited for our particular type of work. Psychics don't need complicated routes to lose a pursuer, not when they can read the pursuer's mind. And it's not hard to tell an asset is lying when their fear of not being believed is woven through their thoughts.

So I am sent to wander Red Square, that massive pool of people and noise in the Kremlin's shadow, in hopes of feeling— something. A fresh memory, trailed behind our traitor like a spelunker's cord. An overwhelming sense of wrongness, of betrayal. I will not be alone, of course. I have a pet spider of my own now, Pavel—ox-shouldered, with a grim reaper face. I suspect there will be others anchored through the crowd. But they are also sending Sergei with me, for reasons unexplained. He won't be using his remote viewing powers—Masha will cover that from back at the mansion—and his skill at reading the average person's mind isn't much better than mine when I'm not touching them. I suspect it has more to do with the smug little grin that wedges onto Kruzenko's lips when I listen to *The Promise*, Sergei's favorite radio drama, with him in the evenings.

Two guards—rifles in hand, naturally—swing open the door to the van. With late autumn sunlight glaring down on us, I stagger out of the van behind Sergei, cupping my hand over my eyes so I can see, and my breath falters a little. We're at the bottom of Red Square, staring up the spiraling, swimming slope of cobblestones. The high-walled Kremlin fortress bounds us on the left, while the white filigree Universal Store—a grandiose shopping arcade, a memorial to our indulgent Imperialist days— lines our right. Over the horizon are the Easter-egg turrets of Saint Basil's Cathedral and the jagged ziggurat of Vladimir

Lenin's crypt, where he lies stuffed with formaldehyde and wax, preserved and displayed in glass like our saints of old.

And in between it all: thousands upon thousands of people, all their thoughts ready to crash and break upon us like waves, drowning us in their unfiltered, uncensored monologues.

"Well," Sergei says, turning up the collar on his wool coat, "where should we begin?"

"If you were planning to commit treason, where would you go?" I reply.

He strokes his chin, feigning deep thought. "Probably not Lenin's tomb. That might be in poor taste."

I smile despite myself. "Or maybe that's what they're hoping we'd think."

Sergei looks me over, some of the brightness ebbing from his grin. "You're nervous, aren't you?" He nudges me with his elbow. "Don't be. You know how to stay in control of your power."

"Not like this," I say. But it's not just the crowds. I want to perform well—convince Kruzenko and Rostov that I deserve to see my family. I just wish I didn't have to destroy someone else's life to do it. Someone else's attempt to stand against the Party. I watch Sergei through the corner of my eye, wondering if he carries this same sense of guilt—if he helped them track me down.

Old women hobble past us with anemic bread loaves and browning lettuce clutched to their chests. Their pantyhose sag around bloated ankles; their scarves are threadbare and frayed. They smell like beets, like the fallen bits of food that cling to the range and burn when it's turned on again. But then they brush against me.

Summers—they think of summers in the wheat fields, when

they were young girls kissing their beaux, and praying before gilded icons of the Romanov emperors and the Holy Mother. They don't like to think of how things are now, fifty years later, but they must sometimes; one worries about whether her grandson's boots will last him for the winter before he outgrows them, and prays (very quietly, without a bowed head or folded hands) his ration comes up in time.

The men are few. They are the ones left behind by the Great Patriotic War, whether by cowardice, fate, or dumb luck. They don discolored furry hats, and are much heavier with their worries. They try to store those thoughts in vodka, pickling and preserving them like Lenin, but I touch their arms—I know what they fear. Marching boots on the stairwell in the middle of the night. Black vans with no headlights. Jail cells. Wetting themselves. And the endless cold, white cold of Siberian prisons, if they're lucky enough to survive.

"Anything?" Sergei asks, watching me with a playful grin. I shake my head and plunge ahead of him.

I hold my hands at my sides, fingers splayed, trying to touch everyone who passes me. I'm like a gypsy thief, but instead of pickpocketing, I'm snatching up thoughts. Hopes and loves and hates and fears and sorrows and blessings and curses and prayers—it's churning, it's thrilling, it's taking over *me*.

But there are only tiny acts of defiance around me: black market traders, ration swappers, resentment of the whole Soviet system shuttered away. Nothing as drastic as what the *Veter* team member intends.

Pavel shoves through the crowd and snatches me by the arm. He doesn't say anything, but I hear him thinking; he believes

I'm trying to run. "I'm here," I say, yanking my arm free—though I don't believe I could if he didn't let me—and march determinedly through the crowd.

Sergei jogs up to me. "Trying to lose me?"

"Not just yet," I say. "You haven't told me what happened on *The Promise* last night while I was practicing with Kruzenko."

He laughs, big and brassy. "Ahh, so that's why you put up with me. Well, Grigorii was taking the night train out of Leningrad, right? Only Natasha woke up and realized he was gone . . ."

Pavel hovers behind us as we push toward the northern end of Red Square, watched over by the red crenellated historical museum. I'm still coming up empty-handed; no spies leap out of the crackle and hum of workers around us. But if I can't bring back a prize for the KGB, then at least I can conduct an exercise of my own.

Hypothesis: Our guards are not psychics themselves.

Experiment: I let down my Shostakovich shield as Sergei chatters on. I feel exposed without it. Kruzenko was right; it really does become a basic brain function. No matter. I steer toward the pink and green confection of a church at the northeast corner of the square. I concentrate all my thoughts on an imaginary tunnel leading out of there, on ditching them in the crypts and slamming the gate closed between us.

Result: Sergei's narrative dissipates in a puff of his breath and he tilts his head. "Yulia, what are . . ." I hold up one finger to silence him and peer over my shoulder toward Pavel. He's close on our heels, but nothing in his granite face indicates suspicion—more than normal, anyway. I turn back from the church as Shostakovich rushes up around me.

Conclusion: Further testing required without Sergei second-guessing me.

"I thought you were through with that," Sergei mutters, turned away from Pavel. He speaks down toward his chest so only I can hear.

I shake my head. I don't owe him an explanation, but I don't like the dull glaze to his eyes. Like I've betrayed him somehow. "It isn't what you think."

My fingertips trail the ridge of a concrete barrier. If I were selling secrets to Russia's enemies, how would I feel? What would I be thinking? Fear, certainly. But determination, as well. Hope—for I would feel there was some good to be gained by my act, or why go to the trouble? Why else do traitors risk their lives, their minds?

I stop so suddenly that two old ladies crash into me and shuffle off, muttering curses that only God is meant to hear. Then a woman's voice prickles at me, looping and looping on itself in a hysterical chant.

I have to find them. Why can't I find them? He said they'd come for me!

I press deeper into the echoing memory and see a woman, lugging a leather case at her side. I can't focus on her face—it shudders and warps, like there's something buzzing under the surface—but she has to be who we're searching for. I can't explain the certainty that settles like a stone in my gut, but I know it's her. Who is she looking for? The spies she's selling secrets to? Something in her frantic thoughts hints that there's more to the exchange.

"This way." We weave back in the direction of Saint Basil's

Cathedral. Its pastel onion domes are flaking, washed out from the Northern sun's angled stare. Scaffolding clothes the church's lower portion, though no workers climb around on the rig. It's like a censor blacking out a past we're not supposed to see.

We move alongside the Universal Store's façade, each column shedding a fine powder of the woman's voice. I see her in fragments, like the shattered tiles in a mosaic. Blond hair, ghostly eyes. She moves like a marionette, too frail to direct herself, guided instead by her obsessive chant.

Hypothesis: There is more to our hunt for scientist traitors than Rostov has said.

Experiment: I must find this woman. If not for Rostov, then for myself.

Sergei trudges beside me, hands buried deep in his coat pockets. "I just thought you were coming around," he says. *Bozhe moi*, is he still hung up on this? "It's not a bad life we have. And it'll get even better once we're full members of the KGB."

"Are you joking? We're *prisoners*. How is that not a bad life?"

"You would rather live in a concrete apartment cell like these people?" He waves his hand around the Square. "We're prisoners because they can't trust us yet. It won't always be that way."

I nestle into the flowery eaves of the Universal Store's entrance and press my fingertips into the carved stone grooves. She was headed this way—I have to find her again. Memories tumble upon memories, amplifying like waves, coiling up like genetic code. Airplanes soaring overhead as boots strike the cobblestones in unison—the Red Army on display. An American pilot dragged from his plane and paraded across Red Square.

Women sobbing as they bid their soldiers farewell. The crowds roil in the sea of changing fashions, changing leaders, changing governments. Drab worker's garb and frothy silk gowns and fur coats. Stalin screaming at a podium; Lenin pacing the stage with predatory grace. The last Romanov emperor, stiff-backed and trembling. It's harder and harder to part the smoke. The woman has to be buried in here, somewhere—

"Yulia!" Sergei grips my shoulders, shaking me from the past. "What's wrong with you?"

My hand's twitching to some phantom rhythm. Decades and decades pump through my veins. But something's wrong— they're rattling through me, tinged in shrill, ear-piercing noise. It reminds me of the sonic churn around Rostov. I try to focus on Sergei, but he only appears in stuttering images, the Square shifting around me.

"I'll be fine." I swallow, my throat parched. "I lost her trail. She has to be nearby . . ."

Sergei shakes his head. "You're pushing yourself too hard. Take it easy, all right? There's no hurry."

Easy for him to say. If I don't find her, then I won't get to see Mama and Zhenya, and then—and then . . .

Her image flutters over my fingers, slipping up my coat sleeve like winter chill. She plays a game of her own. She lugs the bag behind her, a black-market barter for her freedom. There she was, just minutes ago, along the concrete risers behind Vladimir Lenin's tomb.

"It should be here." I sink onto the bench, palms grinding into the concrete. "She dropped the briefcase here." I see her leaving it behind, but immediately after is the electrified fence of a missing memory. Rostov? It couldn't be. Why would he block me from finding the traitor?

Sergei sits down beside me. "It's all right. You can describe her for Rostov. He'll understand." He claps me on the shoulder, like I'm his little sister. Like I'm keeping him from whatever he'd rather be doing—sleeping, or practicing at the rink.

"Finished?" Pavel asks.

I nod, swallowing down my rising frustration. I let them guide me through the crowd once more. The line of—mourners? pilgrims? thrill-seekers?—winds around Lenin's ziggurat. I wonder what I might see if I touched that waxy face. Is a man like Rostov, calling for war, just what Lenin had in mind for the future of his great communist experiment?

Sergei frowns. "Do you hear that?"

As soon as he says it, a wave of static crushes me, sending the world spinning. "Rostov," I say. The noise needles at my brain.

Sergei's curled over, wincing. "No. This is . . . different. Stronger." He exchanges a look with Pavel. "We need to leave. Now."

Pavel moves behind us to usher us along. The woman's thoughts lash out again, clawing at my skin as I push through the crowd. They resemble Kruzenko's after she's been around Rostov—that crackling live wire. She can't be far from us.

They aren't coming. Oh god, it didn't work. How dare they use me as bait? Where are they? He swore they'd come!

I scan the crowd, but her frenzied thoughts force everything through a shattered-glass view. I can't focus; I can barely see through the black spots darting across my eyes. A hand shoots out. Snatches me by the wrist.

It's one of them. Bozhe moi, *I've found them. Come quickly, she's here—*

The woman stands before me, jumbled thoughts crackling around her. Blond curls spill out of her pale blue scarf and chalky lines cut through her too-young face. She stares at me with eyes guilty, haunted, dark.

Her mouth works silently. *Wait*—she thinks, grip tightening on my wrist. *The Americans are hunting you, little girl. Stay right here. It's you they want. You can set me free—*

Sergei steps between the woman and me. "Is there a problem here, comrade?"

Come with me! She screams at me, static sparking over her words. *Don't you get it, little girl? This isn't a game!*

But Sergei breaks her grip, throwing a nasty glare over his shoulder. "Are you all right?" he asks me, rubbing my wrist where her nails left little crescents of red. "Where's that awful noise coming from?"

Hunting us. Her American allies are hunting us. The words stamp into my skull. "I—No. She's not—" But I don't know what to say. I want to turn her in to Rostov to earn a visit with Mama. But if there's a man like Rostov controlling her . . . The only thing that scares me more than Rostov might just be a man like Rostov who *isn't* on our side.

A dreadful new hypothesis comes to me: Rostov and Valentin aren't the only ones who can wipe things clean.

CHAPTER 12

"MASHA, HAVE YOU SEEN my gray sweater?"

I tear through my duffle bag of laundry once more, then dig into the pile at my feet. My wardrobe is only what the KGB has provided for me—five sweaters, three wool skirts, a pair of trousers, and cream blouses to wear underneath. But now there are only four sweaters. A small problem, I know. But the ration rat in me is panicking, parceling out future clothing options, budgeting survival under new constraints. The gray one was the warmest—a necessity for fleeing into the face of oncoming winter.

I try to keep the hysteria building in my lungs from rising up and choking me. It's too soon to run, I know, but after what I saw yesterday in Red Square . . . I have to be ready. The Americans offered that woman a trade—the *Veter 1* design plans in exchange for a way out. *A way out.* They can be reasoned with. Bartered with—just like my black market games.

Masha shrugs, flipping through an old issue of *Pravda*. "Maybe someone mistook it for a dishrag."

I roll my eyes. "Larissa? How about you?"

"It happens," is all Larissa says. She keeps doodling in her notebook.

Wonderful. I toss one last look at Masha and scan her bunk for potential hiding places. I'm sure she's taken it, but if I go digging through her belongings, she'll go crying to Kruzenko. There are worse things she could have taken from my stash. Military rations I won from Sergei in a card game. A heavy blanket swiped from the linen closet. I scoop my laundry into my arms and storm toward the basement to use the washbasin and drying racks.

"Yulia Andreevna. Just the young lady I was hoping to see."

Major Kruzenko blocks the rickety basement stairs as I climb them after leaving my laundry to dry. Light spills around her so she is only a dark form. I stop a few steps beneath her, arms folded across my chest.

"Colonel Rostov would like to speak with you. We need to follow up on yesterday's Red Square mission."

My blood cools, though I've improved my musical shield enough that she shouldn't notice. "Sure." I follow her to the study through its double doors. The guards stay outside, which somehow frightens me more. I hear Rostov's awful churning sounds before he even turns to face me.

"Major Kruzenko's care is agreeing with you, I see," Rostov says. His polished boots click together at the heels, and he tucks his red-banded hat under one arm. "You are no longer a starved dog, hmm?"

"It's more food than we need," I say. Though I could use some extra padding for my escape. Winter's already laid an icy base coat on the ground.

"Nonsense. Growing girls and boys . . . and we must feed the mind, too. It is our greatest treasure, isn't it, comrade?"

Right now my mind is shredding apart from the sound and feel of him—his thoughts, his focus, his *power*—but I manage a pitiful nod and sit in the lumpy armchair he offers me. Kruzenko stands watch at my side.

"So." Rostov sits opposite me, wispy fingers laced on his knee. "In your report, you state that you were trailing someone you believe belonged to the *Veter* engineering team, but you were not able to locate him, and when you reached the location where you believed he dropped the bag full of documents, it had already been removed."

"That's right," I say, my ribs knitting together. I can't breathe. Shostakovich's music crashes around me, Yevtushenko's voice rumbles; he can't possibly miss my panic right now.

"You said that the location of the documents had been wiped clean? That you believe the Americans have someone like Valentin and me. A 'scrubber,' as you called it." He shares a tiny laugh with Kruzenko, like he's flattered by the name.

I manage to jerk my chin in a nod. "A segment of time had been blanked out. Just like you did with my mother's necklace."

Anger flashes across his face, lightning striking and then gone. "You deduced all this from a few seconds of missing memories?"

"N—no. There were thoughts, too, with the same sound to them. The sound that you make . . ." I'm cringing, inward and out. But I would be anyway. Just being near him is enough for that.

He leans toward me, breath heavy with cabbage stew. "But you did not see this person. This . . . traitor." I shake my head, sinking back into the chair. "But I am not convinced of this."

Rostov's noise blasts through me like warring radio frequencies. "Anton, you promised—" Kruzenko says, but her voice fizzles out. I can't help it—the blond woman leaps out of my thoughts, graceful as a deer leaping from the birch trees, and I can't force her back in. Brass blaring, strings sawing back and forth, Yevtushenko's words ringing across the forest. *Oh, my Russian people; those with unclean hands have made a joke of your purity.*

I have to protect her. She stares at me with frightened fawn eyes and her panicked words knit themselves into the music. I can't tug them free without the whole symphony crashing down around me. She's stolen documents, she's trying to escape. She made a bargain with the Americans and they sent her to find *us*, the psychic team. Her darkest secret ossifies, it is clay and bone, it's there for Rostov to see, jutting from my brain, waiting for the harvest.

"There she is." Rostov isn't angry. He doesn't even sound surprised. "I thought she might be in there somewhere."

I'm trying to cram her back into a drawer much too small. I won't let them use me this way. I try to stand, but my legs are numb. Major Kruzenko holds me down as bile singes my throat.

"You should be happy. You are helping the State. And you are paying your debt." Rostov reaches for my chin, and his touch is glass shattering inside my brain. Deeper, deeper—an icepick lobotomy, every note of my musical shield splitting apart like atoms. He reaches right through the wall of Shostakovich and wrests the traitor out me. Notes, fragments of words, images crash down on him. There's nothing I can do to stop it. He's brushed aside my only trick like sweeping snow from the windowsill.

I slump back into the chair, my thoughts tender and bruised where something's been pried out of them. My heart pounds like I've been running for hours through a blizzard.

Kruzenko clears her throat. "Well? Is she part of the *Veter* team? We'll have a sketch made. Compare it to the *Veter* scientists' records."

Rostov stares through me. Veins dance on his forehead; his Adam's apple strains against the collar of his shirt. "I'm more interested in her handler. Another 'scrubber.' That fraying around her thoughts . . ."

"And this other scrubber is hunting us?" Kruzenko asks.

I manage a weak nod. A look passes between Kruzenko and Rostov: a hasty widening of the eyes, quickly stopped. "I will deal with this scrubber myself," Rostov says.

Kruzenko rocks on her sensibly low heels. "Shall we send a team for the traitor woman once she's identified?"

"No, not yet. If these American spies think they are hunting us, then let her play bait a little longer." He stands, hands swinging to his sides. They're too long, even on his tall frame—his fingertips nearly reach his knees. He's too wiry, too intense; he's a man boiled away to his base part, that awful, powerful brain. A scrubber. The word itself rubs me raw. "Surely Khruschev himself cannot ignore so blatant an American violation of our truce as this. And if he does . . ." Rostov looks back at me, oozing a cyanide-sweet smile. "Well done, Yulia Andreevna."

Major Kruzenko pats me on the shoulder. "You mustn't hide things from us. This is how we maintain order and keep you safe from our enemies." But she's breathing too sharply; when she touches me, I sense her unease as well.

Rostov's spindly fingers pull something from his pocket—Mama's necklace. My throat clamps shut as he hands it to me. "Funny that you should mention this," he says, curving a serrated smile. "I thought you might like to have it."

My fist clenches around the medallion. Of course it's been wiped clean. It feels less like a reward, coming from him, and more like a warning.

CHAPTER 13

I MAKE MY WAY OUT of that room somehow—I don't remember what combination lock of pleasantries get me away from them. Yevtushenko and Shostakovich rage in my head, my own shield scolding me for my failure. *I am but one soundless scream above the thousand thousand buried here.*

I charge for the staircase, nearly plowing headfirst into Sergei. "Watch it!" he cries, catching me by the shoulders in his solid grasp. "What's the matter with you?"

"I want to be alone," I growl.

Actually, what I want is to grab the supplies from my stash and scale the walls of this prison. But then I think of the American scrubber coming for us and remember those walls keep him out as surely as they keep us in.

"Come on, Yul, you'll feel better if you talk about it. Right now your head sounds like an angry . . . storm cloud. Of anger."

Distant piano music fills the silence between us as we stare at each other. Finally, I crack a grin.

"Okay," Sergei says, "so I'm no Pushkin."

"I'm sure Vitaly Davidov isn't much of a poet, either."

"Good, maybe I'll join him in the Hockey Hall of Fame someday. Really, though—what's wrong?" He takes his hands off my shoulders, but their warmth lingers.

"Nothing." I crumple into the banister, which groans back at me. "Everything. I don't know."

Sergei starts back up the stairs. "I know just the place to cheer you up. Somewhere not on the official tour."

That piques my interest. Do the guards know about it? I am Yulia the ration rat, after all. I'll stash away every crumb of knowledge that I can.

He leads me deep into the house's bones: an inner hallway somewhere within the second floor. He opens the door to a narrow linen closet, reeking of mothballs and dust. "The nobles who lived here in tsarist times built this passage," he says, fiddling with the sidewall of the closet. "Supposedly, they hid here when the first wave of the communist forces swept through the city." There's a soft click and the wall pops back. A hidden panel. Sergei squeezes through—no mean feat, given his bulk—and I follow through with more ease.

"That's a better history lesson than I'd expect from a hockey hooligan," I say with a smirk.

He rolls his eyes before slipping deeper into the darkened passage. "I'm not all muscle, you know. Not that anyone believes it. Even my parents . . ." He trails off, tension rising in him like steam, and Tchaikovsky's *War of 1812* overture marches through the air. I feel a pang of embarrassment for my selfishness. I'm not the only one kept from my loved ones.

We fall into an uneasy silence as we feel our way down the dark corridor. I tug my sweater sleeves down around my hands to keep from touching the narrow walls; I'm not ready just yet to see the nobles' fate at the hands of Lenin and his Bolshevik army. "Who else knows about this passage?" There's a hope beating its wings inside me, but I don't dare open its cage just yet.

He scowls. "Enough people. So don't get any ideas."

"The guards don't follow us in here?"

"Nah, they know it's a dead end. Here we are." He stops abruptly in front of me, and in the dim light I crash into him, our arms tangling together as I try to push off. "Careful there." He brushes a lock of dark hair from my face, my skin radiating heat where he touches me. I swallow hard and turn away.

"Great," I say. "So it's dark and smells like mold." I can make out vague shapes lurking around us, but little else.

"So impatient!" There a sharp click, and dull amber light floods the room.

Dozens of ornate frames lean against the far wall of the expansive chamber. Fringes of canvas dangle from their interiors where paintings have been cut out, and the wood frames are scarred where looters—or Lenin's thugs—stripped away gold leaf, but even ungilded, the frames are beautiful. I stride across the room and run my hands along one carved with interlocking seashells. A vibrant painting springs into my mind of tsarist-era Moscow, the hills ablaze with autumn leaves. Beyond the frames, bits of furniture are shrouded like cartoon ghosts. Sergei peels back the cloth on a sofa like he's unwrapping a mummy; green and gold brocade shimmers in the light.

"The old owners' leftovers," he says, before plopping onto the sofa, issuing tufts of dust into the air. He pats the spot beside him.

I saunter over and perch on the far end of the sofa. "I'm surprised there's anything left."

He shakes his head. "Just stuffy bourgeois junk. Hey," he says, face lighting up with a grin. "I wonder if you can read this stuff. You know." He runs his hand along the fabric. "Their memories."

The blond woman flickers through my mind, chased around by her desperate thoughts. If it weren't for my powers, Rostov wouldn't be plotting right now to use her as bait. "I . . . Some other time."

Sergei leans toward me, though he's far from touching me. I'm grateful for that. I've met too many Russian boys who, like all us ration rats, long to take what's not been given. I learned early how to fend them off with sharp words and flattened fists, but it didn't keep the shame at bay when a black market trader offered a barter I wasn't willing to make.

"I know you're only going along with this for your family," he says. "But it's what's best for you, too. You have to be safer here than you were on the run."

He's right, and that's without knowing about the American scrubber out there. I'm safe from starvation, strange men, and the hungering cold. But like most tough trades, the cost is far too steep. "I worry about my brother," I say. "He didn't get all the care he needed when we were fugitives, but he had my mother and me. His mental difficulties . . ." Gooseflesh rises on my arms.

I can't bear the thought of Rostov dealing with him, ripping out his thoughts like he just did mine.

"What's he like?" Sergei asks, still half-grinning. It thaws away some of my fear.

"Zhenya's brilliant. I've seen him write down the score for an entire symphony after listening to it once. It's only that he's . . . He's not quite engaged with the world around him. He lives in his own world inside his head, and it's very tough to pull him back into ours." I shake my head. "My parents were working with him at their old lab, researching his disorder or whatever it may be. He was better then," I admit.

"You must be good at coaxing him out, though. You can hear his thoughts, see his world . . ."

"I didn't have enough control over it at the time, and everything about his thoughts was so foreign, you know? Like another language."

Sergei pulls his knees up on the couch. "Sure, but foreign languages can be learned. I speak a little German . . . *Eine kleine Englisch*, too—I'm learning it for our work." His German is like chewing stale bread. "Listening to the Beatles helped me."

I stare at him blankly. "Beetles?"

"You're joking, right? You really have been living under a rock. Everyone knows who the Beatles are, even in Russia." He shakes his head, sending a spray of blond hair across his forehead. "This wicked British rock band. Valentin's got their record if you want to listen. All the lyrics are simple, but so clever."

"How did Valentin get their record? Isn't Kruzenko worried it'll brainwash him into a British sleeper agent or something?"

"Rostov gave it to him for good behavior. Some project they're working on." He shifts abruptly on the couch, his face tightening though he's still grinning. I'd taken his charming smile for a weapon, but I'm starting to think he uses it as a shield instead.

"Listen . . . When I first saw Rostov . . . Through the training exercise we did." I swallow, hard. The Russian thing to do would be to cling to every crumb of knowledge I've got, but information is currency, and Sergei seems like a good source. If he can lead me to the knowledge I need . . . "He was thinking about making our minds 'belong' to him."

Sergei shrugs, like this is nothing new. "He resents what the psychic program has become. Most of the spies from the Great Patriotic War are gone. He doesn't think we'll live up to their glory days. Stopping the Germans, saving thousands of lives. Now we pick at the bones for tiny victories here and there. I suppose he wants to make us in his own image, like the old guard."

"Hunting down spies and making dissidents vanish are only 'tiny' victories?" I ask.

"Compared to singlehandedly saving an entire city by guiding food supply trucks into Leningrad during the siege? Of course." Sergei drops his voice. "He's not a fan of Khruschev— says we appease the Americans too much now."

My eyebrows raise. "You mean he doesn't agree with the Party line? That sounds dangerous."

"It's not that he disagrees; he takes a more extreme approach. He's too impatient for cold wars. Thinks we should confront the Americans now, get it over with." Sergei leans back. "He wants the Party to do more to police our own, too. You know the old-guard types—they long for the glory days under Uncle Sta-lin, when people did as they were told, and didn't complain about 'freedom' because they had better things to worry about, like gangrene and Nazis."

Stalin, who—if whispered rumors are to be believed—sent more of his own people to die than Hitler ever did. Yes, a perfect model for reclaiming the Soviet Union.

"I don't see why he needs us at all," I say. "He's a much stron-ger psychic than any of us."

"Ah, but you're wrong. He's good at what he does—ripping people's brains open—but it only goes so far. He can't read the past like you or see the future like Larissa. And he can't spy on Johnny Kennedy getting a little kiss-kiss bang-bang in the White House, eh, if you know what I mean?" He elbows me in the ribs.

"*You* can remotely view inside the White House?" I say, du-bious.

That half-grin. "All right, so not yet. I'm working on it, but I have a harder time with places I've never been. Anyway, my point is, Rostov is only one man, and the more power he gets, the more people working for him, the more he wants. You know what they say about the security services—we have a third of the country keeping an eye on the other two-thirds."

"The more minds out there searching, the better," I say.

"Exactly. And between you and me, Rostov has always had one big problem. He never sees what he's not looking for."

I tuck that ripe little morsel away. Stamp it, seal it, wrap it in Shostakovich.

"Yulia . . ." Sergei stares at a tacky headless cherub sculpture for a long, heavy moment. The longer it takes for him to speak, the more his music swells. "I know you think there's a better life out there, somewhere, but it's safer here. I'm lucky—my parents always prepared me for what I was. I know it's harder for you, but won't you trust me?"

His music is suffocating me, crowding out my own music and thoughts until nothing is left. "It's not my parents' fault. They didn't know. I—I'm a wildling. Like Larissa."

"They didn't tell you," he corrects me.

"They didn't know!" I cry. "They would have told me. They couldn't have known."

A phantom dreamscape: Mama and Papa, bickering at the kitchen table. They're talking about monitoring someone. About me.

"Fine, so they didn't know. Is that what you want to hear?"

"No. I want to be rid of this," I say. "I don't want this power. All it's good for is hurting other people."

He tilts his head at me, studying me with the vacant, yet all-knowing stare of the saints on old Russian religious icons. "Is this about what happened in Red Square?"

I jam my fisted hands into my thighs, kneading away the static haze surrounding her memories. "She had a chance to escape, and I've ruined it for her."

"Yul. She's a *traitor*. It was the risk she took when she decided to break the law. At least this way, you get to look like a hero for the KGB, right?" He twists toward me, reaching for my knee. "You can't be afraid of what you are. You'll end up like Valentin, barely talking to anyone because you're afraid of yourself. That's no way to go through life."

"You told them," I say quietly. I want rage to flood my veins, but I feel nothing. I'm all hollowed out. "You told them that we saw her."

He winces and scoots back. "Rostov would have found out one way or another. I didn't want him to hurt you."

"Maybe that's not for you to choose," I snap.

"I only reported what I saw, all right? Nothing more. It's not like you asked me to lie." He scrubs a hand through his hair. "You've got to make peace with what you are, Yul. People with our abilities . . . we aren't fit for life outside of here. Can you imagine working at the factory, surrounded by the noise of machinery and everyone's dumb thoughts? What good would it do? You'd go mad like Anastasia did."

I slump back onto the sofa beside him, and a memory pricks me like a hidden straight pin. Images of women huddling in this room; the stifling pain of a corset packed with jewels, rubles, fine silverware. Panic constricts their chests tighter than the corset lacing.

I close my eyes and suck down a deep breath. He has a point. I don't want to be so vulnerable, waiting for the memories to overtake me, waiting for Rostov to pry them out of me.

"Those aren't my only choices. There has to be another way." I stand up. The narrow walls of the room are closing in. This isn't a hiding place. It's a morgue.

"*Bozhe moi*. Forget it. You want to be miserable, you go right ahead. Just thought you might like to have a friend."

"I don't need friends." I shove off the couch toward the concrete hallway. With the light on, I can see the mouse droppings lining the floor, the dead insects in stagnant puddles of water around the leaking pipes. I squeeze my way through the half-open panel into the back of the closet. I don't need anyone. When our livelihood is prying away secrets, I have to cling to every last scrap of me that I have left.

CHAPTER 14

"YULIA? YULIA. DARLING, wake up."

Mama shakes me out of a milky haze. Her face is only light and shadow at first; slowly, my eyes focus on her plump lips, her narrow nose, her sparkling diamond necklace like a smear of stars between her collarbones. I'm dreaming again, I tell myself, but it feels like a memory, just out of reach. We are still Party members. I glance down at my hands, punctuated with knobby little wrists and the countless phantom scars and bruises accumulated from playing childhood games with Zhenya. I can't be older than twelve.

"I'm awake." I force a smile through my stupor. But she doesn't smile back. That wrinkle appears between her eyebrows, hitching my heartbeat. "Mama? What's wrong?"

"It's time for us to go." She stands up from my bed with a twinkle of jewels, and that's when I see that she isn't just wearing her prized diamond necklace. Her strand of pearls, another ruby pendant, her St. George medallion, an emerald and gold bracelet, her Swiss watch . . . Her thick wool coat bulges with several layers of sweaters and blouses, and little round circles along its hem hint at kopecks tucked into the lining.

I struggle to sit up. My muscles aren't yet working, and my synapses are firing as if through tar. Outside my bedroom window, the night is still thick with indigo. "Where are we going?"

"I've already packed your things. Come on, Zhenya's waiting for us in the car."

"What about Papa?" I ask. My feet thud against my heavy winter boots at the side of my bed. Mama holds out a heavy dress and tights for me.

"Your father has already left. He won't be going with us." Her words catch as she says it, like someone tugs on them with a bit of string. "He'll be looking elsewhere. Finding us help."

I stare at her, arm tangled up in the dress's sleeve. "Finding help," I echo. I try to reach past the fog in my brain. I'm certain there's something important here that I should already know, but my thoughts keep glancing off of it.

"There has been a change in our situation at the clinic," she says, voice flat, like when she transcribes charts into her Dictaphone. "Your father will be looking for a way to change it, but in the meantime, we're going to go on a little trip." Her lips twist strangely, though maybe it's just the moonlight. "Don't you remember?"

Remember. The word feels like a taunt, like another tendril

of fog added to the heavy mist already shrouding a part of my brain. Why can't I shake off this exhaustion? "No."

"Good," she says. "Let's keep it that way."

An empty mind is a safe mind, Papa always said. As the dream scatters and fades, I wonder how safe my mind really is.

CHAPTER 15

A GRAY SWEATER APPEARS in my clothing trunk the next day, identical to the one that had gone missing, but where the old one had a moth hole in the left armpit, this one has none. That rules out Masha as the culprit. She'd never have bothered to find me a new one.

It's late October—I've been here five whole weeks—and the snow is growing, mounting, sudsing up like a washbasin about to overflow. It won't go away till April—possibly May. I'm surprised it came this late. I'll have to wait for it to pack down and ice over so I leave no tracks. Now I can't look out the mansion window without shielding my eyes with my hand; everything glares back with a harsh overtone of gold, like it's been washed with too much bleach. Nothing in Russia is so headache-inducing as a sunny snow-filled day, the kind that makes you hate yourself for wishing for clouds.

After Sergei showed me the vault, I've taken to walking the mansion at night, while Larissa is distracted by Ivan. I can't listen to the radio with him anymore; all I feel is the strain on his face as he tries to show me that this is enough for a life, that everything worth living for can be contained in these four walls. So I excuse myself after dinner and start in the left front corner of the attic, working my way down the back right of the bottom floor, one room at a time. I sweep my hands along the walls, the floor, everything in the room, calling up memories like a summoner searching for ghosts.

Surface memories—of my comrades, going about their lives— are easy enough to sift through. I push past them quickly. I don't want to see Larissa's stolen moments with Ivan, or worst of all, Anastasia's looping madness. I shove it aside and dive into history. The worker housing, the thirty-some families who shared the mansion with its bourgeois owners after the Party took control. I go deeper. Beyond forty years, it gets hazy, and I'm not sure I can trust what I see. A man who is dead is alive in the next layer of memories. Lives run out of order, interrupted with more recent static bursts.

But I won't stop looking. Sergei's tunnel may be a dead end, but there has to be another. There are walls that don't add up, there are whispers among the memories. There has to be another way.

Sometimes my feet linger in the ballroom doorway just a little too long, like gravity pulling me toward Valentin's music as he plays. The mathematical etudes ease the knots out of my mind; I like the way his long fingers dance across the keys, and I like the crease that appears between his eyebrows when he comes to the tricky parts. He watches me, but if he knows what I'm doing, he doesn't mention it to me. It's just as well. I'll never trust a psychic like him—a scrubber, just like Rostov, making lacework of peoples' thoughts.

Larissa gives me a sad smile when I return from searching. Does she see my future? Me succeeding in my escape, or failing? I'm afraid to ask. But we talk, some, when Ivan's not around to suck up all her attention. Under night's blanket, she sits at the foot of my bed and tells me stories from her life at school, a normal life full of blue jumpers and white dandelion barrettes. She passes down tales from her grandmother about life under the tsars, before the Soviet Union. There were no lines to wait in, she said, but often there was no money or food to be had, either.

I'll take that uncertainty. Uncertainty is my constant companion, the shadow always underfoot. Whether I'm safer in here than on the run. Whether my parents knew what I am all along. It'll be worth it, I tell myself, as I sweep the mansion's walls. But there are a few more answers I need first.

"Natalya Petrovna Gruzova."

Major Kruzenko points to the black-and-white passport photograph streaming onto the wall from the slide projector. It takes me a moment to recognize the woman because her blond hair looks white and is pulled into a stern bun; her face is fuller in the picture, as if the exhausted woman who grabbed my wrist in Red Square was only her withered shadow.

"She is one of the engineers designing the secret *Veter 1* capsule that will give us the first flight around the moon. If the mission is a success, then we will be sure to achieve a moon landing long before the Americans." Kruzenko's face tightens; her brows draw down. "Unfortunately, we believe Gruzova has been compromised by an enemy team of American psychics. In addition to stealing *Veter 1* design documents for the Americans, she appears to be assisting them in hunting us."

Natalya's eyes in the photograph are glazed with excitement, as if she is staring beyond our world, into the stars. That yearning was gone from the woman I heard in the Square. What happened to her light? Is that what these "scrubbers" can do?

Masha's hand shoots up. "If we know she is a traitor, why haven't we arrested her?" If she and Misha had their way, the Siberian gulags would be fuller than the cities.

"If we arrest her now, we can learn everything she knows, but her accomplices, this scrubber who is working her, will burrow into the earth."

"Then we should find out what she knows," Ivan says. Larissa nods beside him.

"Very likely, she only knows one piece of the puzzle, and the scrubber has carefully controlled the contents of her head to keep her from discovering more." Kruzenko folds her arms. "We will observe her, instead, as she plays her little game, then spread our net from there. We must find more information connecting the Americans to Gruzova, whether it's memories or thoughts in others' heads."

"We're using her as bait," I mutter. Valentin turns toward me, but I keep looking ahead.

"But do not worry. We also have additional agents monitoring her, in case she tries to flee." Kruzenko smirks. "So let's begin."

She splits us into teams again, so we can play off each other's strengths. I'm paired with Valentin this time—I'm relieved it's not Sergei, but terrified nonetheless. I can't shake the knowledge of what he can do. And in case I was harboring any thoughts of escape during our mission, Pavel, my guard, is joined by the slimmer but no less imposing Lev, who wears a pair of scars across one eye like a medal of honor.

Valentin and I are shuttled to the Metro, Moscow's underground artery of trains. We ride a packed car one stop to the Kievskaya station, surrounded by exposed armpits as their owners clutch at the handles overhead. For once I'm thankful for winter and its smell of salt and radiators instead of sweat. Somehow, Valentin finds us a seat—I can't help but suspect he's mentally coaxed this loud man in expensive blue jeans out of it—and Pavel and Lev flank us.

We have other guards. Valentin's voice flutters against my mental shell.

I flick my gaze down the length of the car. *Can't they hear our thoughts?* But Valentin taps a finger to his ear without looking at me. It takes me a moment to catch on, then I realize— Shostakovich is still going strong in my mind. A warmth spreads along my spine. He could have dived right in and grabbed the thought from me. Rostov would have. I look casually to my feet, strip away the strings section, and repeat myself, burying my words in the low tympani. *Are the guards psychic?*

Lev is, but the rest, definitely not. I caught Kruzenko thinking about it.

My jaw slackens. *You can hear her thoughts? But her gypsy music is so loud—*

Hear them, casually? No. But I can take them. In my peripheral vision, he cocks a smile on his face like a loaded gun.

I flinch and raise Shostakovich around me.

Valentin swallows audibly beside me; the next thought he passes to me carries the warmth and the fragrance of spring. *Yulia . . . I'd never take your thoughts without permission. Not yours or—or anyone's, who wasn't a Party supporter.*

I want to believe this. Truly I do. But I can't find the right words for what I'm feeling. Even if we only steal thoughts from our oppressors—the KGB, the Communist Party, whatever Russian entity feels like taking its turn putting soles to our necks—we're no better than they. Are we? And there's Valentin himself, his dangerous skill. Will he savor this power with Rostov's same hunger, where the more power he acquires, the more he craves? Will he use his abilities just as ruthlessly?

I don't talk to him for the rest of our Metro ride. Shostakovich pulses to the steady clanking of the rail car.

We reach the Kievskaya station and squeeze out of the car at the last minute, swimming against the rush of people trying to board. I don't care if our guards make it off the train or not. We can't be blamed for the morning rush.

"Take my hand." Valentin's gloved fingers catch mine. His voice is soft, the command almost a question. "Stay close."

The station itself is palatial—a palace for all the workers, as Stalin once called the Metro stations, and he spared no expense in their décor. Phony plaster molding, chandeliers, marble floors, elaborate mosaics, and of course hammers and sickles everywhere, as if sprayed there by some terrible explosion. The grimy factory film that hastens to cover up such finery is thinner here than in most stations. I can actually see Lenin's coy smile on a painted mural, and the shine on a soldier's boot as he waves to farmers in a field of golden tiles.

We cram onto the escalator. Waves and waves of *nomenklatura*, the Communist Party elite, pass us on their way down. Tailored suits, fur coats, Turkish scarves; the women wear absurd heeled boots under their billowing skirts, the leather already stained with a rind of salt. Unlike the solemn industrial-park station where we boarded, the air crackles with rapid-fire conversation, giggles, grins.

Valentin peers over his shoulder, to the base of the escalator far below. We've been riding for three minutes, but we're only halfway up the tunnel. *Can you see them?* I ask, pushing the thought against him gently.

They're just now boarding. He looks upward at the glowing circle of daylight ahead. *You need to add another layer of music to your thoughts. In case Lev can hear us. Something we both know, so I can understand you.*

I grimace. An arms race of thought. They are trained to penetrate one, so add another. They can penetrate two, so add three more.

This Tchaikovsky song. Do you know it? Valentin closes his eyes behind his fogged lenses and for a moment, all I hear are girls chattering, the elevator squeaking and churning. Then the low, mournful piano chords start. Thick notes, but somehow soft, patient. I think I may have heard Papa and Zhenya playing it together once. It doesn't fit the beat of Shostakovich, but somehow, they meld together into a sturdy fortress of sound.

Keep it in your head along with our usual barrier, he says. *We'll use it to speak to each other. Safely, without me having to dip into your head.*

Like a code. I nod, the tightness in my chest unclenching as we finally reach the escalator's crest. The clouds have reappeared to shield us from snow blindness. The street is a soothing gray, tipped in white. Elaborate apartment buildings of plaster, marble, and stone stand in rank on both sides of the street, bolstered with red columns. Unlike the crowded-teeth concrete blocks in most districts, the boulevard is wide and trimmed with well-groomed trees. No streetcar cables forming a web against the sky; no factory slime blackening the walls. I take a deep breath, and I can't even smell the pickled fish stink of the Moskva River. "This looks nothing like the Moscow I lived in," I mutter aloud, as we stride onto the plaza.

Valentin puffs out a phantom of breath and rubs his hands while surveying the street. "That's because the Party members live here. Rumor has it, there's even a secret Metro line that runs through here for the top officials."

"And where did you hear that?" I ask.

Tchaikovsky's somber chords echo the rest of his thoughts. He slides his thumb up my hand; wriggles it into the hem of my glove so our bare skin makes contact. I flinch at his cold touch, but this is the shortest distance for his thoughts to travel. *I lived here once.*

The winter air doesn't bother me, but that thought certainly does. It slips through my coat and chaps my skin. I'm not so sure I want his hand on mine, but those words lure me in. *What happened?*

My father was Party. We had a private car, a custom apartment, a piano, maids . . .

Was, I echo. We squeeze past a pair of hound-faced men, and I catch an unwelcome thought of sex clinging to one of them.

He doesn't live here anymore.

And then I feel his thoughts tear away from mine. The shine to his deep, dark eyes is gone. He lets go of my hand. Like Colonel Rostov, his thoughts are a negation of thought, a painful noise. They grate against me, brittle and sharp, until he takes a few steps away from me.

I pull off one glove and concentrate on drawing out the memories dormant on the trees, the street signposts, but it's so crowded and noisy in the recent history of this sidewalk. How will I ever find Natalya Gruzova in this crowd? I try to envision her blond hair bound in a scarf: not with the full, healthy cheeks of her passport photograph, but the worn-away face in Red Square, her thoughts strung together with crimped wire after the scrubber interfered.

There. A trail of her scattershot thoughts; it runs from the apartments the next block down to the station we just left. "This way," I say to Valentin, and as I usher him to the crosswalk, our four little shadows follow.

It's Stalinist architecture, same as the rest, a five-story structure that runs flush with the Ukraina skyscraper—one of the Seven Sisters. A quaint grocery store sits in the bottom floor. No rations, no lines. I peer through the glass, and its shelves are actually stocked. They have white toilet paper, real toilet paper, not the standard-issue sandpaper brown.

We pass through the red and gold building's entrance under a stained-glass blue globe. The foyer is flawless. The gleaming granite floor, columns, and ceiling are all full of shadows; our figures play across them as dark blobs with no distinct edge. The Metro stations may be the palace of the people, but this is truly the palace of the Party. The door latches shut behind us, as satisfying as Gagarin's space capsule sealing shut. Kk-ssshhhhsss. We are as safe from the rest of Moscow here as we would be from the vacuum of space.

A head appears from behind one of the columns, ant-sized against the massive portrait of Lenin at the far end of the foyer. "May I help you?"

Doormen? I push my thoughts against Valentin's. *They have doormen here?*

"I'm Igor Gruzov, Natalya Gruzova's brother," Valentin says. "She asked me to fetch some things from her apartment."

I look at Valentin, and in a fuzzy, glowing moment, even I can believe he is this brother, and not the meek, silent boy who hides behind his glasses with a head full of painful noise. I force my eyes away, strip off my gloves, and run one hand along the smooth column, smearing its glistening surface. Where are you, Natalya? Let me glimpse at your secrets. Tell me why you need my help.

"No, you aren't. I've met her brother, and you don't look like him." The man darts back behind his desk. "Show me your papers or I'll call security."

Natalya's curly hair gleams in a glamorously lit memory, her back to me, facing a man in a suit and hat. They converse in the foyer—this morning? Yesterday? Recently. I lean into their words. They speak Russian, but there is something off about the man's voice, the slightest clip to his words. They're too formal. Too stiff: I can see him practicing in the mirror, stretching his lips into those awkward Russian *oo*s, those deep guttural churns.

She calls him little brother, but if she's working with the CIA, he must be one of them.

"What do you mean, you do not know about his orders?" She's hysterical in the memory. She won't let her voice pass a certain volume, but it hisses and crackles. "He said the documents weren't enough to buy my way out. He said *you* wanted me to find these people!"

"Calm down, Natalya. This is all just a misunderstanding. We're gonna get you out of here, okay?"

"I found the girl in Red Square, like he said she would be. I know she saw me. And I found two more. One works at the ZiL auto factory—"

The man looks over his shoulder. There—narrow, long nose, bushy brows—I have him. I let go of the column and toss the man's image to Valentin. *This man poses as her brother, but he must be one of the Americans. The doorman's already suspicious. We must go.*

Come to my side, Valentin murmurs, and I'm startled by how seductive the words sound in my head, inviting as a stretch of sunny beach. My cheeks smolder. I replay it in my head with a tingle along my spine; yes, I want to hear him say this again. But logic intervenes. This isn't really Valentin; it's just a role he's stepped into. I sidle up alongside him, on guard, questioning my sudden craving for this gorgeous, dark mystery whose eyes hold mine gingerly like he's afraid they'll break. Through our thick coats, I feel an electric crackle in the quickly vanishing space between us.

"You don't recall? I told you I'd come back. Here, you remember my wife, Svetlana—you gave her those mints."

I creak back my lips in an awful sturgeon smile as Valentin lopes his arm around my shoulder. I'm liquid Yulia, hopelessly lost like I've never been lost before. His touch is suave, but not overly so. The only boy I've ever kissed—Vovan, such a terrible plodding name—was too bland a kisser, lips factory-stamped to fit with anyone else's. If Valentin's careful touch is any indication, his lips were tailored just for mine.

My face burns crimson. What am I thinking? And *bozhe moi*, do I ever want to think it some more.

"Of course!" The doorman clasps his hands, and the soft leather of his white gloves snickers. "I am so sorry for not remembering, comrade. Here, this is the spare key." He unhooks it from the rack and holds it out to me. "May I take your coat and hat?"

Valentin isn't wearing a hat, I think, looking up at him with dopey batting eyes. But couldn't he be, maybe? Can't I almost see a black fedora perched on his head, with its grosgrain ribbon band, just like the American man? Yes, I think I can, it might as well be there; it makes sense for it to be.

"No, thank you, comrade. We won't be but a minute." He turns toward the elevator bank, and I'm eager to follow, pulled along by this sudden radiance about him, a confidence he's never before bared. Lenin smiles at us from the end of the hall as the ornate hand above the elevator clicks down the floors toward us. I'm bound to his side by the electricity dancing between us, me and this luscious man who has shed Valentin like a cocoon and taken flight.

CHAPTER 16

THE ELEVATOR IS SO WIDE we could stand on opposite sides without touching. But we don't. We stay shoulder to shoulder as it whisks us to the fifth floor. Valentin smiles at me—it might be the first genuine smile of his I've seen. My mouth hangs open as I gawk at this gorgeous, confident creature. Those gorgeous, confident lips. He brushes a clump of snow from shoulder. A need too desperate for words makes me want to snatch his hand and kiss it hungrily.

The elevator stops. Too soon we're stumbling out, and the strange man who slipped out of Valentin begins to buckle himself back in, one strap at a time. Someone snuffs the light out behind his eyes, and he hunches forward once more, closing himself off to the world. We are once again Yulia and Valentin; I'm an idiot with a flush on my cheeks like a scummy film, and he's a monster like Rostov, buzzing with static. Realization slaps me like a blast of cold wind.

You just did it to me. I shove him against the wall, in the fathomless space between apartment doors. My forearm braces across his collarbone. *You swore to me you wouldn't mess with my thoughts, and you just did it!*

I didn't, I swear! I showed him what he needed to give us access. You might have caught some of that, but I wasn't targeting you. Those sad, pitiful eyes, barely able to meet mine. Like he's not even the same man at all. *I promise you, Yulia. I won't do anything to you.*

Anger burns like a furnace in my mind. How can he be telling the truth? He made me feel so ridiculous, made me pathetic with admiration for him. I knew he couldn't be trusted—no one can touch a power as strong as that without wanting to use it more than they should.

But there was something else about him when he tapped into his ability. It was the first time he seemed—open. Whole. For the first time, I saw those beautiful parts of him that he keeps safely hidden away, too dangerous to expose anyone to for long.

I don't like this line of thought. I hate his power—it makes him like Rostov, like the American who's hunting us down. There's nothing beautiful in being able to cause such confusion, such pain. I let go of Valentin and look away from him, down the hall. *Make sure that next time, you keep it from reaching me.* Then I crank Shostakovich as high as I can and storm down the corridor.

We reach Apartment 512. As I jam the key into the brass knob, Valentin drops a hand on my arm. *Kruzenko assigned Sergei and Masha to remotely view in here, as well. Be careful what you do and say out loud. They can't read our thoughts remotely, but they'll be watching us.*

I take a deep breath, pushing down my anger. *All right. Let's get this over with.*

Gruzova's apartment is one part Hermitage Palace and two parts firebombing wreckage. I drop the key on her entry table as stale panic and terror crawl up from the floor on spider legs, barely dampened through my boots. Valentin steadies me with Tchaikovsky humming along his hand, then charges past me. *Bozhe moi, has she been robbed?* he asks, searching from side to side for intruders.

The windswept parlor is cluttered with half-eaten meals on plates, scattered papers, discarded clothing, and stacks and stacks of rubles and Deutschmarks both. Just out in the open for taking! *I think she did this herself.* I pluck up a discarded creamy wool skirt with a careless footprint stamped onto it. Natalya Gruzova flits before me, stripping the skirt off in haste, changing attire after a long evening in the office, and storming from the apartment just as quickly. *Looks like she's barely been living here.*

Then where is she going? Valentin asks.

Somewhere with the CIA handlers? Our boots squeak against the parquet wooden floors as we cross the parlor toward a closed door. I keep my fingers out to feel for more memories, but I find only cobwebs of thought: no substance, no weight, no context. Gruzova has spent very little time here, at least recently.

Wait, Valentin says, urgency fraying the musical barrier around the thought. He's hunched over a coffee table, looking at, but not touching, a stack of folders. *They're all empty, but there's a rectangle cut out of the top of each of them. Looks like someone tried to cut away whatever was written on it. There's some red ink on the edge.*

Act like you haven't noticed anything, I tell him. I want to stay a step ahead of Masha and Sergei; as much as the American scrubber frightens me, I have a theory about his teammates that I want to test. *I'll look at them in a moment, and see what I can read.*

My hand rests on the bedroom doorknob. Finally, I get something tangible. Natalya hesitates here each day before entering; she tucks back a lock of hair and presses her ear to the door. After a few moments, she opens the door slowly, staying pressed against it like it's a shield, and listens for breathing—for the click of a cocking gun. Her American handlers have made her paranoid this way. But she doesn't fear the KGB, awaiting her in silence. She's resigned herself to that fate. It's the one American—the one with the vanishing, noisy face—who scares her most of all.

I open the door.

It is as tornadic as the rest of the apartment. A bed so big it could fit my whole family sits, sheets rumpled, against the far wall in an eave framed by plaster molding of wheat and gold-flecked stars. The French reproduction dressers have been ransacked, and an ashtray bears a fully ashed cigarette corpse.

A heavy gold ring rests on the nightstand, bearing a symbol that looks like the Russian Orthodox cross. Why would a Party member, one as obviously well cared for as Gruzova, wear something so boldly religious? It seems dangerous to me. But then, everything about her is. I pluck up the ring and roll it around in my palm.

I see a handsome, smirking man in a soldier's flight uniform—there's a hint of Sergei, of Russian bluster, in that grin—wriggling the ring off his finger and dropping it in Natalya Gruzova's hand. "Hold onto it for me, will you?" Don't want it flying off during testing."

"Comrade Gagarin, I insist you not go through with this preposterous idea."

I gasp. Gruzova knows Yuri Gagarin? But of course she does—she works for the *Veter 1* team. Are they sending him into space again?

"Premier Khruschev has forbidden you to enter space again. We would not want our national hero . . . damaged," Gruzova says, voice stiff.

"Damaged." He snorts. Even through the memory, I can smell the vodka on him; already he's preserving himself from the inside out, preparing himself for a waxy sainthood. "These are my friends you're sending up in your death machine."

"I assure you, comrade, we are doing everything to make the *Veter 1* safe—"

Gagarin reaches past her to flick switches on the control panel. "It doesn't matter. If it were truly safe, why not publicize the program? Why keep it such a big secret?" He laughs, dry and bitter, and heads for a large metal crate that looks like a testing capsule. "I wasn't the first man in space, comrade." He tilts his head toward her, the charming grin gone, replaced with a look so sad it aches. "I'm just the first who lived."

I set the ring back on Gruzova's nightstand and back away. This won't lead us to the Americans. Her private memories should remain her own, even if they are about the most famous man in the Soviet Union next to Khruschev himself.

Valentin stands in the bedroom doorway. "Anything interesting?" he asks, his voice steady but not demanding.

"It depends on your definition."

He leans back, eyes hooded. *You can share your visions with me. You don't have to let me through your shield to do it—just open them to me, like how we speak in thoughts . . .*

My first instinct is to scream *No!*, but something in the look on his face pauses me. He's not the confident beast he was before, but he's relaxed against the doorframe, watching me. His shoulders are taut, though. Like he's expecting me to snap at him. I choke down my initial reaction.

All right. But stay out of my shield.

Understood. He musters the tiniest smile.

I run my hands along clothing, sheets, chairs tucked into the alcove overlooking Kutuzovsky Prospekt. Only the dirty clothing—which is most of it, thanks to this madwoman—points at anything about the Americans. Unfortunately, what it points to is the scrubber. A sweater chafes with the scrubber's static like it was woven with steel. The coat dangling from a lampshade is painful to touch, overwhelming me with that chaotic noise.

Valentin purses his lips. I sink against the window, the frosty glass numbing my forehead. The alcove window is narrower than the rest, and I see a flash of metal bars beyond it—a fire escape. My heart races, and a primitive need deep within me cries for me to go, go, go. I squeeze my eyes closed, hard, until spots dance on my eyelids. I can't. Not yet.

I open my eyes, heart pounding, and see Valentin staring back at me. He's not inside my thoughts—I've got Shostakovich woven ironclad; surely I'd feel him prying that hull open—but the tight line of his mouth, his widened eyes tells me he knows what I'm thinking all the same.

Yulia . . . You don't understand. You can't run.

I grip the windowsill, cold and clotted with dead gnats. Somehow, it scares me more that he can read me *without* looking inside my mind. *I know, I know. Sergei and Masha are watching.*

That's not all. Yulia—Rostov, he has this . . . man. His thoughts waver. *The Hound. What he can do—it's not like the others, it's not something that can be outrun.*

My nails bite into the windowsill. Natalya's memories flood past me—receiving the apartment as a gift for her work on the *Sputnik* satellite designs, lovers past, endless dinner parties with other party elite—but I don't care, I don't care, I just need a way out.

Valentin moves beside me, carefully, and his hand hovers above mine. *I know what you're going through. Please—let me show you.* A sad smile traces his lips. *I know you won't believe me any other way.*

I lower my eyes from his. *Fine.*

His grasp is firm, but not hateful or controlling like Rostov's. I sink through his music until Natalya's room is completely washed away.

I'm standing in Valentin's skin, under the rusted abutment of a bridge, watching the Moskva River flow past. Starlight twinkles in its choppy waters. He is—I am—breathing furiously, made all the more difficult for the desperate need to stay silent. My hands—I feel Valentin's hands as if they were my own—sting from razor wire's bite, and blood smears the front of my trousers where I've tried to wipe it away. But my trail is clean. Between the psychic eraser in my head and the rushing water that carried me a kilometer downstream before I crossed to the other bank, not even Rostov could trace me.

My heart rate slows. The Moskva River water evaporating off of me leaves raised gooseflesh in its wake. Overhead, the Metro cars chatter as they race across the bridge, and gravel cascades around me.

Safe. I am almost safe. All I need is a soft, simple mind—one of Father's old friends, perhaps—to draw up the documents I need.

The train fades, but the sound of gravel continues. It crunches under heavy feet. My heart lurches as blood races through my veins. They can't have found me. Not even Rostov is so clever. But then my thoughts are ripped away, my shield disintegrated. It's not Rostov—he can split open my skull, sure, but he doesn't suck me dry this way, soaking up all my energy. And yet my face feels numb despite the late summer swelter. Every silent step takes exponentially more strength.

Ahead of me the gruesome curve of a jaw catches the moonlight. It's the man, the thing, or whatever it is that's sapping me away. I am hunted. I am prey who thought myself free, and instead I've hidden right in a trap. The man's massive fist opens, sucking away the last warmth from my bones as everything fades—

Valentin pries his own hand away, like it's some wicked lure that must be slid carefully from my flesh, and I stagger out of his memory and back into the chaotic room, only a few seconds after the memory began. His eyes are pure black behind his glasses. No, only a trick of the light. But I'm afraid of him, of this darkness he collects like I collect memories. He stares down, haunted like Dostoevsky's Raskolnikov—like he's just hacked an old woman to bits.

I let go of the windowsill. *Tell me what happened, Valentin.*

Another time.

Who is this man?

Valentin's music shifts, like a mental clearing of the throat. *You should check the folders on the coffee table.* He strides across the bedroom at a steady clip and vanishes back into the living room—as if the horrible thoughts he's shown me never happened. But even now I see that hand sucking away at my life.

There has to be more. I sweep through the room again, tossing clothing aside without bothering to replace it where we found it. Dull daily routines. Static emptiness. She met with the fedora man in the lobby downstairs without the scrubber around. Surely she's done it once more. I'm growing heavier and heavier with all the emotions I'm soaking up, Natalya's frenzy overflowing.

Valentin watches me with infuriating calm. *You draw up more and more emotions and memories,* he thinks. *Don't you ever push them away?*

I follow him back to the living room and run my fingers over everything. I try not to linger on the folders with their tabs clipped off; I want it to look like I'm examining each thing in turn, from the wadded tissues to the old issues of *Pravda.*

But it's the folders that have my interest. I slip my thumbnail against their edges, seeing a memory of the tabs stamped with a big red SEKRET. Natalya shoves documents into them at her office. Her thoughts are wound too tight; her mental clock is running fast. She has to buy her way out.

But I don't see anything more about the American team.

I knock the folder off the table, making it look like an accident, but I press deeper into the memories as I put it back. My heart leaps into my throat. What I see is not the documents she smuggled out of the laboratory. Instead there are dossiers. Black-and-white photographs, paper-clipped to typewritten fact sheets. The first photograph, I don't recognize. But the next one—

Our guards are coming. Hurry, Valentin says.

The next one is of me. It was taken on the street, when I was still free. I look two steps away from the grave, *bozhe moi.*

I close the folder but slip my finger inside.

Natalya Gruzova sets the documents beside her on the park bench, and a man settles down beside her. Not the man in the fedora—this man has no face, no thoughts but a frenzied swarm of noise. The scrubber. He yanks her documents out of the folder and shoves them into his attaché while Natalya stares dead ahead.

"These are a good start," the man says. His voice scrapes like metal on metal.

Natalya's lips twitch. "I will bring you more. It takes time to get the necessary accesses—"

"Yes, I know. But I have an additional task for you."

"Your boss didn't mention anything else." She laces her hands together, over and over. This conversation must have taken place before the one I saw in the lobby, when she confronted the fedora-ed man—this "boss"—about these extra demands.

He laughs, cruel and empty, then slips the dossiers into the folder. "When you bring me the next batch at Red Square, some of these people will be looking for you. Memorize their faces. Watch for them. Let me know when you see them." He laughs again. "Let them fear us."

I stumble out of the memory, vomit burning at the back of my throat. He *wants* us terrified.

The front door crashes open, and Lev and Pavel, our guards, spill into the parlor. "What's taking so long?" Lev asks.

"Nothing." Valentin shuffles backward. "We haven't found much yet—"

"You've had plenty of time. Let's go. Before that idiot doorman comes to his senses."

They herd us toward the front door. I catch the wink of brass on the entry table where we left it, and my ration rat instincts kick in—my hand darts out, back into my pocket, too fast for even Sergei to see what I've grabbed. So I hope.

I admire Valentin for trying to escape, once. He must have craved it—the razor wire slicing through his hands—his beautiful, pianist hands—cannot lie. I know he thinks it's safer on this side of the wall, and he may well be right.

But I can't leave well enough alone. I have to approach the Americans—I have to at least try. Surely they would make a deal with me. Whatever this man's reasons for wanting us scared, he has to be interested in what I can offer them. Like the games at the market—my information on the KGB's psychic training program must be worth more than whatever else they might have in mind.

It might even be worth helping me rescue Mama and Zhenya.

I reach back into my pocket for my gloves as we head outside, and permit myself a tiny smile as my fingers close around Natalya Gruzova's spare key.

CHAPTER 17

THERE'S A TREMOR DEEP within me all through our debriefing the next morning. It started in my shoulders and hands, but I had to bury it when I heard how my teacup rattled against its saucer. Masha glanced at me once, sharp—like she could hear my fear. Like the plan rattling around inside me had set me shaking.

But as she gives her report on their remote viewing, there's no knowing glance or hint of deception. If she saw what I did, she's hiding it well. Much better than I've seen her hide anything thus far—her pride isn't fond of gathering dust. The safe bet is that I'm safe. It'll have to be enough. The answers I need can't wait.

After lunch, Sergei tugs on one of my braids as I'm about to head upstairs. "Hey. Yul." He's wearing his dazzling grin and leaning back against the doorway, hands tucked behind him. "Look what I found."

He holds up a record sleeve featuring a brooding, flinty-eyed

Russian man with a woman hovering behind him, eyes heavily mascaraed. *The Promise*, reads the loopy lettering across the top. Then, in smaller letters: *The promise is only the beginning . . .*

"It's the very start of the series," he says. "When they're talking about their lives back in Yekaterinburg—this is it."

I grin in spite of myself. "Larissa told me the first few episodes are the best."

Sergei tweaks my braid again. "And tomorrow night, you shall find out."

"What about tonight?"

Sergei rolls his shoulders, leaning back into the other room. "I've got some special training mission with Masha and Larissa. Trust me, I'd rather stay here, listening to radio dramas with you, but what can you do . . ."

I swallow hard, feeling that tremor rise up out of my bones once more. What can you do, indeed, with only a skeleton crew of guards for the night? With Rostov and Kruzenko gone? With a brass key humming in my pocket, ready to unlock just the answers I need?

As soon as the door clangs shut that evening, I drag my duffel bag into the restroom and layer on half my wardrobe. Trousers under my skirt, three sweaters piled one over the other. As many socks as I can wear and still lace up my boots. The inner lining of my coat is heavy with military rations and pumpernickel bread.

Silence thickens the hallway, stagnant and heavy. No scuttling guards. I know the others are listening to the Dinamo hockey game on the radio. Now or never, Yulia. I take a deep breath of the moldy air and hope I won't breathe it for much longer at all.

I head back to the walls that don't quite add up, the mismatched rooms I'd founded during my night walk. A hallway near the kitchen and the two rooms off of it meet at odd angles. I can hear humming through the walls, a drone like electricity. The memories hum, too, but they're lurking on the other side. On whatever's in that hollow space.

I head to the basement in search of an entrance. Usually, our guards keep us out of here, but the skeleton crew doesn't have the manpower. It isn't until I reach the kitchen that I spot the trail—Rostov's static carving a swath through history. What was he trying to erase?

I follow the path of scratched-out memories. The kitchen is dark, animated only with the purring industrial refrigerator. There's a long range fit for cooking fifty meals at a time; a chain of baskets hangs stuffed with vegetables. One whole corner of the kitchen is an oven, floor to ceiling, wide enough for five to stand inside comfortably.

If our meals are prepared here, then the cooks must come in and out from somewhere else. But where?

The kicked-up trail of ash gives it away before the memories do. Footprints, hastily swept over, leading in and out of the oven. I duck my head and touch my gloved hand to the hearth whose chill permeates the wool. There's a gap just inside the archway, so you wouldn't notice it unless you're looking from inside the oven. Only half a meter wide. I squeeze through and find a set of stairs that curves up and down.

Upward will likely only lead me back up through the mansion, through that initial mismatched wall I'd found. No use escaping off the roof. I'm not Valentin, with the brute strength to throw myself over the wall, or however he got up and over. Down it is.

The sweat building on my back chills as I descend the seemingly endless spiral stairs. For a good twenty feet or more, I'm submerged in complete darkness, but then electric sconces start to appear at regular intervals. They hum, industrial, immutable. Every few minutes, I hear a rumble deep below me, like the earth turning over in its sleep.

And without warning, the stairs stop before a metal door. No lock, no lettering. The lack of a lock raises the hair on the back of my neck; there must be some other form of security nearby. I steady myself with a deep breath, one laced with hard water and concrete dust, peel off my glove, and press my palm to the door.

A soldier strolls past the doorway on the other side, AK-47 in hand. I choke back a gasp. Before I can press deeper, the room quakes again. I press my ear to the door as wind rips through the room on the other side. A train—the brakes shriek against the rails as it pulls to a stop.

"Station Number 19," a woman's voice announces, muffled as if beneath water. "Ascending."

What Metro line is this? All of the Metro stops are named, not numbered. The closest Metro station to the mansion should be Sparrow Hills, but that's above ground, hanging over the Moskva River. The next stop would be University Station for Moscow State, but that's too far southwest—I traveled straight down.

I press against the door again. The guard was walking away from the door, and his back should be to me now. Sure enough, he's at the far end of the platform, and now he's pulling a pack of cigarettes from his pocket, his attention absorbed. The train humming on the tracks is only two cars long, and it's covered in golden filigree, red stars, and swooping lines that radiate from boughs of wheat. This station is like the inverse of the plain cars and elaborate stations on the normal Metro lines.

This must be the Party-only secret line that Valentin mentioned.

The train's doors slide shut, and with a roar, it rockets away. The soldier's back is toward me, but I don't have long. As the air vibrates from the departing train, I throw open the door, charge across the platform, and fling myself into the darkness of the train rails. The noise recedes just as my boots hit the gravel.

With one long crackle, the soldier strikes his match.

I unravel the floor plan above me in my mind. The last train should have been coming from the north—from the direction of Kutuzovsky Prospekt. I'm afraid to touch the walls—the claustrophobic smell of the tunnels alone is enough to ward me off—but I'll check at the next station to see if I'm off-course. I head north, keeping to the shadows.

I'm almost to the next station when I see the headlights, swinging suddenly around a curve.

I check the tunnel alongside me for alcoves. It's tight—really tight. I'm not sure there's enough room for me, even if I flatten myself against the wall. The headlights wash over me. I shove off the tunnel wall, hard as I can, and go flying across the tracks in front of the train, into the other lane.

The breaks scream, too late, as the train careens across where I just stood. It skids to a stop over my shoulder. I've been seen. My heart hammers in my chest. I start running, as fast as I can in my bulky gear.

"Attention. Attention." Loudspeakers crackle to life, flooding the tunnel with a booming voice. "Unauthorized personnel spotted on the tracks between stations 18 and 19."

I keep running. Red lights flick on and off through the tunnel, timed with a low foghorn blast. A stitch twists the side of my gut. All the layers of sweaters are trapping my body heat, and I'm awash in fresh sweat. Please, please, let the next station be Kutuzovsky.

Finally I reach the platform of Station Number 18. I launch myself at the platform's edge, just barely hooking my elbows on the lip, and swing my legs until I can roll safely onto the concrete platform. A bank of propaganda posters stare down at me from the far wall: a smith with his hammer slung over his shoulder, standing proud as sunrays erupt at his back. Smiling farmers, peasants with arms full of wheat. A woman snarling at me with one finger pressed to her lips: DON'T TELL!

"Hey! You!"

I don't stop to look. I leap toward the door and slam it shut behind me. One breath, I just need to catch one breath. I don't have powers like Valentin's or Rostov's to turn these soldiers away from me. I can't predict their behavior or hear their thoughts from afar, like Larissa or Misha and Ivan. I can't rely on my powers to get out of this. I can only rely on myself.

The stairs split into two. I take the left, then they split again. I'm touching the railing at intervals, trying to keep the gold and red building in my mind, hoping I'm picking the right path. I see it in flickers and gasps. Granite hallway, giant mural of Lenin. Please, be the right way. Enough Party officials live there. Surely they have their own entrance to the secret Metro line.

Boots thunder in the distance, drawing closer as I climb. I reach the final door and burst through the other side to the ornate main lobby, Vladimir Lenin's mosaic beaming down at me, then slam the door shut on the approaching guards. Quickly, quickly, *poshli*. I jump into the elevator and sweep my hand across all the buttons, all eight floors.

My breath wheezes through tight lungs. The doors open and close on empty floors, each one another wild goose chase for my pursuers. Finally I reach the fifth floor. Only a few more steps until freedom, until I can get the answers I need. The possibilities I've worked so hard for. Nervous energy crackles along my skin as I unlock Apartment 512.

CHAPTER 18

I OPEN THE DOOR to find Natalya Gruzova pointing a revolver at me.

"Oh, god," she gasps, as the door opens fully. "It's you." She lowers the gun, but not all the way. "Come in. Quickly."

The door clicks shut behind me. "You know who I am?" I ask.

She beckons me across the parlor, into the kitchen. A bottle of vodka and at least five filthy glasses crowd her breakfast table. She holds up the vodka bottle, one eyebrow up as a question mark. I shake my head. She shrugs and takes a swig. "He said this might happen. Please, sit."

I slide onto the bench. Nothing feels out of place in the table's memories, the bench, the glasses. There are only echoes of this tornado madwoman, storming in and out of the kitchen, drinking, smoking, pushing around her uneaten dinner as her nerves overwhelm her.

"Why are they looking for us?" I ask.

She sits down opposite me, with a sloppy sandwich of melted

cheese and fish. "You think I have answers for you? We are all pawns." Her hands quake as she tears off a corner of the bread. Something's wrong with her thoughts; too much anxiety pulses through her hand to the table to me. Is this the scrubber's work, or the work of paranoia, eating away all sense?

"I know what they offered you," I say. She reaches for the revolver again. "No—please. I want the same thing. I'm not going to turn you in. You can . . ."

I was going to tell her she can trust me, but it's not something I can guarantee. If I am caught, Rostov will rip her secrets from me again.

"They came to *me*." She jabs her finger at me. "I didn't ask for this. It was obvious to me what they were. I could have reported them, but I didn't. They could see how unhappy I was."

I spread both hands on the table. Her thoughts frizz like there's an electrical short in them. Every time she circles a truth, it darts away from me. What a mess she is. Does she deserve this insanity? She sold her secrets for money, for safe passage. Envious though I am, it's a fundamentally selfish act, when she already lives better than nearly every Russian citizen and is respected and regarded for her hard work. She's put satellites, dogs, men into space, and for the most part, reeled them back to Earth safe and sound. Why subject herself to this pain?

"So they asked you to steal design plans for the *Veter 1* space capsule." I have to keep her on track.

She tries to nod, but it sets her whole body shaking. She fumbles with a box of cigarettes. "They promised me they would get me to the West. Smuggle me out through Berlin, they said—it's too hard to get someone out of the heart of Moscow. But then their new team member showed up."

I lean forward. The scrubber. She can't hold the match to her cigarette. I take it from her and wait as she puffs it to life.

"I knew him from . . ." She trails off, looking through me as she searches for a memory that's no longer there. "He gave me these photographs, said they were priority targets, that he wouldn't let me leave unless I helped him draw them out."

"Why couldn't he find them himself?" I ask.

She taps her temple with two fingers. "Something about his head. They could hear him? Were looking for it. I'm sure you understand better than me."

"They. The KGB, you mean."

"Of course. There was always this odd noise—" She taps herself again like she's trying to break through the bone. "Like a drill—after we'd meet."

"But what did he want with them? Us," I correct myself.

She shakes her cigarette ash into one of the dirty glasses. "How should I know? He wants to eliminate you, I assume."

My heart pounds in my chest. "But I could offer them information."

"You're not a scientist, a politician. What do you know? You stop the CIA from stealing our space technology. You turn in your comrades for thinking unsafe things. That makes you a threat, a tool with a very specific purpose." She shrugs—a deft jab of her bony shoulders. "Who knows, maybe they could put you to work, but why would they use a man like that if not to scoop out your insides?"

The kitchen and all its filth spins around me. The plan I was so sure of two hours ago, climbing down those endless steps, feels more and more like a death wish. How could I think the Americans would help me? She's right. My powers are poison to everyone around me, condemning them for their thoughts, their histories, and offering it up to monsters like Rostov whether I want to or not. I am a liability. At best.

"Where is he now?" I ask, suddenly drained. Sleep, I need sleep. But I have to keep moving. I have no other choice but to try my luck with the Americans, convince them to take me in, and to rescue Mama and Zhenya . . .

"They operate out of some shops near the embassy, mostly. On Tchaikovsky Street."

I pull off my hat; run my fingers through my hair, sticky with sweat. I've come this far. I can do this. "Thank you. I—I'll find some way to repay you, someday."

She gulps for air. *Hold on hold on just a few more minutes* her thoughts roil on themselves, a whirlpool of panic.

"It's safer for you here," she finally says.

"No—I have to leave. Why don't you come with me? We'll demand they find a way out for us both." For my family, a voice in me pleads. "I've risked my life to come this far. We have to keep going."

"I cannot leave!" Her voice is raspy with exhaustion. "I'm just another pawn."

My hands contract into fists. "Pawn?" I ask, staring at her. Her eyes won't meet mine. "I—I don't understand."

She stands up, knocking the chair over with an ear-shattering crack. A tear squeezes from her shut eyes as she takes one more drag on her cigarette.

"Rachmaninov," she says—like it's a prayer. Her head is a yawning void. No more fear. She might as well be dead.

The kitchen door crashes open on a wave of static. Colonel Rostov strides in, surrounded by a swarm of soldiers.

My blood is on fire, starting in my gut and spreading out through my veins. Every protestation in my head is cut short before it can become a full sentence. But she. But I. But why.

I lunge for the revolver, but my body isn't listening to me. Something foreign fires the synapses in my brain now. My arms are cemented to my sides. I'm locked up like an unoiled hinge; a rising tide of noise fills my head.

"Do not bother to fight, Chernina. You will not be escaping us again."

I pry open my jaw, but my throat is too dry, too unwilling to speak.

"I'm sorry," Natalya whimpers. "I had no choice. Trust me, I know the Americans—it's safer for you this way—" A sob chokes off her words, and she takes another swig of vodka.

Rostov wipes the tear from Natalya's cheek as she flinches away from him. "Well done, comrade. I am certain the Tribunal will take your cooperation into account."

"You'll only put one bullet through me instead of two," she says.

Rostov chuckles, then turns back to me. Against my will, I stand up and move toward him. I'm begging my body to obey me, but I'm gliding along. "Chernina, dear Chernina. How could you think I wouldn't find you? You've been planning to escape since you first arrived. Why do you bother? We know everything."

"You didn't know about the CIA team. That they have psychics, too." Every word is a struggle, though I don't think for a moment I could speak if Rostov wasn't allowing me to.

"You barely know them, what they're capable of. Who knows what they would have done to you? You are much safer with us." He flicks his hand back to the soldiers. Then he looks up, at no one in particular. "Thank you, Sergei, that will be enough."

My stomach lurches like the floor's dropped out from under me. Sergei. I fight the urge to vomit. Hot shame, molten shame flushes my face as the soldiers clamp shackles around my wrists. My mouth tastes coppery, like I've bitten my tongue. This body is not my own. It marches along behind the soldiers, Rostov behind me, guiding my moves, his steel wool confidence chafing at what's left of my mind.

CHAPTER 19

NATALYA'S SCREAMS KEEP ME awake all night. Our cells are side by side, and the walls are too flimsy to keep anything out: noise, rats, smell, thoughts. My cot is pressed against the shared wall, so every fingernail they pull from her sends her agony shooting my way. Rostov drills into her brain with his powers, but her head is already Swiss cheese. There's nothing left for him to find.

He is looking for the names and descriptions of the CIA team and their scrubber. He is looking for any accomplices she may have on the *Veter* team, who might have helped her steal the documents. He is looking for the names and faces the Americans sent her to find—other psychics they wanted to hunt down.

But the scrubber anticipated this. Despite his apparent wish to kill us, I almost admire his thoroughness. She is perfectly censored, perfectly blanked out. A perfect Soviet citizen.

Somehow, I succumb to exhaustion, and when I wake, the

cell next to me is silent. No thoughts, no whimpers, no scrubbing, bleaching noise. I won't ask why. Rostov is coming for me next, I'm sure. I won't scream for him like Natalya did. I won't mourn the loss of a finger, my kneecaps. I will tell him everything. I won't fight it.

The KGB will kill me if I stay, and the CIA will kill me if I leave. I'd rather sink into that grave now, than wonder if I'll stumble into it with every next step.

All I will ask is that he set Mama and Zhenya free.

My cell door opens.

It's not Rostov, but another man, with fish-eyes that refuse to settle on me. He's been trained to shield his thoughts. "You are wanted this way." He takes me by the arm—not as gently as he could, but not as rough as I expected—and pulls me from the cell.

They're going to execute me. I'm certain of it. No questions, no second chances. I will stand against the wall and crumple. Clean, quick. I welcome it. A small mercy.

He pushes me into a room and locks the door behind us. "You have five minutes," he says, and he melts into the dark corner.

I turn to my left. The room is divided in half by a partition wall, the top half made of plexiglass. A woman steps forward to speak through slots cut into the glass, right at mouth level. "My Yulia."

My heart plummets. "Mama." Her eyes are black holes, but her wispy frame looks softer, all the jagged angles of starvation smudged away. She has pulled her black hair into a bun, showing off her perfect clavicles peeking above her sweater. Cashmere. "Mama. Where have you been? I thought you were—"

She smiles—a tired, well-fed smile. I'd never seen those dimples in her cheeks before. They used to be just divots.

"I am fine. Better than fine. We're getting Zhenya the treatment he needs. I've been working with a wonderful doctor from the old clinic, and we have developed new methods—no more electroshock therapy or sedatives."

I can't hear Mama's thoughts. No static, no shield, just a great emptiness. "Mama, I need you to listen to me. You've been brainwashed—Colonel Rostov, he's—" I take a deep breath. How to begin? "I don't know how to explain this to you, but I've been . . . I'm a psychic. You know, a mind reader. I can pull memories off of people and places."

She laughs. I'd already forgotten how beautiful her laugh is, swimming and sinking like an arpeggio. "Yulia, darling, I know. I'm proud of you. Really."

I stagger backward as if shot. "You're *proud*?"

"It's a good, solid future for you. What we should have done from the start. Much better than hiding, begging, and trading for food . . . I've been a terrible mother, Yulia. I'm so sorry."

"No, Mama, you don't understand. Put your hand to the glass—"

"No touching!" barks the guard from behind me. I grimace and take a step back.

"I spoke with my old lab director," Mama says. "They're going to let me resume our research. I never should have quit.

Your father left his notes with them before he ran—We were so close to breaking through."

"You quit for a reason, Mama. You and Papa ran away from something—from what?"

She shakes her head, a stray lock of hair sticking to her embarrassed grin. "Your father had such foolish ideas. Running for help, as if anyone in the West might care about our plight. Leaving me with this mess. He didn't know how dangerous it would be for us over there. And you—you have no idea how much more dangerous it is for you, with this power. There are people who would kill you for what you can do, when all the State wants is for you to be happily employed—"

"Happy? *Happy?*" I screech. "Mama, what have they done to you? Why are they making you say these things?" Memories bubble up to the surface through my exhausted haze. "How do you know Colonel Rostov? What does he want with you?"

"He and our old research academy and Khruschev want what everyone wants: a better Russia. I was on the right path, once, before your father got his dangerous ideas." For one flame-flicker second, she looks remorseful. But she blinks it away. "And now I've found it again."

"Time's up." The guard snatches at my arm again.

"Please, wait!" Tears run down my cheeks as I pull against him. "Mama, you have to listen to me—"

"No, Yulia. I beg you—listen." Her tone freezes me where I stand. There's pleading in her words that belies her placid smile. "It's not safe for you beyond the Colonel's grasp. I know this is all very confusing." She squeezes her eyes shut. "But promise me you won't run away again."

The guard stands, waiting, his grip still on my arm. Mama stares right through me.

I hang my head. I can't even look at her as I mutter, "I won't."

I sit across from Rostov in the back of the van. He hasn't stopped grinning. I want to punch him, shatter that smug look. He's waiting for me to say something, give him some hint of acquiescence. But just because he's the safest choice for me right now doesn't make me his ally. I heard Natalya Gruzova's screams—I won't forget what he's capable of.

"It is for the best that you went through this," he finally says. He picks at his fingernails. "Sometimes we need to learn our limitations. Open our eyes to the reality of why things must be the way they are."

"You didn't have to kill Gruzova," I say to my feet.

The back of my head strikes the hard metal wall. My legs kick out from under me, and my wrists lock up, sealed to my sides. I try to turn my head, try to look away from his boiling, scar-red face, but my head won't obey. My thoughts scatter like a flock of birds, flapping in terror.

"What do you think the CIA team would have done to her, if I let her live? Would they continue to work with her, knowing they'd been betrayed? Would they keep poking holes into her thoughts until her brain crumbled?" The words hiss through the gap in his teeth. "She was not living. She was a walking shadow."

I hate him—every nerve ending on my skin burns with hatred for him—but I stay locked in place. I can't push this hatred out of me. I am too weak. I soak up his fury, letting him fill me with his emotions, his control, his contempt. Why can't I push these feelings out? I'm like a waterskin stretched to bursting.

And the worst of it is I know he's right.

"Traitors, dissidents, cowards like your father have the luxury of looking down on our Soviet way. They have never known true suffering, and therefore don't see its purpose. They cannot fathom why we must resort to such measures because they've never witnessed the consequences of too much liberty."

Again, that pain in my heart at knowing he's right. Our family was always privileged, we always had plenty—food, soft toilet paper, clothing, holidays on the Black Sea—until the day Papa ran for help and left us to live off the streets.

"He infected your mother with these foul ideas. He would have us be like America. But why?" Rostov sneers. "We have no orphans, no mentally ill living under bridges. Everyone who wishes a job has one. Our artists are celebrated, not shunned. University education for all who wish it, food on every plate. We do not segregate our people by race, by gender. Look at the top women scientists, like your mother, unhindered by their sex. And we are winning the race to the moon! Our *Sputnik* satellites peer down on the Americans, where they are helpless to stop them.

"She had forgotten the importance of her work. Lost herself in his fanciful dreams. But she remembers now. We are forgiving, when one deserves forgiveness. The Academy has forgiven her for abandoning her important work. And so I forgive you, too, for the impulsiveness of your youth."

Forgiveness? The very word, from him, tastes like rancid meat. Maybe he's right about Papa, about the cost we pay to live in a country like ours. Maybe, in time, I will not despise my gift and the work it has led me to.

But I will never bow to him.

"She knew," I say. "About my ability." I don't expect him to answer me honestly, but even lies have a way of peeling a few layers back on the truth.

Rostov smiles like he's savoring this moment. "They both did. We monitor all Party members' children for the markers of psychic abilities. As scientists themselves, it appears they were able to suppress those results from reaching us, but nothing stays hidden forever."

His words strike at a tender spot in my mind, like an old bruise. My thoughts edge around it, trying to imagine Mama and Papa keeping such a secret from me. It's as if, because I didn't know what I was capable of, it stayed hidden just under my skin until there was nowhere left to hide.

"Those records," I say. "What if the CIA got access to them? And that's why they're hunting us now."

Rostov nods. "It is possible. We are conducting an internal investigation on the matter. Our top priority is keeping you and your teammates safe from whatever foul plans the CIA has."

"But it's not just our team." My voice sounds thick. I'd only glimpsed a few photographs, that day in Gruzova's apartment; but perhaps Rostov has salvaged memories of the rest from her shredded brain. "There are others they're hunting. These wild-lings." I swallow hard. "I want to protect them, too." At least I can sense the scrubber coming for me, screaming like a tornado or a falling missile. The wildlings, with no control over their powers, don't have that luxury.

"So you will continue your work for us?" I know it's not a question, but he pretends it is. "We will keep you safe from this scrubber, and you may lead our efforts to protect these wildlings from the Americans. The less you fight us, the happier we are to accommodate your wishes. A place of your own, in time; visits with your brother."

He relinquishes his physical control of me. I slump down on the bench. My rage is gone, crushed under its own weight. I think of the fire that smolders behind Valentin's eyes. Now I understand that he has not given up, but he knows there is no other choice.

"I'll do it," I say, my voice rough as burlap.

Someday, I promise myself, I will be strong enough that Rostov can't pull my strings. I can no longer despise myself for this power. I must make it my own.

CHAPTER 20

MASHA WASTES NO TIME in seeking me out to gloat. "Look at the ration rat, caught in the mousetrap again." She flops onto the cot next to mine and crosses her arms behind her head. "You know, most rats learn not to get caught twice."

"Most rats don't survive the first time," I reply.

Masha sucks in a deep breath, then lets it out, a blissful smile overtaking her face. "If only you could have seen your face when Rostov walked into Gruzova's apartment. I bet you thought you'd been so careful. But you can't trust a traitor, especially not one as screwed up in the head as that."

Larissa catches my eye from the far end of the room. It hurts to look at her—I really believed she was different from Misha and Masha, and even Sergei. Masha, I'd expect to stop me at every opportunity. And Sergei—I ignore the pang in my gut. I don't want to contemplate why he helped them. But Larissa, who must have seen my plans to seek the Americans' help in her visions of the future, stings in an entirely new way. She has no loyalty to our captors, none that I can discern, or the slightest hint of interest in playing their games. She must have had a good reason for doing this to me. That, or she's the most devious spy of us all.

Which means—I shake my head—of all people, the one who didn't betray me was Valentin. I'd been so worried about the dangers he posed that I didn't see he's my only ally.

Larissa raises one finger to her lips: *Shh.* I glance down at Masha on the extra cot, eyes still closed, humming boisterously to herself as she basks in victory. Larissa slowly raises her other hand, dangling a dead mouse by the tail. Easy, Shostakovich. Larissa moves slowly, deftly enough to keep the floorboards from squeaking, and tucks the mouse into Masha's bed.

Masha's ear-bursting screams after dinner, ringing throughout the house and rattling the windowpanes, almost make me grin. Larissa may not be my ally, but there's clearly more to her motives than I'd first guessed.

"Check." Ivan knocks Valentin's pawn with a heavy click. "Again. Stick to your jazz music, Valya."

Valentin fiddles with his black frames and studies the board for a long moment, then finally claims Ivan's bishop with his knight.

"You've fallen into my trap!" Ivan slides his rook across the board, sending the knight flying. "Check and mate. You're really terrible at this game."

Valentin shrugs. "I never trust people who are good at chess."

Sergei nudges Ivan. "Move over, it's my turn." Ivan lopes off to join Larissa on the couch, and Sergei plops down at the chess board. My chest tightens at the sight of him. He'd been carefully avoiding me since I returned yesterday. "Yulia, want to play?"

He flashes me that half-formed grin, hair glittering gold in the afternoon light, but where it might have made me smile before, now it leaves a taste in my mouth like ash. I narrow my eyes at Sergei and point to the textbook in my lap. Valentin's gaze flicks from Sergei to me.

Sergei's smile falters. "All right," he says, "your loss. Let's play, Valya."

The book is *An Introduction to the History of Genetics*, my "welcome home" present from Major Kruzenko. She'd given it to me along with a list of the dates for Moscow State's entrance exams this spring. "You'd better start studying now," she'd said. As if like that, my escape had been erased and the conclusion foregone: I *would* continue my work with the KGB. I *would* be permitted to attend courses at Moscow State. And just like that, Kruzenko ties onto me a puppet string of her own. As if Rostov hadn't attached enough.

"You should have forced Ivan to lose," Misha says to Valentin, as he heads toward the doorway.

"Get in Ivan's head and force him to make a bad move," Masha adds. Her delicate legs are slung over her chair arm as she flips through a newspaper.

"I wouldn't use my powers like that." Valentin shakes down his rolled-up sleeves. His eyes catch Sergei's, and my heart twists when he speaks again—"It would set a bad precedent."

Sergei jumps up from the table, chess pieces scattering everywhere. "Do you have something to say, Valya?"

Valentin's eyes dart toward mine, then away again. "No. It isn't worth it."

"Oh, let me guess," Masha says, voice reeking with sarcasm. "He thinks you owe his little girlfriend an apology."

My cheeks sting like they've been slapped. I'm frozen, uncertain whether I should deck Masha across the face with this heavy textbook or shout a refutation of what she's just said, but neither seems like a good option just now. Fortunately, Valentin leaps in for me. "It's nothing of the sort." I'm relieved I don't have to speak, but a sick, vile part of me, one I wish I could smother, feels disappointment at his words.

"I don't owe anyone an apology," Sergei says, words whistling through gritted teeth. "I was trying to help her. Save her from far worse. Better than end up like old whats-er-name, right, Valya?"

One of the spider-guards crawls out of the shadows. "Sergei Antonovich." A look passes between them, then Sergei shrugs them off and storms from the room without so much as a glance toward me. Valentin watches me for a moment, head lowered like he's embarrassed by the whole affair, then shuffles off. I expect to hear him banging around on the piano within minutes, but silence hangs thick as fog in the mansion.

I turn back to my textbook. A chapter on eugenics—the practice of selectively breeding a human population for desirable qualities and keeping those with undesirable qualities from procreating. Americans and Germans have long taken part in eugenics programs, the book claims. But it says nothing of the perks given to obedient little children like us, or to couples who meet in the Komsomol, the youth members' group of the Communist Party. Lavish apartments on Kutuzovsky, healthier rations, prompt medical services—I wonder if it's really so different.

The goal of most eugenics programs is to eliminate unfavorable mutations, but some programs embrace them as welcome additions, much like dog breeders shaping a new breed.

Or turning a fox into a pet or a weapon, I think.

There's a commotion on the couch; Ivan hovers over Larissa, arms plunging around her, but she pushes him away. "Not now," she murmurs, looking back at me.

Ivan sighs and gets up to crank the volume dial on the brand-new television set: Larissa's reward for selling me out. *KVN*, Larissa's favorite show, is too loud, making it hard for me to read. It's an endless parade of bulbous Russian men performing lopsided comedy routines. All the jokes are safe, boring; the audience laughs at the ridiculous antics the performers get into while waiting in line for rations, but no one is laughing at the lines, the rations, the absurdity of our daily life. Ivan wheezes and chuckles along with the audience. The laughter crashes and swells in my head, like a wave sloshing back and forth. It emits an endless too-bright color display of teeth and throats rolling with laughter, and Ivan's laughing with it, and the fact that they're laughing only makes them laugh more—

A hand closes on my arm. "Yulia." Larissa peeks up over the chair arm, watching me with wide blue eyes.

I narrow my eyes at her, though the look she's giving me is an achingly good mirror of Zhenya's when he knew he'd disappointed me in some way. "What do you want?"

Ivan laughs again at *KVN*; Larissa tugs at my wrist. "Let's talk somewhere else."

I let her guide me out of the living room and into our classroom, where Major Kruzenko has taped up photographs of all of Natalya Gruzova's colleagues and friends on one side of a blackboard. Larissa flips the blackboard over and starts scratching out names on the reverse side: Chernina, Yulia Andreevna. Sorokhin, Valentin Borisovich. She adds the rest of our team members' names, then lists out code names for John and Jane Does.

"The dossiers you saw in Gruzova's apartment," she explains. "I want to help you find them."

"And who says I want your help?" I ask.

Larissa starts scribbling additional information in a grid: profession, address, last known location. "No one." She shrugs. "But you won't get far on your own."

She passes me a stack of folders: Rostov's typed reports on everything he recovered about the wildlings from interrogating Gruzova. They're all around our age—fourteen to twenty. Young enough to be aware of their powers, but likely without any real mastery. Factory workers, a railway technician, polytechnical students—nothing high profile, just cogs in the Soviet machinery. Just remote enough that the KGB can't find them and bring them in without our help.

Larissa twirls the piece of chalk between her fingers. "When I was ten, my math teacher held me after class. He was convinced I'd cheated on my test. I hadn't—I just saw strange things happen when I wrote down answers. I could already see the teacher's writing on the test, marking it correct or not."

"So you reworked your answers until you got the right mark?" I ask.

"Yeah. I wasn't the best student, so of course he was suspicious. He started lecturing me, but I found I knew the words he was about to say right before he said them. I started answering accusations he hadn't yet made." She gazes off, lips easing into a smile. "I'm sure it was his report that tipped off the KGB. I didn't know well enough to hide what I was."

I stare at the grid again. Factory workers. It's far too broad. We'll need a way to narrow it down. "You think these wildlings have probably slipped up, too," I say.

She nods. "Exactly. Not enough to get brought in, but I'd bet there are *some* reports that could point us in the right direction. Let's you and I figure out what we're looking for, then we can present it to Kruzenko."

"Good idea." I smile—then stop myself. "I guess you're pretty good at bringing people in."

Her hand tightens around the chalk; I hear a soft snap. "I'm doing this to keep those wildlings from getting hurt. You know that, right?" She shakes her head. "It was the same for you."

"Spare me."

"Yulia. You don't know what I saw." Her gaze is hollowed out. "The American scrubber—he's not like Rostov, ripping your thoughts out all at once. He's corrosive. A slow poison. You don't understand what I was saving you from. All I could taste was blood when I tried to see you going to him . . ."

Anger surges through me, but I'm haunted by Natalya Gruzova, her thoughts sputtering out as she tried to cling to sanity. I try to swallow down this constriction at my throat—this emotion at the crossroads of anger and relief. "We can't live like this forever," I say.

161

"No," Larissa agrees. Far more readily than I'd expected. "But there's got to be a better way than *that*." She smiles. "That's a puzzle for another day. Today, let's see about keeping these wildlings from that fate."

After a few hours poring over records and maps, we've compiled a list of possible wildling locations for Major Kruzenko to compare to neighborhood KGB post reports. I catch myself smiling at Larissa, laughing at her jokes, even discussing our upcoming operation at the Revolutionary Banquet. How easy it could be, for me to surrender to this life and accept my place in the machine.

If only I could forget the way the wind felt on my face in the Metro tunnels; the taste of possibility in the air.

CHAPTER 21

THAT NIGHT, I DREAM OF my old life again, a strange lens skewing it like a memory I'd forgotten until now. Papa sits in a sterile room I'd never seen before—white, smelling of bleach and menthol, with an undercoat of stale cigarette smoke. He hunches over a soapstone countertop, jiggling one foot as he lets ashes tumble from his unsmoked cigarette. They land to the left of the ashtray, flecking the stack of charts before him marked SEKRET.

He swivels on his stool to face the two dark-haired children tussling over a ragged bunny doll on the floor. The scene isn't familiar, but the bunny sparks my memory instantly—I'd had it from birth, but it vanished when I was nine. Papa told me I'd probably left it somewhere, but I never bought his excuse. Most likely, Mama had decided it had endured enough trauma for one lifetime and threw it out. In the dream, it looks on death's doorstep.

"Sorry, Antonina," Papa says to himself, watching us. The

cigarette dangles precariously off his lower lip, held in place only by spit. "It stops here."

He plucks the cigarette free and lowers it to the corner of the charts. It crackles at first, resistant; but soon the flames blossom across the paper's edge. As orange laps at the page, I can see a name at the top of the charts:

CHERNINA, YULIA ANDREEVNA

CHAPTER 22

IT IS THE SEVENTH OF NOVEMBER, the forty-sixth anniversary of the October Revolution when Lenin's Bolsheviks seized the Winter Palace, shot up the royal family in a basement, declared all land to be state property, and promptly let millions of peasants starve to death when the new centralized government was unable to distribute food. (So the history Papa taught me goes—my schoolbooks tended to skip over the dying parts.) They also pushed the Russian calendar forward by twelve days, so we could emulate the Europeans we one day hoped to convert to communism, which is why we celebrate the October Revolution in November.

Premier Khruschev has been shouting angrily on Red Square all day, punctuating his statements not with the thwack of his shoe on the podium (as he often does), but with artillery fire, which sounds as if it's exploding directly over our mansion. Red Army Sukhoi fighter jets burst forth from the Moskva River on the hour, tearing through the sound barrier, and circle overhead before strafing Red Square to our north.

Masha and Misha are watching the live broadcast on television, but I grow bored with it once Ivan starts fighting with them for control of the dial. Larissa helps me lug the big electric samovar next to the door of the back deck, and we pour ourselves mug after mug of hot tea so we can watch the aerial show in person under the threat of fresh snow.

Finally, the time comes to prepare for the Communist Party celebration at the Tchaikovsky Conservatory. There are actually seven official Revolutionary Banquets, and we are attending the third most prestigious gala, posing as honored Komsomol guests. Of course, we are actually on a mission. If Gruzova wasn't working alone, we must dig through the thoughts of her colleagues and acquaintances, searching for signs of treasons.

Dresses and suits were dropped off for us this morning. Mine is a warm shade of blue, with a sash in the back that won't stay tied. Larissa and I curl each other's hair, and I can't resist a little twirl in the mirror, to great applause from Larissa. After years of baggy clothes belted onto me as I root around in the streets, the glide of satin against my skin does feel nice. I look like a dark-haired doll in the mirror, like the child of lavish Party members I once was. But the more I look at it, the more it churns my stomach, and I smear off most of the lipstick Larissa has applied to me, so the rosy stain is only a ghost on my lips.

Major Kruzenko summons us for a pre-operation briefing, reviewing the names and faces we'll be seeking out tonight. She wears not her usual green KGB uniform, but some tiered pink monstrosity trimmed in floppy lace. She's positively radiant as she warns us about our targets' potentially dangerous, treasonous thoughts.

The van deposits us a few blocks from the conservatory, and we must trudge through the snow past a long line of old women, shivering in their threadbare coats. The building they are lined up for reads "Pharmacy." I think of Mama and her makeshift clinic. She helped so many in our neighborhood who couldn't have gotten to the State clinics on time. But I also know our supplies had been smuggled or stolen from state-owned pharmacies like this one, which only meant a longer wait for these old women who follow the rules. I turn my head away from them, as if they might somehow recognize my shame.

Red velvet banners frame the conservatory entrance, and its already ornamental façade has been further spangled with bronze sickles and hammers and sparkling stars of crystal. We slush through the snowbanks to the staircase, and Major Kruzenko promptly loses us in the press of fur-clad partygoers that carry us up into the entrance. I can sense her, though, at the back of my mind; Pavel and our other guardians never feel far enough away.

Inside the main atrium, we are greeted with even more red bunting and a massive bronze statue of Vladimir Lenin. He is mid-stride and holds one hand out before him as if testing for rain. Perhaps it's just the sculptor's doing, but there's something too crooked in his grin, too assured; his eyes are unfocused and his legs seem too long for his body. I am glad when the crowd—suddenly radiant with heat as they shed their fur coats—sucks us into the next room.

Where is the food? I'm starving.

I can't believe Natasha got invited to the second-best party. I've done that bitch's work for years . . .

Oh, great, here comes Boris with another glass of vodka. I'd better stay sober.

Aren't those Rostov's kids? Better keep my thoughts to myself. What was that trick he showed me . . . ?

My gaze follows the last as he drifts past us with a smile that never dims. He wears a trim, well-pressed suit, but something about his gait and his hair suggests KGB. I file away his face in case I need to remember him.

Others' thoughts build around me frantically as I push deeper into the hall, searching for Larissa—I know she's probably working with Ivan, but I don't want to work on my own. The negative remarks and ugly fears are like splinters pricking my skin each time I brush against someone; they twist into me, impossible to wrench free. These are the *nomenklatura*, and they have everything and yet they worry over money, love, work; their lives just like the rest. I wrap my arms tight across my chest, hoping that if I make myself small enough, people will stop brushing against me, wrinkling my gown, leaving their nasty little thoughts behind.

A hand closes around my shoulder with a familiar tune. "Hello, gorgeous. That's a good color for you."

I spin around to face Sergei. He smiles and scrubs at his hair, like he's a little kid about to charm his way out of a scolding. Well, I won't give him the satisfaction. I shrug his hand off of me and turn away.

"Yul, wait. Please."

And there it is, that pitiful twinge in his voice like a kicked puppy. I stand still, not facing him, and wind Shostakovich tight around my thoughts.

"I know you think I owe you an apology. And—and you're right, I probably do. But I—"

"*Probably?*" I hiss, trying to keep my voice down.

He takes a deep breath. "Sorry. I'm no good at this. Let me try again. I know you think I betrayed your trust by telling them that I saw you take the key—"

"Oh," I say. "So that's what happened."

I turn back again, and his face is completely wilted, his smile drooping. "It wasn't *just* me," he says, voice pitiful. "Larissa saw it, too. She saw that now that you had the key, there was a high chance you'd make a run for it when the opportunity presented itself—so they made sure it did."

So my entire escape had been orchestrated from the start. I want to be furious, but the more complicated the situation becomes, the less I know what to feel. I study his rumpled tuxedo, twisted awkwardly around his sturdy frame. The sleeves are too short for his long arms, so his forearms creep out whenever he moves. "I'll let Larissa speak for herself."

"I just want you to know I did it to keep you safe, Yulia. If you had gotten caught by the Americans and gotten your thoughts scrubbed out—or worse—and I could have prevented it . . ." The smile dies. "Well, I never would have forgiven myself."

I let Shostakovich harden around me. A protective shell. "Well, I'm glad your conscience will be clean."

"So . . ." He extends his hand toward me, holding it more like a question than a handshake. "Truce?"

"We'll see," I say.

He snatches two champagne flutes from a passing waiter. "Great! Good to hear it. I'll drink to a 'we'll see.'" He slaps one of the glasses into my hand. "Of course, it's Sovietskoye Shampanskoye, which tastes like stale bread, but we'll make do."

I eye my bubbly glass. "We're supposed to be working. We have to find Gruzova's co-workers."

"And nothing loosens the thoughts like a little sip, eh? Come on, times are hard enough." He gestures toward my gown. "You look too pretty not to enjoy yourself."

I scrunch my face at him. When I concentrate on it, the secondhand satin feels filmy with guilt against my skin. Kruzenko said the dresses came from the KGB's wardrobe department, which explains the sleazy details of honeypot operations—pretty KGB girls plying secrets from male targets—that occasionally sink in. I clink Sergei's glass and down my champagne in one gulp, though I try to look none too happy about it. It's mostly bubbles, anyway. The cottony taste is gone as quickly as it came.

"Where shall we start?" Sergei asks, weaving us around the various banquet spreads. "I'll help you brush against some of the *Veter* scientists, then maybe we can slink off to a nice dark corner where you can help me . . . uh . . ." His grin spreads. "Remote view."

Heat creeps up my face. I summon up my best indignant look for him, though the champagne fuzz in my head betrays me, and it dissolves into a stupid smile. "How about you go work on that by yourself, and we'll meet up later."

He holds up his hands. "All right, I had to try. Try not to miss me too much."

"Sure thing, comrade." I offer him a sloppy salute, even sloppier than I'd intended courtesy of the champagne, and plunge back into the crowd.

I'm trying to remember Sergei as the jerk who betrayed me, and not the well-meaning jerk who wanted to keep me safe. But it's wearing me down, dulling my musical shield and letting every thought and memory flood in. I don't have the energy for all this anger anymore. Just like the easy path is playing along with Rostov's and Kruzenko's plans, the easy thing to do is to let go of my rage.

If I have to laugh at another one of Comrade Colonel's stupid jokes . . .

He always does this to me, off talking to Irina again—

I don a smile to match my strand of fake pearls, and before I know it, I've circled the whole atrium, and my second glass of Shampanskoye has disappeared.

"Find anything?" Masha asks, slithering up alongside me.

A moment later, Misha appears at my other side. "And we don't mean an escape route."

"I'm just learning my way around." I clench a fist around my necklace. "You know. Establish a . . . a baseline." I suppress a giggle. The bubbles are making me sound like a textbook, though I feel like a soft summer cloud.

"Oh. Right. We—we were doing that too." Masha scoops up a tiny square of bread smeared with salmon from her plate of *zakuski*—little bites. "But I already found one of the *Veter 1* scientists hanging on some man's arm during the last number. Irina, I think her name is."

"What did the man look like?" I ask.

Masha doesn't hear me. She pitches a smile over her shoulder in the direction of the band, which has been playing a blend of folk songs and jazz improvisation. Then I spot who she's smiling at—Valentin, tapping his foot along to the music. When he notices Masha, he glares back at her like we're ants and he's the magnifying glass.

"Valya's shaping up to be quite the spy," Masha says, turning back to me with a fake flirty smile smeared on her lips. "Once he stopped trying to run away, he's really learned to make the most of his gifts."

"A little moody still," Misha says. "But I think he understands now the value of our work."

Masha shares a smirk with her brother. "Don't worry, Yul, there's always Sergei. Nothing on upstairs—he's perfect for you, really. But even he has the good sense to enjoy the privilege we've been given."

"You were an idiot to try to give this up," Misha says, and Masha nods. "Look around you—isn't this a better life? Khruschev may make concessions to the Americans now, but Colonel Rostov's plans will return the Soviet Union to its glory. You should stop fighting it."

"I'm not fighting anything," I say. "I'm just doing my job."

"Khruschev and his guard are fading out. It's time for the Soviet Union to be great again." Misha's eyes focus on me—they could be carved from slate, that cold, callous pair. He's way too close to my arm. Masha is, too, for that matter. They're closing in on me from both sides. It's hot in between them, in this packed room; I'm flushing like at our old dacha's bathhouse sauna, where the only relief came from diving headfirst into the snow.

I take a step back, but the twins follow me. "I'm not interested in playing political games. I'll fulfill my obligation and be done."

Masha flicks her head to one side with a flawless swoosh of hair. "Our work has no end. Not until the workers of the world are united. We have to protect Russia from these monsters who would kill us for what we are."

Brilliant pinks, blues, reds spin across the dance floor before us, and thoughts and smells spiral away in the dancers' wake: sweat, eagerness, acrid perfume, regret. One thought is faint, but unmistakable to me—the hum of a brain that's encountered a scrubber. My stomach churns. Who is this poor person, who has no idea what's being done to his brain . . .

Valentin catches my eye from over by the bandstand. He must have sensed it, too. He marches toward us with tightened fists. "Yulia. You're looking lovely as ever. Are you enjoying yourself tonight?"

"Could be better." I sip my champagne, fighting back the blush on my cheeks. When did I get another glass? Is this my third or fourth? I'm losing track.

"How about a dance? I can't promise to make your night better." A dark, false smile tweaks his lips as he looks at the twins. "But it can't make it worse."

Masha glares at him for a minute, then shrugs her shoulders. "Your loss." She slinks off toward the buffet table, Misha trotting after her like a puppy.

I hold my hand out to Valentin. He clasps me gingerly in his arms, and we start the dance steps, slow and careful at first. "I don't suppose you're here to say 'told you so' about my escape attempt as well."

"Actually," he says, "I've been dying all evening to do this." He tips me backward as the music spikes, then pulls me back up against him.

My dark curls bounce around my face as we whirl along the dance floor, thankfully concealing the rush of blood to my head. We dovetail together nicely; I can feel his chest rising and falling. Normally I'd fend him off with a snippy comment, but with a horrible sinking in my gut, I realize I don't *want* to fend him off.

"Unfortunately," he says, "we also have some investigating to do." He steers us into the throng of dancers, and we fit seamlessly into the gears of the dance.

A fresh number begins—a folk song, the kind where the tune starts slowly, but then repeats, growing more and more frantic with each round, coiling up like a spring until it snaps and everyone collapses, unable to keep up. Valentin establishes our steps early, simple enough that we should be able to stay in the game for several rounds while searching for the person with the scrubber-touched thoughts. Those who aren't dancing circle the floor, pinning us in, clapping in rhythm with the song.

Valentin's lips lower to my ear, and a thrill shoots up my spine, unbidden. "There are things I feel I must tell you," he murmurs, "but this isn't the right place for it."

I pull my head back a fraction from his. My skin is bubbly, but his breath smells curiously sober. "Seems as good a time as any."

"Are you still looking for a way out?" he asks.

I can barely hear him in the frantic music—surely I've misheard. I untangle my feet just in time to avoid crashing. "Are you asking me what I think you are?"

"The side project I've been doing for Rostov. Some new information has come to light." He whirls me under his arm, and my skirt flares wide. "But I'll need your help to make sense of it."

The music clicks up in tempo; our feet fly beneath us. "I'm afraid I'm not as good at playing these Soviet games as I used to be," I say. But I like the idea of being a confidant, a co-conspirator. I've been fighting alone for so long, and this inscrutable, sobering boy . . . In one dangerous instant, I think I could share a secret with him.

"You say that like it's a bad thing." Valentin looks at me sidelong before he swings me away, then catches me in his arms. When I face him again, the whites of his eyes gleam—is he afraid? "I like you when you're Yulia—the real Yulia." He looks away. "Not the battle-hardened mask you usually wear."

I want to smile, but my head is too much like a cotton ball, soaking up everything, without a brain to make sense of it. Do I want him to say these things? It takes every ounce of my dwindling sobriety to process my thoughts about Valentin. He sends me into another twirl. Before I have a chance to stop myself, I slide a quick kiss onto his cheek, natural as breathing, as the music steps up the pace again.

Valentin continues through the steps, but with a stunned look on his face. The clapping around us turns violent, frantic to keep up with the music as it zips along. My feet turn to rubber. "What?" I ask, squeezing his hands. "Did I do something wrong?"

First, my foot lands on top of his; then my knee tangles into his thigh. The heel of my shoe threatens to snap. Valentin tumbles toward me. As my tailbone strikes the marble floor, he throws his arms wide, so even though he lands on top of me, we scarcely touch.

The dance floor rolls with laughter as the musicians let the song deteriorate for comic effect. Several other couples have collapsed as well. Some of the older men stoop down to help us to our feet.

"I'm sorry." I suppress a hiccup. "I couldn't keep up—"

"It wasn't you." Valentin's hand is still closed around mine and squeezing tighter. "The *Veter* team member you thought had been talking with the scrubber. I think it's more than just—"

I catch a flash of lightning in the crowd—feel it more than see it, ripping through my mind. I spot a dark-haired woman I recognize from our briefings on the *Veter 1* team. According to the records, she and Natalya Gruzova were close friends. Is her mind so thoroughly scrubbed that she stings like this? But then I try to look at the man she'd been dancing with and he sets my eyes on fire—

I double over, nearly falling again. Valentin holds me firm and turns me away from the dance floor. "Don't look at him."

I force my eyes shut but the man's brilliance is reverberating in my brain, it's ricocheting like a bullet, it's throbbing through my veins. Waves of white light crash across my eyelids. I try to reach out with my thoughts to sense him, but he sends my mind scattering. Logic and words peel off of me.

"Come with me." Valentin swallows loudly. "If that—that *thing* . . . is the American scrubber . . . Well, he makes Rostov look weak." Valentin's face is pale under a veil of sweat. "And Yulia?"

"You saw something," I whisper.

Valentin drags me off the dance floor, shoving through the drunken crowd. "He's not here just to work on Natalya's friend." He pulls me into a stairwell and licked his chapped lips. "He's searching for *you*."

CHAPTER 23

PAVEL, MY GUARD, hovers over me. Watching him is like hearing an echo; his face trails behind his movements, and his words dot his face like breath in the winter air. The American sunshine man radiates somewhere over my shoulder; my bared back is already peeling with a burn.

"Get her out of here." Pavel's voice dances before me. "Don't let her back into the main room. I'll alert the others."

Someone's hand closes tight on my arm and faces swirl before me like little galaxies, exploding into balls of nothingness and radiation. "Too much Shampanskoye," another guard says from the end of a comet's tail. We're orbiting the party like a *Sputnik* satellite, snapping little spy photographs.

"Please, Yulia, you have to shake it off." Valentin helps me sit on the stone steps; we're facing a massive painting of Tchaikovsky, surrounded by Karl Marx, Stalin, Lenin, and a sea of faceless farmers harvesting wheat as rays of sunshine and music soar overhead. They fly through the cosmos with me, shrouded by a planet's umbra, safe from the scrubber's glow. "Focus on your mental shield—try to keep it in your head—"

"What's going on?" Footsteps pound down the staircase toward us. I flop backward against the sharp stairs and see Sergei from upside-down. Shostakovich cinches around my thoughts.

"The scrubber's here with one of Gruzova's co-workers." Valentin's voice turns stony. "I think he hurt Yulia."

"I'm *fine*," I say.

Sergei pushes his hand under my shoulder blades and props me back up. "Scrubbers are dangerous. She should steer clear of them. All of them." There's an edge to his voice, cutting through the haze.

Valentin's cheeks burn darkly. "I would never do that to her."

"But you could. Maybe you did it by accident." Sergei crouches down on my other side and snaps his fingers in front of me. "Yulia? Null, one, two. Follow the sound of my voice."

There is no galaxy, no blinding sun. My head throbs and the marble is too firm against my hipbones, and I'm sinking back down to earth. I smack Sergei's hand out of my face. "I'm fine. Just a little dizzy, is all." I nestle into Shostakovich's sawing strings section. "I didn't even get a good look at the guy."

"As well you didn't. If he was targeting you . . ." Valentin grimaces.

"Don't scare her." Sergei won't take his hand off my shoulder. It weighs on me like lead. "Bad enough she had to dance with you, flatfoot."

Valentin sets his lips in a straight line. "I'd better get back. I want to help our guards hunt him down."

"I'm not some weak thing you have to protect." I rub my temples. Now that my adrenaline has faded, there's a sharp pain rooting around in my skull. It treads a familiar path through constricted blood vessels, though I can't recall ever feeling this pain before.

"I know you aren't, but I'd rather he try to scrub me than get ahold of you. You work with touch, and if he were to . . . grab your arm, or something—"

I nod, halfhearted, at Valentin. "Fine. Do what you have to do."

Valentin stands. "Keep an eye on her, will you, Sergei? Take her to the upstairs lobby, maybe—away from the main hall." Valentin's gaze hangs on me for a moment, like he wants to say more, but then he turns and ducks through the doorway back to the atrium.

Sergei helps me stand up, then loops one of my arms over his massive shoulders. "What the hell were you doing with that weirdo?" he hisses, as we climb toward the darkened second floor.

"It was just a dance," I say. "What do you care?"

"Listen." He jerks his head over his shoulder, checking that we are more or less alone. "I know he's got this moody, broody artist act down, and some girls go for that. Oh, look at the sad puppy. But it gets to be a drag, you know?"

"Not really," I say stiffly.

"And believe me, it's just an act. There's a monster under there. He's got the same sickness as Rostov and this American. He may mean well, but people still end up hurt around him." Sergei's upper lip curls back, menacing. His missing tooth doesn't look so cute now. "You don't know who he is. What he's up to."

I tug away from Sergei's grasp and settle into a dusty chair along the shadowed hallway. "Yes, apparently all of us are keeping secrets from all the rest. Go ahead and spit it out. I'm so tired of everyone's games."

His music storms around him as he kneels in front of me, fists solid at his side. "You want to know? Fine. If he won't have the courage to tell you himself—"

"Get on with it," I snap.

"Valya's hunting for your father, Yulia."

My ribcage constricts; I sink deep into the chair. The pain in my head twists tighter, like a vise closing in. "No."

"Rostov forced him into it after he tried to run away." Sergei's face is dark, his usual charm wiped away, leaving only a sadness behind.

"I don't . . ." I shake my head. "But how?" This fuzziness coursing through me isn't the alcohol anymore; that's long gone, and with it, the panic at encountering the scrubber. I reach out for Sergei's hand, propped before me on his knee. If I don't hold onto something, I'll shake uncontrollably until I'm no longer human, and all that's left is this vibrating, agonized mess.

"I don't understand it entirely. Rostov shows up at the mansion at night, after everyone's in bed, and then I think they slip into your thoughts while you're sleeping."

The dreams. The ones that feel like memories on the verge of being lost forever. I lick my lips and slowly, carefully open my mouth to speak. "I've been having these dreams," I say, "of my parents. My father, in particular." I cradle each word like it'll shatter if I let it go too soon.

Sergei nods, squeezing my fingers. "That's how scrubbers work. And the better he learns your emotions and memories, the easier they are for him to manipulate—"

"They're memories I didn't know I had," I say. "I'm not even sure that they're real."

"They're looking for clues to your father's whereabouts. He was part of your mother's research, after all." His hand lowers, clenching mine. "You deserve to know. Valya's only doing it to protect himself."

I clench my teeth until they ache. What a fool I am. When I thought he was the only person truly on my side, he was betraying me like the rest. "Just—stop. No more. I don't want any part of this madness."

Sergei leans toward me, shadows obscuring one side of his face; the other half is mottled with golden light, like at afternoon's end. "I'm so sorry, Yulia." He brushes my cheek with the back of his hand, leaving a warm trail on my skin. "I should have told you earlier." His forehead comes to rest against mine, throwing him into shadows completely.

I feel nothing, I am nothing. Sergei weaves his fingers into my hair. I don't meet his eyes; I close mine, weighing the momentum that's bringing his face toward mine against the emptiness in me that wants to shrink away from it all.

Then his lips are warm, directly on mine, and a little sticky from the champagne, though I'm sure mine are, too. His lips part as he kisses me again, digging for me this time. No. Too late, my brain finishes its sloppy calculation. I don't want this. I push away, squirming further into the chair, shoving at him with arms that don't work, answering with thoughts that don't come from my throbbing brain.

"Stop, Sergei. No—"

He pulls away immediately. But I'm spinning, whirling like a gear in a machine, and no one can stop me. Not Sergei, for sure. I wade my way out of the chair and stand. He backs up to give me space.

"If you knew, you shouldn't have kept it from me." I wrap my arms tight around me as I suck down sharp, panicky breaths. Sergei tasted of warm wheat bread and dangerous fires; I suddenly yearn to feel cold. "And you—it doesn't excuse what you've done."

"I'm only looking out for you. I want you to be safe."

The wall is cool and firm against my back. I turn away from him and press my cheek into the tiles, exhaling slowly. I don't want Sergei's taste on my lips. His eyes watching me from another room, another building. I don't want Rostov, Valentin, or the American scrubber in my head. I want my flesh and bone and thought and life to be mine, mine, mine alone. I'm on fire and I need an ice storm.

"Maybe it isn't your job," I say. "I certainly never asked for your protection." I've had to take care of myself since the day Papa left, wearing whatever guise was required to protect those I love. Sister, daughter, thief, spy, teacher, student, cook, ration rat. Valentin said he liked me best when I didn't wear any masks, but he must be mistaken. There's no room for the real Yulia under all of that.

Sergei's face looms too close at my shoulder. "You think you don't need protection? Then you're only fooling yourself."

I duck under his arm and slip into the shadows that chase the balcony. I run deeper into the conservatory, alongside the locked entrances to box seats. Even with my spider-guard behind me, I'm alone.

CHAPTER 24

I HOLD UP THE NEXT PHOTOGRAPH for Larissa, and her eyes flutter closed as she sinks into her visions. I don't need to speak for our wildling-hunting sessions. I ignored Valentin's offer of breakfast in the ballroom, which seemed to surprise him, and Sergei's apologetic grin, which didn't surprise him much. I do not talk to Misha and Masha, now or ever, and I have nothing to say to pimply Ivan who only ever wants to talk about himself anyway. I'm lucky to have pried Larissa away from him this afternoon after the ball, since she usually spends the afternoons surgically grafted onto Ivan's lap.

After not speaking all day, I'm finding myself more and more like Zhenya: whistling, humming, mumbling to myself, repeating the same strand of thoughts over and over in my head until they feel just right. I smooth them like sea-tossed stones:

Valentin is out for himself and can't be trusted.

Sergei is out for me for all the wrong reasons and can't be trusted.

I did not like Sergei kissing me.

I liked dancing with Valentin.

I do not like who I become when I drink Soviet champagne.

None of it matters because I am out for myself and can't be trusted, and Larissa and I are keeping tabs on the wildlings so we can use the KGB to protect them from a greater evil, all so I can have a glimpse of my brother someday and keep at least one soul off my conscience.

Larissa's eyes open with a gasp. "Running. One of the outer neighborhoods of Moscow—Zelenograd, maybe, or Khimki. Yes, they're passing a war monument. They know someone's chasing them."

"Is this happening right now?" I ask.

She shakes her head. "Sometime soon—maybe in eight, ten hours. No, wait—they're not running on foot now. They've taken the express bus. The pursuer is following them by car." She flinches. "No, that's not right, either . . ."

I tighten one hand, nails biting into my palm, and take a deep breath. It's not her fault, I tell myself. She's doing the best she can. But I can't bear to think of another wildling evaporating under the American scrubber's gaze. "How does it work?" I ask. "Your gift. Maybe if I understand it better . . ."

"It's like I'm looking at trees, right?" She splays her fingers. "A whole forest of possibilities. But I have to focus on the one tree in question. So I follow it up its trunk, okay, but then it splits. One of the branches is easier to follow than the rest—that's the most likely outcome at the given moment, but this is constantly shifting as people consider different choices. So I try to find the branch with the end point you want, the juicy apple, but it's tangled in all the other branches, and sometimes I have to guess which one will be the most likely path . . ."

"Wow." I whistle under my breath. "That sounds really complicated."

"It's not so bad. I see what's coming, so I never bother to look back."

Major Kruzenko charges into the room, still wearing her snow-dappled coat, a cardboard box clutched to her chest. "Hello, my little dears!" she sings, depositing the box before us. "Any progress on tracking the wildlings?"

Larissa updates her on Artyom, the one she'd been predicting, while I eye the box suspiciously. "Did the surveillance teams find something for us?" I ask, when Larissa's done.

Kruzenko's gaze darts between Larissa and me. "Yes," she says, dangling the word out like it's a piece of garbage. "Larissa, do you mind excusing us?"

Larissa pulls herself out of the lumpy sofa. "Sure, I'll go watch *KVN*."

"Isn't it reruns?" I ask. "I swear, you laugh harder at the jokes on the old episodes than when they were new to you."

"Nothing's new to me." She smiles at me sideways, pausing by the doorway. "I just get better at pretending to be surprised."

Major Kruzenko shuts the double doors behind Larissa, then shrugs out of her coat, melted snow flinging everywhere. "I do hope you are feeling better after your ordeal last night. We had nothing to indicate the Americans would be in attendance, or I would have provided more security for you."

Why bother? She doesn't protect us from the scrubber on our side. But I say nothing.

"I know such people are difficult to see clearly when they don't wish to be read, but did you see anything that might help us identify him?" She flips the spigot on the samovar and watches the steaming tea fill her oversized mug.

"It was so noisy already, and his face, it's . . ." I stare down at my hands as she slides into the chair opposite me, resting her mug on the empty table between us. "I got a decent look at another CIA team member when Valentin and I went to Kutuzovsky. I'm afraid we're better off tracking him instead."

"We already have operatives working on it, but we require your assistance for other matters." She gestures to the box.

A long silence drifts between us. She looks out the grimy second-floor window, and I look at the nicked black-and-white chessboard squares painted on the tabletop. I hold my breath and gather up the words I'd been planning to say, then finally release them in one gush.

"I've been working very hard on this case, and Rostov promised me I could see my brother soon if I did."

Her lips round into a surprised little O and she exhales. "Yes." She traces the rim of her mug. "Yes, he did." Shostakovich bounces through my head like a hockey puck let loose while I wait for her to continue. "But we must ensure the safety of these wildlings first."

She pulls two items from the box and places them on the chess table—a worn leather glove and a rubber mallet. "We recovered these items from the factories you pinpointed as possible job sites for some of the wildlings. I would like you to tell me if they are, indeed, psychic."

And there's the difference between why I'm searching for the wildlings, and why Kruzenko is. I want to protect them from the Americans; she wants to abduct them for the KGB's purposes, just like she did me. After feeling the scrubber so close against my thoughts, grinding into them like broken glass, I can see how Sergei might be inclined to choose the lesser evil of keeping me under lock and key. Not that I'd ever tell him that.

My face hardens. I am a Soviet mural of the Worker as She Grimly Commits Vile Acts for the Greater Good. I slip my hand into the leather glove.

A hot, tangy smell like blood floods through me. No—not blood. Molten pig iron. I'm in the slag works of a factory, handling a pair of tongs, moving a sun-bright rod from the oven to a cooling vat. Where are my thoughts?—Here, a concern over the next factory Soviet meeting—the Party representatives are keeping secrets from me. There, a date with Katia.

So much uncertainty; such ignorant bliss.

I peel off the glove. "No," I say. "This man doesn't have the ability. He should be safe from the Americans."

Kruzenko jots down a note in her folder, then pushes the mallet toward me.

I pick up the mallet and suddenly I'm placing it on the top shelf of my locker. My eyes itch from too little sleep; my nerves are dulled with exhaustion. All my life, I've heard little things, things I shouldn't. But the sounds following me the last few nights, like air raid sirens, scare me more than anything I've heard before.

I let go. I don't like the way this boy's fear pricks into my skin like an injection, over and over. Major Kruzenko watches me with eyebrows raised.

"Is that a yes?" she asks.

"Which one is this?" I ask, checking the chalkboard of profiles. "When did the team retrieve this? Have they found this mallet's owner?"

"We know which factory it came from. We'll contact the operations bureau and send plainclothes officers to track him down." She stands, snapping her folder shut. "Your assistance is much appreciated—"

"I want to see my brother." I slam my hand onto her folder, and she jumps back. "I'm not waiting any longer."

"I will pass your request to Colonel Rostov and see that he carries it further up the chain of command. It is the most I can offer you right now."

My knuckles are white around the table's edge; I feel bloated with too many emotions, both mine and the wildling's, swirling around and frothing up. "I have behaved impeccably since my return, have I not? Over a month with no complaint. I've been a perfect little spy, tracking the scrubber's targets, monitoring the *Veter 1* team. All I want is to see my brother. You *owe* me that."

Too much rage floods my veins. I can't keep this all inside. Don't be an empath, Yulia. Don't bottle it up. I have to get these feelings out of me, can't let them swell like Anastasia's did. I have to find a way to get them *out.*

My palms vibrate against the tabletop like the hangover of a dramatic chord after Valentin's hammered it on the piano. I'm pulled into the wood, an undertow slamming me against it, and just as quickly, my emotions fizzle out. I can't remember what made me so angry, so frightened, though I remember feeling that way.

Major Kruzenko leaps up from the table like she's been scalded. Her eyes are ringed in white. Can she feel what I felt? For a second, I can see my anger's shadow on her face. "Yes! Yes, you have done everything we've asked." She backs away from me. Her fingers tap against her thighs like an SOS. "Your dedication is not the problem. But there are certain difficulties—"

"I will see my brother." The absence of emotion is like the sky opening wide. I can be as cold, as determined as I need to be. "This week."

Kruzenko snaps her heels together and nods, jowls wobbling. "Of course. I will do my best. Your hard work and dedication will only add to the glory of the Soviet Union." That Russian shrug as she backs away, fear burning hot in the whites of her eyes. She leaves in a hurry, a thick slime-trail of gypsy music in her wake.

CHAPTER 25

MISHA, MASHA, SERGEI, and I are riding in the back of
a truck. It sounds like the start of a tasteless joke. Two socio-
paths, a ladykiller, and a paranoiac walk into a KGB van. No
one walks out. Sergei's too close to me. He's finally caught on
that I'm giving him the silent treatment, but I don't like his
shoulder so close to mine, skittering with anxious noise cloaked
in Tchaikosvsky. When I look at him, I taste sticky champagne.

But today I am less concerned with Sergei's misguided affection and more with the feeling like I'm a tool selected for a
specialized task. Colonel Rostov. He brought us into the truck,
though the details are hazy. I don't entirely remember it happening. No matter, we're here now. The truck slows, and the
tires squeal against cement, echoing as if indoors.

Rostov throws open the hatch for us. "Come." We're in a
circular tunnel, streaked with water stains. Only one guard, the
truck driver, marches behind us with his rifle at the ready. The
tunnel is dimly lit from overhead, but to either end of the tunnel

I can only see darkness. I don't think it's near the secret Metro line; no cool rush of air, no rumble in my chest of an approaching train. We are so deep within the earth that there aren't even rats.

"Calm down. You're too worked up," Sergei whispers to me—I feel it more than hear it—as he brushes past. I sink into Shostakovich's music and Yevtushenko's words like a fresh drift of snow. *How little we can see and smell . . . We are denied the leaves, we are denied the sky.*

Rostov ducks into an alcove, his shiny boots scraping across the concrete, and unlocks a metal door. Stark yellow and black triangles on its interior mark the tunnel we just left as a nuclear fallout shelter. I try to imagine living there for twenty, thirty years while Russia rots and festers above. I think I'd rather take my chances in the blinding white forever at the moment of impact.

We climb. We climb like clawing from the earth, up a narrow ladder that flakes with rust under our palms. Twice my snow-soaked boots slip on the rungs; stale air weighs down on our shoulders, daring us to fall. Masha huffs and puffs ahead of me, too frail for this work, while Sergei nudges impatiently at my heels.

Finally we reach the top of the ladder and move through double doors into a metal room that makes me think of the hull of a giant ship. "Mikhail, come with me," Rostov says. Misha sidles up to him. "You will maintain a link to Maria. Maria and Sergei, you will open a viewing where Mikhail and I go. Please be aware of anything in our surroundings that we do not notice."

Masha's hand flies into the air. Rostov's face stretches even longer as he nods to her. "Comrade Colonel. Permission to manipulate the environment?" she asks.

"What, your attempts at telekinesis?" Rostov asks. "Please, Maria, this is a delicate operation. We must minimize our chances of detection. Observe only, please—no interacting.

"Oh. And Yulia." Rostov whirls on me. His eyes are shadowed wells beneath the brim of his KGB officers' hat. "You will observe through Maria and Sergei, and then Mikhail and I will indicate what I want you to read. I believe you are strong enough now that you can use your powers through theirs."

"Yes, Comrade Colonel." I drop my gaze to the floor. I've only linked powers once before, in training. I'm not sure I'm ready to perform under pressure.

Rostov lowers his voice to the guard. "The Hound is where I requested?" The guard gives a tight, anxious nod. "Well done."

Rostov marches away with Misha, leaving me with Masha, Sergei, and the soldier. "Sit," the soldier says, gesturing to the corrugated metal floor. He pulls out a pack of cigarettes and pats them against his palm while Sergei and Masha sink into their visions.

"We're . . . we're inside the KGB headquarters," Masha says, eyebrows wrinkled in confusion. "They're headed into the directorate chiefs' offices," Her closed eyelids twitch. "Taking the elevator to the top floor."

"Why are we conducting a mission in our own headquarters?" I ask. "Shouldn't we be hunting the *Veter 1* traitors?" But my questions hang thick, unanswered.

Somewhere above us, a KGB general is banishing a dissident

to a gulag labor camp deep in Siberia. Perhaps another is conducting a raid on an apartment block, one like Aunt Nadia's, to round up more people whose neighbors have reported on them for sneaking extra rations or trading at the market. Another chief plans the death of American spies in East Berlin who do not yet know they've been compromised. And one more toasts to Premier Khruschev's health as they look down from the Kremlin onto Red Square and smile at the snow whipping against the workers' sooty faces.

I hate these men. But I cannot shake the creeping suspicion that Rostov means them harm—why else would he be conducting an operation against his own people, the KaGeBezniks?—and I would not wish his toxic, jagged thoughts upon anyone.

"Misha's keeping watch outside one of the offices," Masha says. "It looks like he's reading thoughts to see if anyone notices them, while the Colonel turns away the thoughts of anyone who does."

Sergei joins hands with Masha, and reaches out for mine. "Come on, Yul. You heard the orders." He looks tired; bored, even. Like this is one of countless such operations he's done. But this mission feels different to me. We're missing our usual entourage of guards, Kruzenko chirping at us about our progress, heavy documentation, and reporting.

"Why isn't Kruzenko here?" I ask. "We weren't given a specific objective." The soldier's cigarette smoke gusts away from me as I exhale.

Masha groans. "Rostov does this sometimes. The Soviet Union does not always function perfectly, but it's the duty of men like him to correct its course."

Something rattles in my thoughts at that; a broken thought

jarred loose. Perhaps Natalya Gruzova thought it her duty to correct the Soviet Union's course by evening the playing field between America and the USSR in the space race. Perhaps Stalin thought killing several million dissidents was correcting the course. And Khruschev, with his erratic but softer touch, is correcting us once more. What does it make Rostov, to defy Khruschev's will? A patriot? A dissident himself?

"Yul." Sergei reaches for my hand. "We have to do this."

"Something is wrong," I say. I'm not Larissa, but I know the taste of foreboding, like bile on my tongue.

"Did you hear something, Seryozha? All I hear is a ration rat going *squeak, squeak, squeak*," Masha says.

I grit my teeth. "Better than screaming my ass off. Do you still check your sheets every night?"

Sergei snatches my hand and yanks me toward him. "Shut up, both of you." His lax shoulders still look bored, but a shadow of fear crosses his face. I reluctantly lace my fingers in Sergei's clammy grasp.

I plunge through the surface of Sergei's and Masha's viewing. The image is so much sharper than when I just viewed through Masha's when we practiced; everything is overfocused. The slate gray walls look like impending storm clouds. I could cut myself on Misha's scowl as he guards the First Directorate Chief's door. I am standing in the doorway, an apparition, a wraith. I cannot see my hands but I can feel with them through Masha's and Sergei's sight.

You are just in time, Yulia Andreevna. Rostov's voice slithers through the weeds of my thoughts as he appears in the doorway, standing over the Chief's desk. *Come. Sit in this chair.*

What am I looking for? I ask. The words teeter on the edge between Shostakovich's symphony, and the untouched, unfenced parts of my mind where Rostov waits, watching, from the shadows.

Rostov taps his fingertips against a thick folder. *Who typed this?* he asks. I shuffle forward and run my fingers over the folder's cover.

Someone's coming, Misha says.

Then you must hurry, Yulia. Show me who wrote the document.

The officer hunches over a typewriter in an empty office, twisting around to look behind him frequently. He cannot trust this report to a secretary in the typing pool. He has to finish before the office's owner returns. I peer over his shoulder: "Comrade General—I regret that I must compose this report anonymously, but I am sure you will understand. I fear that Comrade Major Anton Sergeevich Rostov is gathering his own army from within the KGB to move against Premier Khruschev—"

Show him to me. Rostov grates his thoughts against mine. The gawky, studious young soldier sloughs off of the memory in my thoughts. Rostov grasps his image, glowing as he recognizes him.

The Chief is coming down the hall, Misha warns. *I can't stop him.*

Let him come, Rostov says. *You have done well.*

There is a thud in the hallway.

"Misha?" Masha asks. Her portion of the viewing stretches and warps as she pulls away from Sergei's. Misha is slumped against the wall, pulsing with the soft thought waves that I usually sense from people in a deep sleep.

Masha screams.

"Quiet!" the guard hisses. My sight darts back to the cramped metal room that smells of stagnant water. Our guard leans over Masha, hand raised to slap.

Sergei yanks both Masha and me toward him. "He'll be fine," Sergei tells her. "Rostov will protect him. Focus." Masha is hyperventilating, gulping down nicotine-laced rusty air; but slowly the viewing returns to its over-sharpened state, and I settle back into their sight.

The Chief stands in the office doorway, looking at Rostov. "Comrade Colonel." His thought pattern changes. I can't tell if he's a psychic as well, but he knows the music shielding trick; it grows thicker and thicker. "I was not expecting you."

Rostov drums his fingernails against the file folder. "I believe that you were." He bristles with intensified noise and I cringe. Sergei soothes me with his thumb over the back of my knuckles. "I understand you received a troubling report."

"I receive many reports," the Chief says stiffly, "few of which a Colonel need concern himself with."

"My results are exceptional. You know this," Rostov says.

The Chief teaks the bridge of his nose. "I don't doubt your results—only your methods. This report—I can't ignore such things. You put us all at risk by threatening the supremacy of Premier Khruschev."

Rostov's static hum is drawing dangerously taut. His power is a molten bar of steel, a blacksmith hammering it to a lethal edge. "What you and Khruschev's lapdogs do is far more dangerous." His words are whisper-thin. "You spit on Stalin's grave. You beg the Americans for food, economic support. Dissidents like that damn poet Yevtushenko run their mouths against Marx's vision and instead of locking them away, we give them medals, treat them as national treasures!"

"We couldn't carry on like Stalin forever!" the Chief cries. "You saw how many died under him. Starved, executed, diseased—the system is broken. The West cannot be our enemy. We can no longer stare each other down like we did in Cuba, fingers on half-pulled triggers."

"What is broken? Only you. Premier Khruschev. And everyone in between."

"I keep the state safe—"

"You keep us weak! You are weak!" Rostov slams his fist on the desk; Sergei and I jump. "Only I can clean it out. I must trim the fat."

The Chief's eyes narrow for a moment as he prepares a retort, but then he eases and his eyes glaze. Too quickly, for an old spymaster. My stomach sinks. Rostov must have drilled through his mental shield.

The young soldier who wrote the report staggers into the chief's office, arms smacking against the doorframe, legs bending unnaturally. He's burning up, he's warped with a white glow that washes out our viewing. I try to pull away from Sergei's hand but he holds firm. The soldier's actions are puppet-like, jerky and unreal, and his mind, *bozhe moi*, it's full of Rostov's noise. I know too well how it feels to be bound to Rostov's strings. The soldier reaches into his holster, fighting with himself as he does it, and rips his pistol free—

Colonel Rostov knocks us back with his static, white-hot, blistering my brain as the remote viewing is severed. But he is a split second too late. I feel two gunshots in my marrow as Sergei's and Masha's viewing tears to shreds. The Chief's chest. The soldier's temple. Like the afterimage of a bright light, I see the shooting even after the connection is lost.

And then a nest of bees is in my brain, buzzing, scrubbing away what I've just seen. Has Rostov done this before? Sleep opens her warm, cozy arms to me, and I stagger into them. Consciousness seeps away from me, but I fight that emptiness. I must not . . . lose my . . .

The fired shots are land mines beneath my skin. I cannot let Rostov know that I have seen this, or they will detonate and tear me apart. I cannot ever think about this. Rostov must believe I didn't see it. *An empty mind is a safe mind,* my memories of Papa claim.

Bang-bang. Buzzing drowns out the gunfire. I can't hold on. *Sleep,* my mind calls out. *Forget.*

I throw up right into someone's lap—in the creeping black of sleep, I hope it's Masha's—and my forehead strikes the metal floor as soft as a pillow, as deep as the Black Sea.

CHAPTER 26

I'M AT THE HIGHEST POINT in Moscow—the upper tiers of the central skyscraper at Moscow University. The grandest of Stalin's Seven Sisters. I've dreamed all my life of standing here, in the red granite hallways, unlocking the mysteries of life. The code inside our DNA; the pattern in the noise of my brother's head. But I never could have imagined the path that brought me here—not a university exam, but a thin smile from Rostov, opening the door for me as he thanked me for a job well done.

The head doctor marches toward me, checking his charts. A scream drifts toward us from the far corridor; it's like a shard of ice in my heart. He utters something to the pretty nurse at his side, and she scurries toward the corridor.

"Please, pay no mind to that. Many of our patients suffer from afflictions more . . . severe than Yevgenni Andreevich's," he says. He smiles at me with suspiciously white, parallel teeth. "Your brother will be out momentarily." He gestures toward a row of wooden chairs, set along the window bank that peers out over the Moscow skyline.

"I prefer to stand," I say.

"I understand you are interested in research yourself. We are all great fans of your mother's work—her techniques for educating the mentally infirm have greatly enhanced the level of care we provide. It would be an honor to add another Chernina to our ranks, you know."

I take a deep breath, despite the fear constricting my chest. This is what you've always wanted, Yulia. A normal girl would jump at this opportunity. Kruzenko is helping me prepare for the admissions test in March, even bringing in a tutor to help me with the advanced mathematics I never learned when I missed four years of school. A cleverer girl than me would be turning this conversation to her favor, securing an internship spot on the research team.

My head tells me to listen to Mama's pleas and Sergei's reasoning. Surround myself in the safety of the thick wool of the Soviet system, far from the scrubber's reach. Embrace my gift, use it well, and live the life I've dreamed of, working within the structure, playing the games until the day I die.

So why do my feet still itch to run, run, run?

Two figures appear at the end of the hall, the tallest leaning on the other for support. *Bozhe moi*, my Zhenya. I swear he's grown half a foot in these past few months. Smile at me, Zhenya. Run toward me. Doesn't he remember me?

"We are working with him on proper socialization," the doctor explains, as if the rejection I'm feeling stings him, too. "But you must understand that he does not respond to new situations as you or I would."

I swallow down the lump in my throat. Sometimes Zhenya would panic if I left the room for more than five minutes, but he could pass entire weeks without acknowledging my presence at all. I cannot take offense. I love him, quirks and all.

He reaches us, still leaning on the petite nurse for support. His face is fuller. We share the same dark features, but his chin juts like Papa's, instead of pointing as Mama's and mine does. That mischievous sparkle in his eyes—I'd nearly forgotten it.

"It's too cold for our walk," he tells me.

I try to smile. Does he mean the daily stroll we used to take? Or am I a random observer to him?

"Have you been working on your symphony?" I ask, as the nurse disentangles herself from him. "I was very impressed with your progress on it." But he jerks his head away from me. All right, he doesn't want to talk about music today, fine. Already I'm slipping back into the game rules of Zhenya, easy as hopping back onto a bike.

"Now, Yevgenni, what do we say when someone compliments us?" the doctor prompts him.

"We don't call them a liar. Even if they are."

I wince. "You know I'd never lie to you, Zhenya. You know who I am, don't you?"

He shrugs. "Mama says you shouldn't come here." His face screws up. "'She doesn't need distractions.'"

"Zhenya." I reach for his arm, then pull back, remembering

that he hates to be touched unless he initiates it. "Zhenya. You've spoken to Mama? Are they letting you stay with her?"

He rolls his eyes at me, but it's answer enough. He hates stating the obvious.

"What does Mama say? Does she really want me to—" I swallow. I've been trying so hard to comply to Mama's wish for me, though it pains me to. "Is this what she wants for us?"

"Bzz, bzz." Zhenya pushes past me and heads to the window, making mosquito noises. He stares out the window, at the pepper flakes of people on the promenade thirty stories below.

"The stress of encountering elements of his old life—like you—can occasionally revert a participant to their previous state," the doctor says hastily, as if he knows my brother's behavior better than I do. "I assure you, he's made substantial progress—"

"Spare me." The doctor falls back, blinking rapidly. I move to Zhenya's side. "Please, Zhenya. What's happening with Mama?"

"She's working hard. Bzz, bzz. Says we can't go outside. It's too cold. It isn't safe. Bad things." He swipes his fingers on the window pane, sketching out a musical phrase. "Said to tell you, but I think it's better not to say it in words. Music is better. Music is math, just like codes."

Bzz, bzz. Like a fan belt whining. Like a swarm of bees.

Like a scrubber, purging his mind.

"I'd like to hear your music." I hold my hand out to Zhenya for inspection. "Is it all right if I touch you?"

He regards my hand, studies all the angles, scrunches up his face. Finally, he nods. "But only because you're my sister."

I laugh bitterly to myself. He does remember me. "I promise this won't hurt. But will you let me see what you're thinking?"

My heart shatters in my chest when he answers. "I wish you always would."

Oh, Zhenya. I wish I only knew how to decipher your thoughts. I twist my fingers in his, and with a jolt, a fractured landscape unfolds. His thoughts are alive and vibrant, like a Kandinsky painting, with great slashes of color and heavy strokes of disparate thoughts. I find myself wanting to reach out and re-order the jumbled-up brush strokes, make sense from the chaos.

But I am not Rostov. I am not a scrubber, out to change his mind. Look, I tell myself, but don't touch.

"Mama," I whisper to Zhenya. "Think about Mama."

Mama dashes between the windswept brushstroke trees. The buzzing chases her, cutting through her, soaking her up when it catches her. It looks like how it feels to be near the scrubbers; Rostov must have done this, desperate to stay in control even when he's granted me this small concession. But if Zhenya knew how to lock away his memories of Mama in his music, there must be some way to bring it back—

"I think that's enough exertion for one day," the doctor says. "We don't want to undo all his progress."

I wave him off and plunge back in. Zhenya's thoughts shift to accommodate the hunt for Mama, and dark colors cut through the bright. He's leading me into the heart of his brushstroke thoughts as his symphony fills the space around us. Trumpets bursting like the rays of dawn as a dart of red paint jags the sky. We spiral deep into the color and noise where Rostov couldn't have possibly seen. *Oh, Zhenya. For once, I'm grateful your mind isn't structured like anyone else's.*

I remember now what Sergei said: Rostov can't see what he isn't looking for.

A memory of Mama, lurking between two walls of knotted-up color. Even as she flickers, she seizes me by the shoulders and refuses to let go. "Tell Yulia," she pleads. "Tell her I was wrong."

"Come on, Yevgenni, it's time for class." They're prying my hand off of him. Please, one more second. I fight to keep contact, to keep Mama's disintegrating face looming in front of mine.

But she lets go, enveloped in a fresh jolt of color and a whirlwind melody as Zhenya's mind covers her up once more. "Tell her," Mama whispers, "to run."

CHAPTER 27

"WE KNOW THE AMERICANS are desperate to best us in the cosmos," Major Kruzenko says to the dining hall at large. "We have a satellite. A man in space. And soon, the *Veter 1* will pave the way for a moon landing! Surely they have not given up their attempts to steal the design. But they have all but vanished from us. Why? Where are they going?"

We've spent a long day beating our heads against various walls: Sergei and Masha attempted to remotely view various suspected safe houses of the CIA team, I wandered the neighborhoods of the two remaining wildlings, Ivan and Misha scanned the thoughts of their neighbors, and Larissa scrounged up a report on the CIA team's plans that was vaguer than a horoscope. To Kruzenko's credit, she didn't berate us, yell at us, or say anything harsh. She masked her disappointment with a grimace and is now drowning it with an extra helping of vodka. Her gypsy music grows louder, more cacophonous as she drinks.

My head has throbbed all week. Perhaps I've inherited

Mama's headaches. The thought of vodka or—my stomach whimpers—Soviet champagne brings bitter bile to my throat. My head pounds. Bang-bang. A gunshot; a heart throbbing angrily. And Mama's words, her chilling plea for me locked inside Zhenya's head, echoes with every pulse. She wants me to run, but is there anywhere safe for me to run to?

Ivan points to Kruzenko as he leans conspiratorially toward Larissa and me. "I heard the other day that she and Rostov used to . . . you know." He makes a circle with his thumb and index finger, then jams his other index finger in and out.

Larissa wrinkles her nose. "That's disgusting."

Ivan grins. "It would explain why she drinks so much."

"How are we so incompetent?" Kruzenko bellows. "How are they stopping us? We must find them before they have another chance to act."

"They have more than just the scrubber," Valentin says, to his plate of Chicken Kiev. "They know what we're doing, and they're blocking us. It's another useless game, another useless race. Space, weapons, psychics. Arms races, all of them, going nowhere."

The doors to the dining room fly open and one of the house guards storms in. "Telephone for you, Comrade Major. Urgent— from headquarters."

She wipes her mouth and stands. "I'll take it in my office."

"No need. Major General Rostov says to turn on the state news channel."

I choke on my sip of tea at the reminder of Rostov's new title—Chief of the First Directorate of the KGB, following the previous chief's bizarre murder-suicide. Bang-bang. The vein throbs deep in my brain, smothering a memory that's trying to rise up.

Fathomless exhaustion washes over Kruzenko's face, slipping into her wrinkles and anchoring them. But the sharp tone of her mind hints at dread as well. She hurries out the door to the main parlor, and we all follow her in tacit agreement. We have just as much right to see whatever's making the news.

The colors on the screen are harsh; pastel in that uniquely Western way. Hot green grass, pink dress, a car so black it radiates blue. The American president holds one hand in greeting while his wife gapes at us. She is perpetually frozen in that fake, wide-mouthed laugh you make for people you have to impress.

And then his head whips back. Her laugh morphs to a soundless scream. The picture freezes. It's fuzzy, but on the side of his face is a glimmer of gore—like a wink, a promise. The air around us thins as we all suck in our breath.

"Less than one hour ago, the American president John Kennedy was shot in the state of Texas," the announcer intones in Russian. "Premier Khruschev has warned the united workers of the world that we will be blamed for this incident. But it is probably the work of restless Westerners, acting on their own accord, in response to the indignities of the capitalist system. The Soviet Union does not believe in murder as a political tool."

I have to bite down on my hand to kill the—the what? Cry? Laugh?—that rattles in my throat. No, we would never murder our dissidents. We send them to freeze in Siberia; we send them to houses like these and turn them into weapons. We seize control of their minds and train their guns on our enemies, then dispose of them like torn paper bags.

No, Yulia. Bang-bang. You must forget.

The clip repeats on the screen, over and over. It has been less than an hour, the announcer continues. He says they do not know if he will live, but with that terrible smear, I can't imagine he would survive. I find myself staring, not at the glisten of blood, brain matter, missing face, but at the pink woman. Her mask as it disintegrates. That false happiness that she can show no more. Her husband breaks, and she breaks apart with him.

"How did we not see this?" Major Kruzenko cries suddenly, after about the eighth loop. "How could we miss this?"

She lobs her vodka to the floor, jerking us from our hypnosis. Glass and sharp, stinging alcohol spray across the room. Kruzenko's red face shimmers with a trail of tears.

"I am trying to protect you all. Keep you from burning out like all the rest. I know you're not ready to take on their responsibility, but how could you not see this?" A gurgle rises from her throat like she's being choked by her own tears. "How can I show you're ready when you can't even sense something like *this*?"

Valentin shifts beside me, eyes smoldering behind his glasses. "What happened to all the rest, Comrade Major?"

Big, fat, unbearable tears pour down Major Kruzenko's face. "We have been trying and trying so hard and it's just too much," she says to herself, as the American president's head deflates over and over. She turns on us and jabs her finger at the screen. "Do not let this happen again. For all our sakes."

"Comrade Major, that's enough." Sergei bounds to his feet and swoops around her. For a moment I see his hockey reflexes come alive, as if he means to tackle her to the ground. "We're working hard. We won't let Rostov down." His thick, corded arms circle her shoulders from behind in a bear hug and he maneuvers her toward the doorway. The stringent stream of vodka wafts behind her.

"Rostov? My dear Sergei Antonovich, you don't understand." Kruzenko wheezes laughter at him. "Rostov will soar to great heights for the glory of the Soviet Union, but what about—me—"

The door swings shut behind them, but her words keep echoing in my mind. If the other psychics—like Misha's and Masha's parents—are wearing out, or worse . . . But I take care to seal up that thought in a Shostakovich envelope. Like all the other Soviet games, information is the dearest thing I can possess.

We're snowed in until the first week of December. The sky is solid slate; as the snowdrifts climb up the windows, I imagine our snow-globe world on the cliff filling up, floor to ceiling. Kruzenko's henchmen carve a path from the gate to the docking bay, so we always have food and tea, but otherwise we are locked up, only able to see the outside world through our minds.

I'm drawn to the ballroom in the afternoons, when Valentin plays, though I do not meet his eyes during this time. He's playing a new jazz theme, kneading it over and over into different shapes and styles, though the piano's quickly coming untuned. I can't bring myself to forgive him for invading my dreams, but I feel safer surrounded in his notes than in any words either of us could say.

I have taken, too, to lying in Anastasia's bed sometimes,

acknowledging her pain. It reminds me that my own troubles aren't so great: my mother and brother live, I'm slowly gaining control of my power, and maybe there's danger beyond these walls and loneliness within, but not so much that it could crush me like it did her. Anastasia's troubles were the taste of wood clenched between her teeth; Kruzenko's face peering over her as she's strapped onto a gurney. "You have not been following our training. Your condition is worsening—"

They filled her with electricity, hoping there will be no room left for her madness. But like the beast of Frankenstein, it only brought a darkness far worse to life.

My project with Larissa offers a distraction, at least, if not much in the way of results. It's strange to watch her work— looking forward, navigating the branching waters of the future in search of the missing wildlings, even as I reel backward against the currents of the past. Larissa convinced Kruzenko to dedicate some of the KGB's resources to the hunt, as long as it doesn't distract us from our *Veter* team mission.

Finally the snow settles enough for us to venture beyond the mansion, and the Americans get a new president, and they kill an American man who they think killed the president, and there is no new threat of nuclear war because they do not blame us, though we feel the pressure of their nuclear missiles aimed our way like the glare of narrowed eyes. Major General Rostov is too busy for our little troupe as he whispers in the Party leaders' ears, telling them—Misha and Masha report proudly—that Khruschev is not protecting the Soviet Union enough.

One more name is struck through on the chalkboard, leaving

only one wildling at large. Only one name. But it will have to be enough.

"The remaining wildling works at the ZiL auto factory, but his shift leader said that he was missing last night," Kruzenko tells us at our morning briefing. Missing. I find the word unnervingly vague. "Their records show a British businessman recently visited the factory under a foreign investment visa, but we have caught many spies using this cover." Larissa and exchange a look; of course Kruzenko has a secondary goal in letting us run our little mission. She's hoping to catch a spy in the process. "His hotel room is where you will go, Valya and Misha—" she gestures to the two boys—"and Yulia, Lara, and Ivan will go to the factory. Sergei and Masha, you will stay here with me to observe."

Larissa bounces beside me on the truck bench as we putter blindly through the snow-walled streets of Moscow. "All the best movie dramas take place in factories," she says. "I wonder if there's a dreamy foreman like the cute guy in *I Love You, Life.*"

"You watch too much television," I tell her.

"I'm all the Russian man you need, my little squirrel." Ivan nuzzles her cheek; I turn away, staring at the empty bench beside me.

The truck deposits us, with our spider-guards, in the back alley behind the ZiL factory. The cold air carries the smell of molten slag, though the snow has muffled the trash bin stink, thankfully. The factory is flat concrete and glass and, save the smoke stains that rise away from punched-out windows, undecorated. We crunch our way to the rear factory door and listen to the chugging of machinery inside, rattling like a caged panther.

"We can search the factory floor unnoticed," Larissa declares.

"The floor manager is on an extended lunch. Ivan, can you ensure no one looks too closely at us?"

"Not a problem, my sunbeam." He tweaks her nose, then looks at me. "What are you going to do?"

"I'll retrace the businessman's footsteps. See what he's been doing here."

Ivan's guard unlocks the alley door for us, and settles in for a lengthy standing session. "Try not to be seen," he grunts from under his scarf. "Best if we don't have to send a team after you kids."

The stench of oil and tar nearly knocks us flat as we pull open the door. We shake salt and ice from our boots, and strip down to our base outfits: the Soviet standard-issue gray that works better than camouflage in factories and ration lines. None of the workers so much as glance up from the assembly line. I take in the alien contours of machinery, the impossible mechanical arms reaching and grabbing every which way—

And suck in my breath. There is no rattle of seamless automation. The clanging noises come from the workers crawling over the metallic, holey carapaces that might someday turn into Party officials' limousines. They ratchet valves into place by hand, with comically large wrenches; at a far station, a babushka with a dowager hump wrestles stitched pieces of leather from an uncooperative sewing machine. What good, then, are these Stalinist monstrosities of pipes and hydraulics jutting every which way?

"They really needed a whole factory for this?" Ivan mutters. "No wonder it takes seven years to get a car."

"Let's be quick. Ivan? I think the babushkas are looking our way," I say.

"Of course." He brings his fingers to his forehead—as if his mind is this great muscle and our work is causing him physical strain—then he motions along the wall. "Move quickly. You're clear."

Larissa and I scamper along the wall, hopping over dilapidated crates and metal bins full of tubes, pistons. I keep my hands tangled in my stripped-away coat, not ready yet to sink in. We find a small nook beside a thicket of metal towers. They look like intricate machinery, but there is no telltale hum of electric currents; a cord is bundled in hooks on one side, felted with thick dust.

Larissa slumps against the wall and catches her breath. "This team will be taking their lunch break soon. Start here, then move toward the foreman's office. He won't return until after we're gone."

I dump my coat at her feet as she twists a lock of hair around her fingers and take a deep breath. I flatten my hand on the cold, silent steel and sink into its memories.

Day after day at the factory, the constant clatter and clang. I see the missing wildling darting in and out of frame, scuffling along as he settles disputes between workers and shuttles to his locker and back. But one day, a white haze blurs the edges of the memories; it pulls me with a familiar, dreaded tug.

The scrubber.

A man is walking the floor, pointing to the various assembly bays and describing their purpose. "The workers are much happier to contribute to the State, you see, than fat cat industry bosses like in your country."

"I'm not here for politics."

The voice nearly jars me out of the memory. At once it sounds so typically Russian, perhaps with a southern Baltic lilt—but as soon as I think that, my mind's infected with doubt. Of course this person is not Russian—he is just well educated. Oxford, probably. Didn't they say something about an English businessman? Yes, it makes perfect sense.

He rounds the corner and it's like an atom bomb going off. I am splitting apart, molecule by molecule, scattering into blissful white nothingness. They say that we are made of stardust, of fragments from the cosmos. His radiance makes me believe. Even with time separating us, his power burns me away, strips me down to raw genetic code.

No, Yulia. Fight past his noise. Concentrate.

"And that is the extent of the factory," the boy says. In the background, someone swears as a faulty valve slices into his arm.

"I'm afraid it is not." The scrubber turns, and the boy's smile fades as the scrubber's glow falls across him. "There is a worker I would like to meet. Dmitri Shadov. You know him?"

"I'm sorry, comrade, but I am the only person authorized to speak to foreigners—"

The scrubber smiles. I cannot describe how I sense this through his white-hot glow, but the smile fills me with warmth. I can see it in the boy's eyes. He, too, wants to trust this man; he will walk headlong into whatever the scrubber asks of him.

"I will make you a deal." The scrubber leans forward. "I will speak to Dmitri today, and you will not stop me."

"Perfect," the boy says, flustered. "Yes, I should have thought of this myself. Hey! Dmitri! A visitor for you."

The missing wildling looks up from the auto body. He's a strapping fellow, dark-haired and packed with hard-earned muscle. He lowers his mallet. With each step forward, his pace slows. Does he feel the radiation, too?

The blinding scrubber's face parts with a glossy white smile. "Let's have a word in here, Dmitri. We won't take long."

They duck into the office. Hot noise flashes from the cracks around the door, jolting me backward, nearly breaking my contact with the machine. I grit my teeth against the static storm and wait it out, wait for that door to open, ready to flinch away from the flash burn of the scrubber's radioactive smile.

Dmitri staggers out first, his head like a ball of shrapnel. His gaze roves the factory, not really seeing it before him. The scrubber—*bozhe moi*, but I can't look at him dead on—claps Dmitri on the shoulder. "We are agreed, then?"

Dmitri's eyes water as he stares, unblinking. "Gorky Park," he says, like he's reciting it. "Thursday. Noon."

"Absolutely not," Major Kruzenko roars. "I am not putting you anywhere near that scrubber. He is targeting us, Yulia. It wouldn't be safe."

I clench my teeth as Major Kruzenko paces her office. "But he's going to do something to the wildling—something more than he already has. Either finish the job he started on his brain in the factory, or . . ." I can't finish the awful thought. "It's our best chance to catch them and help this poor Dmitri."

Kruzenko pinches the bridge of her nose and exhales slowly. "We will send a team. But I do not want any of you near him. It's simply too dangerous."

I can't argue with her reasons. I know how it feels to be wiped clean, even if only at a distance, by these monsters. But there is something compelling me toward this meeting—no. I am not being compelled like a puppet on the scrubber's strings. I want to believe this determination is mine alone, my need to protect Dmitri, and not a seed planted in my thoughts. I don't want to examine it further. I don't want to consider the possibility that the scrubber has turned my thoughts deeper down; set in motion this need inside me, drawing me to him like a moth to flame.

I will protect the last wildling, and Kruzenko won't keep me from it.

CHAPTER 28

WHEN I FIND MYSELF in another vivid dream, the first since I'd learned what Valentin and Rostov are doing, I scream and beg through a soundless throat to wake up. But I am transparent, voiceless, trapped on a train; I feel as pale as the fog beyond the train window that masks the countryside. Papa sits on the bottom bunk in the crowded sleeper car, sipping vodka from the glass and pewter tea mugs—*podstakanniks*—which all Russian trains provide. Moonlight catches the glossy surface of his playing cards, a red glow pulsing between his lips.

"What troubles you, comrade?" Papa asks, in his gruff but quiet voice. I thought that I'd forgotten it, but there it is, hanging in the air, as familiar as his eternal cloud of cigarette smoke.

"A friend." The figure on the bunk opposite him sits too deep in the sleeper cabin's darkness for me to see. "She thinks I've betrayed her, but she doesn't know the whole story."

"Betrayal is a tricky thing. Some might say I've betrayed my family. That I sent them down a treasonous track. But I think they know that whatever I do, I have their best interests in mind." Papa sets one card onto the deck.

"I think the problem is that she resents having the choice taken from her." The figure counters Papa's card, and they both take another sip.

Valya? I whisper, but my voice is drowned out by the alcohol and smoke so thick in the night.

"That's my girl for you. She'd rather make her own mistakes."

Valentin leans forward and catches the glint of moonlight on his glasses. "She may never forgive me for doing this—scouring her dreams under Rostov's orders, sifting through her memories for clues as to where you might have gone."

Papa takes another drag before answering. "Sounds like Rostov, all right."

Valentin scoops up the cards and shuffles them. In the still, dead night, it sounds like machine gun fire. "It helps me, though, that you kept it all from her. It makes my work easy. When I tell Rostov that there's nothing, it's not a lie. I wouldn't tell him anything regardless, but as you know, he has his . . . ways."

"We hid it from her, her mother and I," Papa said. "For her own safety."

Valentin sighs. "It would appear you're not the only ones. There are parts of her mind—I don't know if it's something Rostov has done, or . . ." For a moment, I almost think he looks at me, but it must be the light playing on his glasses. Again, I feel that sore patch inside my head like a fading bruise. Rostov. It has to be. But some of the spots feel older, more battered than the rest.

"You could help her," Papa says, "but I doubt she'll let you." He lays out his hand of cards. "I win again."

Valentin smirks and digs in his pockets. "At least it's only dream money." He drops a wad of rubles on the tabletop.

"And I'm only a collection of her memories of me." Papa scoops up Valentin's bills and deals again.

"I do have an idea," Valentin says. He lays the words out as carefully as he plays his next hand, letting them linger while Papa takes another drag on his cigarette. "Not just helping her recover whatever memories she's lost. I—I know she doesn't trust me enough for that, not yet. But if she wants to escape from Rostov, all this . . ."

"Best not to say too much right now," Papa says.

"No, you're right. But if she can forgive me, if she's willing, then she should meet me in the vault room tomorrow afternoon. One o'clock. We'll have a few hours to talk before I have to go on a mission with Kruzenko."

Papa extinguishes his cigarette in his emptied glass. "Not flesh nor feathers—best of luck to you, young man."

The train rattles around a corner, and the moonlit fog pours in from the window, darkening my view until I slip back into the prickly warmth of sleep.

CHAPTER 29

THE VAULT IS DARK as I feel my way through the narrow corridor. Maybe my dream of Valentin and Papa was just that; or maybe it's all a trap. My fingers scrape flecks of paint from the walls, and an image flits through me of others touching this place—servants, liveried and trussed up, seeking refuge from their bygone rulers decades ago.

Something shuffles at the end of the hall. Scraping sound; smell of sulfur; light. Valentin's face looms out of the darkness as he lowers his match to a large candle, then takes it around the room, lighting further candles from the first.

"Are we performing some sort of ritual?" I ask. "You have Saint George's finger bone on display in here?"

He shakes his head. "I had to use the light outlet to power the record player."

I smile despite myself and sink down cross-legged onto the floor. He appears to have made some effort to sweep up the dust and fragments of disintegrating drop sheets. The record player is open before me, built into a square plaid-patterned suitcase. "And what does this have to do with—"

"Shh. A surprise." He finishes fussing with the candles and sits opposite me. After flipping through his stack of record sleeves, he pulls a black disc out without letting me see the album cover.

"Come on, Valya. I hate surprises."

"Most psychics do." He slides the disc onto the turntable. "Close your eyes."

I wrap my arms around my chest. "I'm really not in the mood for games. What you've been doing to me . . ."

He winces, eyes closing like a searchlight extinguishing. "I know I shouldn't have kept it from you, Yulia. But at the same time, I had to—as long as Rostov trusted me to do it, then I could monitor what he was doing, protect you from facing him alone . . ."

"I don't need your protection," I say, my face flushing "Not anyone's. Why does everyone think I'm so helpless? I can take care of myself."

"But don't you see? That's just it. You can't stand up to Rostov by yourself—none of us can. We have to work together. But they've turned us against each other this way, everyone spying on everyone else . . ."

"Please. Don't. You were right before, when you showed me what happened when you tried to run. It's safest for us in here." I lean back on my palms.

Valentin nods, fingers circling the rim of the record. "For now, yes. But once we catch the Americans . . ."

I tremble, squeezing my eyes shut. "No." His words are

making me sick. He's filling me with the foulest disease I can imagine.

He's filling me with hope.

"I want to run again. Of course I do. But Rostov—" Buried memories rumble deep in my mind. I cannot let them free. The blistering white heat, the thud in my chest and temple—No. There are thoughts Rostov must not see. But their existence, their hearts beating under the floorboard, remind me what he's capable of.

"Yes," Valentin says, "but even Rostov cannot catch everything." He takes a deep breath. "Do you trust me, Yulia?"

"No." I don't even pause to think.

Valentin smiles. "Fair enough. But I think we want the same things—a better use for our powers, a better life than 'good enough.' Do you want them badly enough to try?"

Yes. The answer comes from deep in my bones, etched onto my genetic code. I want answers, I want freedom, I want something more than the comfortable but helpless life that Sergei says is ours. I want to know why Mama has changed her mind; I want to see the soft, tender thoughts under my brain's bruises.

"All right." I shift my weight and squeeze my eyes shut. "I'm closing my eyes."

The needle drops. Scratchy sounds creep from the record like melting ice. "I was given this music as a reward for sifting through your dreams. I think you deserve to have it as much as I do," Valentin says.

Three guitar chords—then they tumble down the scale. Three chords, then back down. The drums kick in, and suddenly three men's voices sing out in simple English, perfect harmony, not just one line but a thick, lush landscape of sounds.

> *And I, tell you something, I think you'll understand*
> *When I, feel that something, I wanna hold your*
> *hand . . .*

We are no longer in the dead of a Russian winter. Instead we skip across a beach, in Georgia perhaps, looking across the Black Sea as sunlight and sand kiss our toes. It's like nothing I've ever heard before. It isn't dark and heavy and crushing like Russian music, nor is it treacly and false like what our comrades put forth as a pretense of pop. It is so real, so unusual, so removed from anything I've ever seen or heard.

> *And when you touch me, I feel happy inside*
> *There is this feeling, and this love . . . I can't hide*
> *I can't hide*
> *I can't hide . . .*

The song rolls into a sour mood, but only long enough to tug my heart from my chest until it turns joyous again. It's over too fast—only a few minutes in length. I open my eyes and find Valentin staring back at me with the same glassy-eyed hunger for this music that I feel pounding through my veins.

"And this—" I wet my parched lips. "This is American pop music?"

"Actually, they're English. Call themselves the Beatles." He smiles, and lies on his side, propped up on his elbow. "I have a few other songs for you, if you want to—"

"Yes!" I tumble onto my back with a laugh, my head angled toward him. "Yes, more. Please!"

"All right." He leans over me to change the records, blushing furiously as he does. "These are the Animals, and they are in the American style called 'blues,' which is similar to the jazz I love so much . . ."

A mournful guitar patters along for a while before a man sings, deep-throated but crisp, and Valentin translates in my head the sad story of a house in New Orleans that chews up lives and spits the souls back out.

Valentin nestles onto the floor beside me again, shoulder hovering near mine close enough that I can feel his warmth. His temple radiates a pleasant lack of thought. There is no fear, no overwhelming responsibility in this room; only wonderful music and Valentin and me.

After that song ends, and he has played a few more—Elvis Presley with a dark chocolate voice who "Can't Help Fallin' in Love," and another Beatles song about a week with eight days, which I joke must be some crazy capitalist calendar scheme—he tilts his head toward me. "You are happy?" he asks, his words flowing across the floor.

"It's incredible. Is this what the rest of the world sounds like?"

"Not all of it." He props one hand on his forehead, and his fingertips touch my hair. "But this is music, music when restraints have been lifted. It's the difference between plants growing in a fenced-in garden, and the same plants left to conquer an entire field."

"Music is very important to you," I say. Stupidly, I know. Music is his soul, and all those afternoons I basked in his piano playing—he shared more of himself with me then than he could ever speak.

He nods. "It's a language for things we can't put in words."

I roll my head toward his and our noses brush together. We have similar dark hair, olive skin; his eyes dark and brooding, mine wide but no less dark. Genetics mark us both as Georgian, he a Sorokhin and I a Chernina. Like most human beings, we share ninety-nine and nine-tenths percent of our DNA. Perhaps even closer—we share whatever strange gene gives us this mental prowess, if it can be explained with science at all. And yet there are things about each of us that neither will ever understand. That we can only admire from afar, like a Fabergé egg under glass whose gears will never be exposed.

"When did your family leave Georgia?" I ask. Papa always spoke of visiting his grandparents back in Tbilisi, before Stalin's days.

"We didn't leave," Valentin says. His chest settles and our noses press closer. "Father and I were taken from there."

"What was it like?" I want his soft, thick hair in my fingers, as though I were sifting through sand. I raise my hand, tentatively; his hair doesn't disappoint. His eyes half-close but he is still watching me, every bit as alert. Yevtushenko's poem bleeds through my music. *We can do so much, denied our earth— tenderly embrace as lovers in a darkened room.* Never mind that he was talking about corpses in a mass grave.

"We lived in a tiny town in northern Ingush." He raises a hand and tangles it in my hair, mirroring me. "I woke up every morning to the smell of sea salt from our back porch. I practiced piano while the sun came up, and at night, I walked the beach. Even after my mother passed, we survived, we . . ." He hesitates. "Her memories were like happy ghosts around us."

"It sounds like a charmed existence," I say.

He shakes his head. "I had no idea, at the time, what work my father did to give me such a life. That there were debts we'd have to pay."

"Debts?"

He looks away. "It was too good to be true. It couldn't last." He twitches under my hand. "I don't deserve such things. This monster that I am . . ."

"No." My hand tightens into a fist. "You aren't a monster. Neither of us is. We have the tools, the power to be monsters . . . but we don't have to use them that way."

"I never wanted to be more. I felt trapped in this fate, until the first day I saw you and knew just who I had hurt by not caring. By helping them hunt you down."

I flinch. I thought I was prepared for that truth, but hearing it hang in the open air gives it a sharpness it doesn't deserve. "We have all done unforgivable things. You had no choice," I tell him.

"We always have a choice, Yul. Some may cost us more, far more than we can pay, but we can choose. After I met you, I swore I'd stop obeying them blindly, but I couldn't undo what I'd done . . ." He sighs. The spark of hope and the blackness of regret is in that sigh. "How can you ever forgive me?"

My lips find his, and it's like kissing the sea. He is salty, cool without chilling me, and fresh as a clean summer breeze. Our mouths snag together, two currents flowing as one, and all the music in his head goes spilling into mine, the thoughts and emotions for which there are no words.

His hands dig deeper into my hair. He is gold-domed Russian Orthodox chapels on the shore and birch forests awash with green. I'm pulling myself onto him, and a new song emerges in the rise and fall of our lungs, in his lips reaching for mine.

"Yulia." He jerks forward beneath me as if he's been startled from sleep. "Yulia."

I kiss the smooth tip of his nose. "Valentin?"

"I don't deserve your affection—"

I slide off of him, but can't keep my hand from running the length of his arm as I try to catch my breath. My blouse is tangled up in my sweater, and the pleat of my skirt won't lay flat. I don't care. Snow is falling outside, but in here I could melt away, just a puddle of craving for the music inside Valentin.

Valentin crosses his legs funny. "I'm sorry," he says, and I like him so much I pretend not to know why he's covering himself the way he is.

"You don't have to apologize," I tell him. "I wanted . . . I mean, I started it—"

"No. You don't understand." He takes off his glasses; the lenses have fogged. "I'm letting myself be a tool for Rostov and his monsters, and I don't know how to break free."

Free. The word shatters against me, too painful to contemplate. I tuck flyaway hairs behind my ear. "Valya. Please." His shortened name is so rich on my tongue. I want to say it again and again. "I understand why you've done these things, but I don't want you in my dreams anymore, all right? I want the thoughts that we share to be given freely."

His eyes squeeze shut; his thoughts hum like a radiator. "You know what Rostov is capable of. I can't simply tell him no."

One, two bullets in my skin. "I know." I lower my head. "But you said you had an idea."

He loads the Beatles record onto the plate and starts it over, ratcheting the volume up. "Focus on the music," he shouts at me. "Try not to think too much about the words I'm saying."

I nod, and scoot closer to him. I stop myself short of reaching for his hand.

His lips tingle against my ear. "If we work together, I know we can escape. I've been testing the guards, getting them to do little things under my command—I'm sure I can distract them. And you can learn the Metro tunnel guards' patrol route . . ."

"The tunnel? There's no way. They'll be expecting it. And what about that, that *thing* working with Rostov?" I ask.

Valentin leans closer. His breath is so warm on my sizzling neck. It's all I can do not to reach for him—but no. This is too important. "I'm still working on that part. But I know we can do it. Think about it, Yulia. If you're willing to work with me . . ."

"I'm willing," I say. My heart beats with the Beatles. *I wanna hold your hand, I wanna hold your hand.*

Valentin draws a sharp inhale, like he's catching one last scent of me, then stands. "We've been gone too long as it is. Please, do your best not to think of this." His fingers trace a piano chord on my arm. "We have to suppress it. I know you've suppressed thoughts before."

I shudder. Just knowing that bad thoughts lie deep under my skin makes me queasy. "I'll do my best."

"Especially around Sergei," he says. "I'm afraid that if he found out, he might—"

"Tell Rostov. Right. They do seem to get on well." I stroke the back of his hand. "I'll keep our plan safe."

"Our plan." Valentin looks at me sideways with his cheeks burned scarlet. ". . . Yes. Don't let Sergei know about that, either."

CHAPTER 30

AFTER VALENTIN LEAVES with Kruzenko, Misha, and Ivan to follow the scrubber's trail, I settle into the parlor, desperate to numb the hyper-awareness coursing through me, the receptors hungry for the taste and feel of Valentin. I can't think about him, or the fact that even now he might be too close to the scrubber, getting his memories stripped away. I let the bland *KVN* skits on the screen wash over me, the heavy genetics textbook anchor me, and Masha's rant floss through my ears.

"It's just not fair," Masha continues. "We don't get any respect, do we, Sergei? I don't think Kruzenko understands the importance of remote viewing because she isn't a remote viewer herself. I mean, you're kind of weak, but I'm mastering telekinesis, too—"

"She respects us just fine. If a project doesn't call for us, she doesn't take us." Sergei's knee tap-tap-taps beside mine. Up and down as he stares at *KVN* on the TV screen.

Masha slings herself over the back of the couch. "But they

can always use us. We're the best anyway, aren't we, Seryozha?" She wedges her shoulders between Sergei and me and I'm more than happy to lean away to make room. "I guess I have to try to run away if I want to choose what projects I get to work on."

Most mutations are recessive, but in a capitalist society that perverts Darwin's "survival of the fittest" to control their citizens, mutated specimens may eventually gain dominance as the individuals lacking the advantageous mutation die out.

I keep reading. I do not think about Masha's words. I will not let any anger bubble up in my head, or let my musical barrier warp and distend as it tries to contain that luscious bow-shaped curve of Valya's lips—

". . . and even though it's Ivan's specialty, I'm probably better at reading thoughts than he is, he's so weak—"

"Masha?" Larissa mutters. "Go walk on a dick."

Masha slithers off the couch and narrows her eyes at Larissa. Their angry thoughts bounce back and forth, practically tangible in the air. "*Poshol na hui* yourself," Masha manages to spit out, and storms away. The guards know better by now than to get in Masha's way, and practically trip over themselves giving her room to pass.

I turn to Larissa to thank her, but instead of smirking at her success, she's glaring at the television as if she means to telepathically turn the dial. "Lara," I whisper, trying to catch her eye. "What's the matter?"

Red stripes from dried tears still run down her face from her fight with Kruzenko this morning—I've never seen Larissa so eager to use her powers. Screaming, pounding on doors, guards dragging her away. "I should be there instead," she says, shaking her hair forward to cover the cut on her temple. Her Vysotsky folk song keeps starting and stopping, stumbling over itself.

"They need you here, predicting what's coming next. Sergei's right," I say. He snorts beside me; I force my gaze to stay on Larissa. "Not everyone is most effective out in the field." With a twinge, I realize that I *am* needed most out there, yet I couldn't be happier to be far, far away from the scrubber's sound.

"*Bozhe moi.*" Larissa's hand goes to her mouth.

I follow her gaze to the comedy sketch on TV. A frumpy comedian, dressed like Premier Khruschev, is arguing with a man in a mouse suit. He offers the mouse a fistful of ration cards—the mouse shakes his head, and the audience giggles nervously. Something is not right in their laughter. They sound too guilty.

Khruschev tries a bottle of vodka; the mouse denies him again. Khruschev holds up a miniature *Sputnik* satellite—a round silver globe, ringed in spikes flying away in one direction as if swept by the wind. Enormous laughter. The mouse looks tempted here, and he almost reaches for the *Sputnik*, but stops himself and shakes his head furiously.

Khruschev reaches down, pulls off his loafer, and starts beating the mouse with it—really wailing on him. The audience is howling now, the kind of unselfconscious laughter when you realize your worst fears have not come to pass, that you are not crazy, that you are right to laugh, and saxophones bleep and blurt as Khruschev gives the mouse chase, and we all three stare slack-jawed at the screen until the image is abruptly replaced with a sickle and hammer and "Technical Difficulties"—

"I—I don't understand." I look at Larissa and her glassy eyes. "What is the mouse supposed to be?"

"Mickey Mouse. Because Walt Disney wouldn't let the Premier onto his roller coaster rides when he visited America—"

"What's a Mickey Mouse?" I ask.

Sergei shakes his head. "They shouldn't have done that. If the Premier finds out—and he will—"

"They're going to cancel *KVN*." Larissa stands; kicks the television console. The sickle and hammer warp on the screen before settling. "And those stupid men will be shot and it wasn't even that funny. Stupid, stupid, senseless. Everything is senseless!"

Larissa thuds out of the lounge, and her boots slam against the staircase. I hesitate for a second, wanting to follow her, if only for an excuse not to be left alone with Sergei. But then I have waited too long, and the moment has passed. The screen is still the sickle and hammer image, and the national anthem blasts through the lounge. One of the guards steps forward and turns down the volume knob on the TV. I stare hard enough at my book that I think I could set it on fire. I try to fill my mind with other songs. Valya's songs.

"So," Sergei says. His knee bounces fiercely against mine.

"So," I say.

He laces his fingers together. "I was given tickets to the Spartak game on New Year's. They're playing Dinamo."

"Sounds fun for you," I say.

He catches his knee in his tangled hands. "I didn't know if you liked . . . If you'd maybe want to go . . ."

Now I'm the one with the Russian shrug of defeat. How easily I can slip into the life the KGB has constructed for us.

Taking entrance exams for Moscow State, going to hockey games. Just when I'm ready to surrender to it, Valentin and Mama spark that vile flame of hope. "I . . . I wouldn't feel right. I don't want—"

"No. No, I get it." He tangles his fingers in his hair, making a fist. "You still won't admit this is your life. Well, guess what, Yulia. You don't *belong* anywhere else!" he laughs, cold and dry. "You think you can function out there, knowing what you are? Maybe you can be a factory girl, queen of the gossip hive because you can peek at your friends' thoughts on the assembly line. But it'll drive you crazy."

"And who's to say it won't drive us crazy in here? Look at Larissa, losing her head over a TV show. Or Anastasia—I know all about that," I say.

He smirks. "Do you? Are you sure about that?"

"I know enough." I stand, tucking my book under my arm. "I don't need you lecturing me."

"But you're so caught up in what you think your life *should* have been that you're not living it the way it is!" He stands, too, towering over me. "I'm trying to protect you, don't you see? But I can't do it forever."

"Enough, already! I'd rather take my chances than have you constantly trying to save me!" I stumble back from him. The ridges of the bookshelf, tacky with cheap paint, press into my spine.

"You're vulnerable to sycophants like Masha. Dangerous revolutionaries like Valentin. He'll get us all killed with his scheming, but he's never let that stop him before."

"Keep your voice down," I hiss, but the guards are already watching us. We're certainly more interesting than the static logo on TV.

"Valya's plans would cost us our lives, when we have so much to give. I say we ignore it all and live a true Russian life as best as we can while dealing with this—this curse." His voice drops low. Pulled taut. "But lately, your thoughts sound just like Valentin's."

The front door bangs open. Sergei and I look at each other—a threat to finish this later—and charge for the stairs. Larissa is already flying down them, her sloppy braid airborne behind her. Realization hardens and calcifies in my gut. Why she's upset today. She knows something. She knows.

Kruzenko, Rostov, and a rash of uniformed KaGeBezniks swarm the foyers, crowding around a long, flat object. A stretcher. The lump on it moves—there is a person on it, bundled in blankets, but I'm not hearing any thoughts, even though I'm close enough that I should be hearing something. Something is horribly wrong. There are too many bodies and not enough voices. A black emptiness on the stretcher where someone's thoughts should be. My chest constricts; my pulse rings too loudly in my ears. *Bozhe moi.* Please don't let it be Valentin.

"Into the dining room. Quickly, quickly, *poshli.* The doctor will be here soon. You—bring in the other boys." Kruzenko herds them out of the foyer and the doors slam shut.

Larissa curls around the banister, boneless, but her face is oddly serene. "What's happened?" I ask, fighting to keep my voice calm. Her eyes, usually brilliant blue, look dead. They're just fixed on the closed dining room door. I want to shake her, bring her back to life.

She unhooks herself from the railing. "Ivan," she says. Her tone is hollowed out. "He's been scrubbed."

And she slinks back up the staircase, with no shock, no surprise, no panic, nothing at all.

CHAPTER 31

KRUZENKO AND ROSTOV DISAPPEAR into her office after the doctor leaves. We can't hear them argue, but the whole space around the door is electric, like if we reach for the doorknob we'd get shocked by the furious, heated thoughts buzzing around inside.

No one will say what happened when they tried to track the scrubber from the hotel room they'd found. Misha sequesters himself in the boys' room; I try to catch Valya's eye, but he retreats to the ballroom to tinker away at a tumultuous jazz melody. I sprawl on the ballroom floor, feeling worse than useless. He stitches new melodies, fragments of songs from his records, and other threads I don't know into the fabric of the first tune, making an endless bolt that spools out as we wait for news. The cracked plaster ceiling overhead anchors me as the sea of notes beneath me rolls and shifts.

This is what it must feel like to wait for the atom bomb to fall. When the American cowboys tire of our angry premiers and our slipshod satellites, when they push a button and our klaxons wail a too-late warning that our molecules are about to pull apart like taffy, time must freeze with anticipation like this.

A guard storms over to the piano and rests his hand on the keyboard cover. Valentin yanks his hands back and the guard slams it down. "Dinnertime." The guard jabs his AK-47 in the direction of the dining room.

Ivan is gone. The stretcher is gone. The table is set with one of the more lavish meals we've had here—smoked salmon, boiled pierogi smothered in sour cream, sturgeon roe caviar spread on huge chunks of bread. Bottles of Sovetskoye Shampanskoye wait at each place setting. I sit between Sergei and Valentin; Misha and Masha are opposite us, with matching glum stares. Neither Larissa nor Ivan appear.

Major Kruzenko doles out pierogi for herself and starts shoveling them into her mouth. No one speaks. I plop slices of salmon onto my plate, but the nervous, fearful energy rumbling through the room keeps me from taking a bite. Even Sergei doesn't do much more than push around his food.

Finally, Kruzenko drains the last of her Champagnskoe and scoots her chair back with an authoritative scrape. Beside her Rostov rubs his thumb idly against his Major General's stars on his collar. I try to read his emotions, but it's too painful to look at him straight. It makes my head throb. Bang-bang.

"Children." Kruzenko reaches to Rostov's free hand and slips her fingers into the gaps between his. I expect him to tear free of her, strike her for such a display. I need him to, just to show that everything is normal. But his fingers tighten upon hers. *Bozhe moi*, Ivan might have been right. Once upon a dismal time, these two monsters looked to each other for comfort, strength.

"Children," Kruzenko tries again, pitching her napkin on her plate. "Today's incident is no one's fault but the American coward who harmed our Ivan. Please do not blame yourselves. Sometimes these things cannot be avoided."

"But what happened?" Sergei asks. "Why isn't anyone explaining?"

Valentin stares down his nibbled bread roll as he speaks. "He'd checked out of the room two days ago. We thought we could glean clues off the hotel workers, but then he was there—he led Ivan away from us, and—"

"Valentin Borisovich, that is enough." Kruzenko stands. "It is not important how this came to be. Now all we can do is hope for the best for Ivan and hunt this beast down."

"You can't keep throwing us at him. We're clearly not prepared," I say. "Why not send the more advanced operatives? Like—like your parents." I gesture to Misha and Masha. "All the rest."

Misha and Masha look at each other; I don't need psychic powers to tell they're communicating in a language all their own. "They are . . . indisposed," Misha says. "Important business."

"The others have more important matters to attend do," Rostov snarls. "It's time you learned to take care of yourselves." Behind his jagged expression, though, white rings his eyes. Is he himself afraid of the scrubber's power? "Comrade Major." He nods at Kruzenko. "I must return to headquarters."

Kruzenko salutes him, and he turns away. His boot heels click away down the hall.

I reach out for the strands of Valentin's thoughts—they're there, tangled up in his jazz music, in our Tchaikovsky song, in the Beatles. *What's happened to the other psychics?* I ask, trying to bundle the thought in the same knot of notes.

Not now. A new song slams around him, locking me out.

But fire is crackling in my mind as the possibilities stoke it on. The idea that I am not a wildling, that my parents have known what I am has smoldered in me for a while. But I fear it's only the smoke of a much bigger fire. A memory, or perhaps just a dream, flashes through my mind, but it is gone in a cloud of cigarette smoke.

"Misha." Kruzenko sits back down. "Will you please report on what you *did* manage to find at the hotel?"

That fire is eating at my thoughts; its crackle conceals all sound. Beneath the table, Valentin's hand falls onto my knee. Perhaps he means it to be comforting, steadying. But I only feel caged.

We are an experiment, I know this. The second wave of what started under Stalin; young, untrained psychics like Kruzenko and Rostov summoned forth to defeat the Nazi threat. But there is a vital component in the experiment that's eluding me, hovering just on the periphery of my thoughts, darting from sight as I try to look at it dead on.

"One of the hotel guests did overhear some of the CIA team members discussing the meeting with the last wildling that they have scheduled for tomorrow," Misha says. "But we couldn't find anything that indicates they've made contact with any other members of the *Veter 1* engineers. We don't know if they've already stolen all the information they need, or—"

"Or the whole *Veter 1* mission was only bait." My heart sinks as I say it. "A secondary scheme to draw in their primary target—us."

The table falls silent again. Silence tugs at us like gravity tonight, trapping our words in its atmosphere. It slumps Kruzenko forward, dulls her one-word answer. "Maybe." Her uniform is too tight; the folds of fat under her jaw have grown more pronounced, and black bags swell under her eyes.

"What will happen to Ivan now?" I ask.

"If he awakens, then we will have to be very careful. We will need to determine whether the Amerikanski poisoned his thought process before scrubbing him blank. If so, then even if he is healed, he could be completely—I don't know, rewired, perhaps, to act as an agent for the CIA."

"*If* he awakens," I echo.

Kruzenko nods. "The best thing we can do for Ivan right now is finish what we have begun."

"I'll go to Gorky Park tomorrow," I say. "We have to stop the scrubber from wiping the factory boy, too."

Valentin's fingers tighten against my knee. "Yulia, please, no."

"It is much too dangerous," Kruzenko agrees. Masha stares at me wide-eyed, almost impressed.

"Please. We can't let it happen again, even if it is to a wildling. Have our teams had any luck finding him?" I ask. Kruzenko doesn't answer. "That's what I thought. If we know exactly where he'll be—if we have this one chance to stop the scrubber . . ."

Kruzenko meets my eyes, and I know she doesn't need psy-chic powers to know how determined I am. "It will not be easy." She grimaces. "At the slightest hint of trouble, I will end the operation immediately."

"Whatever we have to do. Bring whatever backup we need," I say. "Please. For Ivan."

CHAPTER 32

"HE'S WAITING ON the park bench. No signs of the CIA team yet." Masha's brow wrinkles, shifting on the metal bench built into the inside of the van. "He's very antsy. He has a suitcase with him . . ."

Kruzenko glances at Rostov, who nods. She leans back from the heavy microphone kit. "Continue monitoring. We cannot move in until we've located the scrubber."

Valentin runs his finger down my arm. I flush and scan the truck to make sure no one else saw. "You're certain you want to do this?" he asks.

"We owe it to this wildling," I say.

Rostov's grin oozes across his face. "We owe it to the Motherland to stop this threat." There's a dark glint to his eyes; I'm sure he's hungry to add another medal to his uniform after today.

Masha jerks forward. "Someone's coming. Down the hill, off the main sidewalk . . . I think he's coming from the skating rink, though it could be the carnival rides."

Kruzenko presses the thick button on the microphone's base. "Agents, stand by. Comrade Rostov is moving in."

"Do those poor agents have any idea what they're up against?" Valentin mutters.

Rostov shrugs into his leather military long coat and pops his plastic earpiece into place. "They know it's their duty to do whatever I ask of them." He climbs out of the back of the van and slams the door shut behind him.

Masha takes a deep breath, then shakes out her hands. "Rostov is on the right path. There should be a clump of trees that'll give him cover from the bench. The scrubber is—" Here Masha shudders, "He's in a heavy coat, fur hat, and . . . well, I can't get a good look at him . . ."

Major Kruzenko relays the information over the microphone, then adds, "Agents, prepare to intercept."

Masha's face flushes with strain. "It's hard to see right now. The air is too—crackly. I'm not sure where Rostov went, but the scrubber is reaching the bench now . . ." She winces. "I'm not feeling so good."

"What do you mean? Where is Rostov?" Kruzenko mashes the microphone button. "Agents! Report in!"

"I can't focus on their conversation, and Rostov is—"

Major Kruzenko shrieks as static overwhelms her headphones—I can hear it from the other side of the van. She yanks the headset off and leaps up. "Masha? What do you see?"

"I can't look at the conversation, Comrade Major. I'm sorry. Rostov is—he's just standing there, his back turned, and . . ."

I cover my mouth as a drop of blood rolls from Masha's nose. "She needs to rest, Major. He's hurting her."

"No!" Masha cries. "I can do this, I swear."

I shrug and slump back on the bench, trying my best to look relaxed, though my heart is beating out a distress call. Valentin's thigh presses against mine. The Beatles sway back and forth between us. He's trying to slow the spinning centrifuge of thoughts in my head, but it's not much help.

"All right, I can see the bench again. But they're gone—the scrubber, the wildling. Rostov, too. I'm so sorry, there was just too much noise for me to see through—"

Kruzenko looks us over, and as her gaze crosses me, my stomach drops out from under me. "You." She points at me. "Probe the bench. See if you can replay their conversation. Valentin, go with her to find Rostov."

Valentin swallows hard. "I'm not sure I could do very much against the scrubber, if he finds us before Rostov does . . ."

"You'll be fine!" Hysteria curls at the edge of her voice. "Just hurry—please!"

As Valentin helps me out of the back of the van, we hear Kruzenko calling frantically for the agents to report in. "Stay close to me," he says, latching the door behind us. I chew at my lower lip as we wade into the snowy park.

The leafless branches overhead are glazed in ice; the frozen path fractures beneath our boots. Children whirl on the skating rink beside us while their Party mothers chatter nearby. The fresh-fallen snow adds a sense of stillness and beauty all around.

But I feel the scrubber's chaos, crackling in the thin winter air.

Neither of us speaks, as if we fear disturbing the eerie feeling slinking around us. We draw closer to the frozen riverbed lined by empty benches. The carousel's music washes over us; the shadow of the Ferris wheel spins across our path. Valentin raises one hand like a hunting dog and tilts his head, listening. Slowly, the pressure of the scrubber's noise fades.

"He's gone. Headed north, I think—out of the park. You should be safe to check the bench."

"What about the wildling?" I ask.

Valentin's Adam's apple quavers against his tight scarf. "I only sensed one person."

The wind stings at my eyes as we crest the hill and scan the park benches. Only one has been freshly cleared of snow. We trudge down the bank as Red Army trucks rumble past on the frozen surface of the Moskva River. "Not flesh nor feathers," I mumble, peeling off one glove, and press my hand against the bench.

I am greeted, not by a memory, but a message.

Yulia Andreevna. Crisp, glittering sunlight thaws me from the inside out. *You want to visit the Ferris wheel.*

I smile and stifle a childish giggle. I had not admitted it until now, but yes! I *do* want to ride the Ferris wheel. How could I not? It's the most sensible thing in the world. One cannot visit Gorky Park without riding it.

But you must go alone.

But what about Valentin? He won't let me out of his sight, not with the scrubber still on the loose. I sigh, two primal needs warring within me. I have to stay safe with Valentin, but horrible things will surely happen if I don't visit the Ferris wheel—

Alone.

No, the voice is absolutely right. Valentin would worry too

much. Everyone tries so hard to protect me. No sense in troubling him. I'll just slip away . . .

I will distract your partner, but you must hurry.

I pull back from the bench and re-glove my chapped red hand. Valentin is transfixed by the Red Army procession; by the truck beds laden with covered cylinders. Missiles of some kind, or test rockets, perhaps.

Go.

I charge up the hill. Valentin doesn't even stir. I glimpse Rostov in the trees, but he, too, is lost in a daydream. The crowd shifts around me; no one complains when I push to the front of the line for the Ferris wheel. I press some kopecks into the operator's palm. He opens the door to help me in—

—and as I jolt out of my reverie, the scrubber climbs into the car with me, and the metal door slams shut.

CHAPTER 33

THE COILED CONFUSION LOOSENS around my brain, and I find myself caged into the Ferris wheel car with a burning star. I scramble back against the far wall, but I can't escape his heat, his blinding light. He turns toward me with an awful metallic scrape. I only wish it was the sound of the Ferris wheel tearing apart around us.

I pile one song on top of the other. Every American pop song Valya's shared with me. Mama and Papa's Tchaikovsky records, their Shostakovich, their Bartok. Zhenya's symphony. The national anthem, plodding and grim. But the scraping continues, chipping away at the melodies, chiseling straight for my brain.

And then, just as painfully, his brilliance dims into a silence that leaves me hollow and aching.

"You are Chernin's daughter," the scrubber says.

The Ferris wheel lurches forward and we begin our slow rise into the Moscow sky.

"You are not safe here," he tells me.

"Of course not. You're going to scoop out my brains like you did to Ivan."

He chuckles. I can almost look at him from the corner of my eye; speckled black hair, not onyx like Valentin's but like a shirt left too long in the sun. No, wait—is it golden? A blazing red? Trying to pin down this man's substance is like trying to catch a firefly in your hand. As soon as I think I've caught him, I open up to find him gone.

"The foolish boy? He was too close to seeing me. I couldn't have him tattle. No, Yulia, I'm here to help you."

I shake my head. "Please, if you're going to kill me, get it over with. I don't want to suffer like he's suffering." The car's cold metal seeps through my coat; the wind outside lashes at us through the bars.

He laughs like crinkling foil. "I'm offering you a way out."

The spokes of Moscow's streets branch out before us, pinned to the city center by the Kremlin and Lenin's tomb. White and gray slush, split open by drab buildings, dead trees. "Out of what? The KGB, the mansion? Moscow?" I swallow hard.

"You don't want to be trapped forever." He leans toward me. His face is tan somehow in the dead of winter. No, that's not right; it is ashen, post-mortem gray. "You're tasked with protecting the *Veter 1* lunar mission design, yes?"

I nod. My mouth has frozen over.

"They will launch the *Veter 1* in secret just outside of Berlin in a few weeks. Your team will be in attendance—ostensibly to protect the launch and the high-ranking Party members in attendance from dangerous men. Like me."

"Will we?" I ask.

He nods. "You *will*." Sunlight glints off his smooth teeth. I must comply.

"Rostov is a dangerous man," I say. "He will do whatever it takes to stop you. His powers, they're just like yours—"

"But I am better." The scrubber grins again.

"Why Berlin?" I ask. "If you really mean to offer me a—a way out." *A way out.* Three words focusing my thoughts like a lens.

He shifts, jostling the seat; our car crests the top of the Ferris wheel with a lurch. "Because even I am not that good. Besides, there is still much more fun to be had."

He leans forward and pushes his ungloved thumb against my forehead. Metal screams all around me, as if the Ferris wheel is pulling off its axis and our car will go tumbling into the frozen Moskva. There is something inside my brain—slivers of ice. The man that was the scrubber has flared into molten whiteness once more.

"Chernin," I say. "You knew my last name." I can hardly think around this new presence in my mind, but I'm replaying his words, desperate for meaning.

He doesn't answer. I don't know if my head can carry all this weight.

"Please," I whisper. "Tell me what you know."

The car sinks. Moscow swells up to greet us. I slump against the wall as this alien thought buries deeper into my head. The operator tears open the door.

"I will see you in Berlin," the scrubber says, all brilliance fading from him as he steps out of the car.

Valentin pushes toward me as I stagger off the Ferris wheel platform. The air smells like death and cold; it's too sharp. Too real. He seizes my arm and all the pain and fear in him rubs off on me. Too much. I shake him away.

"Yul, what happened? Are you okay?" He puts an arm around my waist, but I tug away from him again.

"Please, don't touch me. My head is . . ." My head is what? I look across the park, listen to the children scream as they run between the rides and the skating rink. Where have I been? Did I fall asleep on a bench and dream of sailing through the stars?

"You vanished. We were standing by the bench, and then . . ." He stops and rubs at his eyes. "*Bozhe moi.* Did he come back?" Valya's voice turns hard. "Did he hurt you?"

"No. He was right there, and I—" I what? I couldn't see his face. I heard his voice, but the words were like drops of water, and once they'd come together, I could never sort one from the other.

"You saw him?" Valentin cups my face in his hands. Even through his gloves, his hands are scorching. "But you're—all right." He swallows hard. "Aren't you?"

The noise in my head turns sharp and acrid. "He could have killed me," I say, throat clenching up. "But he didn't. What if he doesn't want us dead at all?"

"Yulia. You saw what he did to Ivan. To that wildling boy."

"This is different," I insist. "He was trying to tell me something." The mass in my brain starts to unwrap like a wad of tinfoil, one layer at a time. I stand up a little straighter and sift through the thoughts that flake away with the first layer. "He wants us to go to Berlin."

Valya and I look at each other. It's as if we're hearing the same song—I've never heard it, but it is suddenly familiar; I know its contours just before the melody glides along them. I remember flying through the air, a thumb pressing on my forehead. But I don't remember this song or what it means.

"We can find a way out there," Valya says, at the same time the exact same words ring in my head. But of course we have to go. Why would we ever consider anything else? I squint against the too-bright snow. Escape; I dream of running free. No guards or scrubbers or spies tethering me.

Suddenly I crave this escape more than anything, more than a hot meal in the coldest depths of starvation, more than the taste of Valentin's sea-breeze lips. It's not the frantic escape plan of a caged animal, like when I ran through the Metro tubes. This has weight to it. Crisp edges.

Valya presses his finger to my lips. "Please. Do not say it, do not think it. Whatever you know . . . we must keep it safe."

"How?" I ask. "Rostov's pried thoughts from my head before, even when I tried to suppress them. I don't know if there's anywhere safe in my head."

"You'll just have to fill it with other things." He sighs, his breath hanging white between us. "I'm sorry. I wish I had a better suggestion, but anything else I might do could hurt you—"

"Perhaps not everything." I circle my arms around his waist. I'm hungry for escape. For freedom. For the music that swells between us. "I can think of a few thoughts to fill my head with."

I kiss him fiercely, my gloved hands gripping clumsily at his sides and his fingertips cradling my jaw. His thumbs trace my cheekbones as his mouth slips open and absorbs mine. We part to gasp for humid breaths that cling to our skin, shielding us from the sapping cold. Our eyes lock for a second before Valentin's lips inch up my cheek, to my earlobe, kissing it faintly. "Yulia," he whispers, savoring the vowels. "I'd follow you anywhere."

Snow crunches behind me. I whirl around, untangling from Valentin's arms. Major General Rostov staggers down the snowbank, fists plastered to his thighs as he fights for balance. "Children. What are you doing out here? It is not safe."

"We were looking for . . ." Valentin looks from me to the bench to Rostov again. "Well, I think we were looking for you. Kruzenko was worried—"

"Nonsense. I'm perfectly all right. Come, quickly, we must report back." He turns back onto the path toward the van, walking in jerky, piston-like steps. Valentin and I stroll along behind him. I find myself whistling a strange tune—a silly song, really, meandering around yet repetitive. Perhaps it's something Zhenya made up a lifetime ago. Or maybe I heard Valya playing it. I smile at him and his blushing face. I have this music in my head and his taste on my lips and I feel grand.

But Valentin hunches his shoulders tight, jamming his fists down in his coat pockets. "What happened to you, Comrade Rostov? You went to find the scrubber, but then you wandered off, and—"

"What? No, of course not. Why would I do such a thing?" He barks a dry laugh. "No, I overheard the conversation perfectly. The vile CIA team means to attend the secret *Veter 1* launch in Berlin next month." The strange three-note melody swells around us. "I fear they may attempt to sabotage the launch. We must stop them."

Yes. *Yes.* Yearning grabs hold of my spine and yanks me forward. I want this, too—to go to Berlin, to find the CIA team, to witness the launch. The melody fills every gap in my brain, caulking up the empty, bruised hollows and concealing the faint shape of something I think I'm trying to forget. "You're absolutely right, Comrade General. We will stop the scrubber in Berlin."

Rostov's smile cuts through his face as he looks back over his shoulder. Normally, it might send a shiver through me, but now it matches the phantom melody. "I am so glad you agree."

CHAPTER 34

SERGEI CLUTCHES THE CARDBOARD TUBE, brandishing it overhead like a claymore before swinging it down and around. It strikes the plastic chess piece in a direct hit, sending it tumbling end over end until it cracks against the plaster wall and sticks.

"And just like that, I scored on our top goalie!" he roars, throwing down the tube and tossing his hands in the air. "The crowd went wild! Luzhniki Stadium shook to its foundation!"

"I thought you said this was during practice?" Masha asks.

Sergei wiggles the chess piece out of the cracked plaster. "Well, if there *had* been a crowd, it *would* have gone wild."

"Congratulations," I tell Sergei. "Now could we have our chess piece back?"

He looks toward Valentin and me, and his grin vanishes. "I didn't think you liked chess, Yul."

I scan the chessboard, trying to remember where this bishop piece belonged. "It passes the time." Killing time. Passing these interminable hours, waiting for a chance to plan with Valentin, steal a moment to speak and kiss and *exist* with him without guards and Kruzenko and our classmates hovering over us . . .

"Sergei Antonovich!" Kruzenko's shrill voice splits the air. "What on earth are you doing to our maps?" She rushes into the parlor and snatches the tube out of his hands. "Not studying them for the mission, I can see!"

"We still have time to prepare," Sergei says.

Kruzenko shakes the maps out of the tube and unfurls them with a crack. "We depart the day after New Year's. Misha and Masha, have you practiced your drills?"

"Yes," Misha says, chiming with Masha's "Of course."

"Valentin? You have been keeping your mind limber?" Kruzenko tapes the maps over the now-completely crossed out list of wildlings.

"As much as I can, without hurting anyone." Valentin's gaze falls to his hands, tucked into his lap.

Kruzenko smiles. "Good to hear it. Larissa will . . ." Kruzenko looks around us, tongue clucking, then shrugs. "Well, I'm certain that when she is feeling more like herself again, she will be up to the task. I will see to it. In the meantime, Yulia Andreevich, might I have a word?"

I jump up from the table. "Did you approve my request?"

Her back is to me, but her finger beckons me from over her shoulder. "We'll discuss it in my office, please."

My pulse thrums as I follow her through the mansion. If Valentin and I succeed in Berlin—no, I scold myself, *must bury that away*—then this may be the last time I see Mama and Zhenya for a while. Not forever, though. It can't be. No matter where we run for help, we have to find a way to rescue them, too, eventually. I just want this last glimpse, this memory that I can tuck in the darkest corners of my mind for safekeeping.

Kruzenko closes the door behind us, keeping even the guards outside. Her face is too flat. Her gypsy music shield races around the room. Is it stronger than usual? I'd never noticed before the subtle shift in her shield when she's working hard to suppress her thoughts. I dare to hope I'm getting stronger, shrewder in my skills.

"I have tried, Yulia," she starts.

Everything collapses inside of me. Crumpling up, shriveling.

"I have begged and pleaded, but Comrade Rostov will not allow it. You must understand, your mother is very busy with her research . . ."

I'm numb, deadened to the rising tide of emotion inside me. "Surely she can take time away. And Zhenya, I know the doctors think he's doing better, but I don't want him to—" I strangle back a cry. "—Forget me."

"Perhaps when we return from Berlin, and she completes the next phase of research, then something can be arranged." Kruzenko laces her fingers together. "I trust that will be sufficient."

"Of course it's not sufficient." Tears burn in the corners of my eyes, ready to blaze a hot trail down my cheeks. I have to see them once more, I have to. I have to know what Mama is afraid of. Why she told me to run. I have to hug my brother one last time and hear him tell me, matter-of-factly, that I have no reason to be upset. "What is so damned important about her research? Why can't she step away for just a few hours?"

Kruzenko rubs her temples, squishing her skin around like it is dough; she looks so much older now than just a few months ago. "Yulia . . . There is something I must explain to you about your family."

A warning shot fires in the back of my mind. Bang-bang. There is something that I know, but it lies broken in my mind, flattened under layers and layers of thought. I probe at its edges, like I'm probing an aching tooth with my tongue.

"Rostov does not feel it is necessary for you to know these things in order to do your job, but I do not always agree. Sometimes we need reasons more than mere orders." She swallows; the whites of her eyes gleam as she leans toward me. "Your parents . . . You know that your mother is a geneticist and your father was a developmental biologist for the State."

"They were working with children with genetic disorders," I say. "Trying to train them to be functional workers."

"Yes, that came afterward. But before that, they worked on a secret research project for Stalin." She sucks in a deep breath, hands quavering. "Our program, Yulia. They helped create it."

I don't answer. Jet fuel burns through my chest: shock and utter inevitability all at once.

"They isolated the genetic markers that carry enhanced mental powers, yes—at least, a few of them."

Their old research. The cabbage soup from lunch creeps up my throat. The dream I had, one Valentin stirred up, of my parents arguing about returning to their old research. The room sways beneath me. Did they know I had this ability? They had to have known.

But why keep it from me?

"We founded the program during the Great Patriotic War,

when Hitler betrayed our treaty and invaded. Stalin demanded that we never be caught off guard in such a way again. Your parents' team was already renowned for their work in genetics, studying an unusual mutation that had been found in cross-sections of the Soviet population . . . including . . . themselves."

"You meant that my—my parents were . . ."

Kruzenko purses her lips. "Your mother knew her gift for what it was—foresight, premonition. A bit like Larissa. But it also gave her painful headaches, and she wanted to isolate the cause. The research had already caught the Red Army's attention before the war, then when it began, Stalin approached her about military uses for the people with this mutation."

"But what about my father?" At some point, I sank into a chair; I feel as if I'm sinking still.

"He worked in the biology department, but when your mother collected samples from the other university students, he showed the markers. Turned out he had some latent remote viewing powers. Your mother convinced him to join her team." She closes her eyes as a quaver works its way into her voice. "When the war started, all able-bodied psychics worked in their own military unit under Rostov and myself. Afterward, we decided to continue the program for espionage purposes, and your parents were to conduct further research, including, ah, how shall I put this." She smiles with the pained look of someone about to cry. "Including how the ability passed on to subsequent generations."

A program. A genetic program. We are silver foxes, being stripped of our teeth and claws. "A breeding program, you mean."

"Not precisely, but yes, it was . . . encouraged." She purses her lips. "Misha's and Masha's parents met through the program as well, and there have been others—"

"Just tell me." I'm bloated with all the emotions I want to feel, but I'm afraid of settling into my own skin. Afraid they'll drown me, swallow me whole. I hover within myself just like I hover over an object whose memories scare me. "My parents were really in love, weren't they? My birth wasn't a . . ." The word lodges in my throat. *Experiment.*

Kruzenko smiles for real this time. "Of course they were. If you could have seen them together, during the war . . ." She sighs. "But they did grow troubled after your brother's birth. He bore some of the genetic markers, but other mutations that pointed toward a different disorder. There's no guarantee of psychic ability at birth, you see. One can't be certain until age nine or so."

"So they knew what I was when I was nine. But . . ."

I stop myself, that thought chewing at me like acid. But I didn't start experiencing my powers until I was twelve or so. No. There's something else missing, something Kruzenko isn't telling me.

"What happened to the program, then?" I ask. "You make it sound like Stalin recruited dozens."

"Just over a hundred, actually. But the Great Patriotic War was a very messy thing, you see. Only a few dozen survived. And of those—some could not cope with various aspects of their condition. Some took their own lives, others lost their hold on reality. Some, like your parents, could not cope with the requirements of the program itself, and had to be . . ." She shrugs. "Dealt with accordingly."

"Is that why my parents went into hiding?" I ask. "You were threatening them to come back?"

"Rostov approached them about it, yes. The program is so small now, and yet the threat we face from the Americans is so great. We are continuing to search for wildlings, naturally, but we were shrinking every year. Now that your mother has returned to us, however, she has restarted her research."

"You're monsters. All of you." I am shaking; it's the only outlet for all this emotion humming inside me.

She smiles at me, unfazed. "And always we need new test subjects, too. We encourage the fraternization, by the way—that is why Larissa and Ivan were never a problem to me." She arches one brow. "I suspect you have a fondness for Valentin. He would not be my choice for you, personally, but if it will produce results—"

I can't disconnect anymore. The dam bursts; my rage is drowning me.

"You crazy bitch. You monster, treating us like your laboratory rats." My heart hammers frantically in my chest. I stand up and lunge over the desk, hands reaching for her throat. "I swear, I will kill you before I let you use me like some show pony to be bred—"

A heated blade twists into my skull, jarring my thoughts, splitting them apart and sending me to my knees. She stands over me with a laser-guided glower.

"I think you forget too easily, Yulia Andreevna, that this is not a summer camp. A fancy academy. You are the property of the Soviet Union, and when I tell you these things, when I permit you to see your family, it is a *privilege* and not a right." Her weepy-gypsy song scrapes me raw like a dull razor. "Remember your place. Who you are speaking to. Remember your purpose." She laughs, more to herself than me. "Because there are far worse things you could endure."

We are not permitted to access the third-floor observation deck, mostly because it is too dilapidated and dangerous, but tonight is New Year's Eve and I don't want to drink champagne and vodka downstairs with the rest. Valentin and the twins are on a mission for Rostov at one of the Party celebrations; Larissa is still in mourning; and I can't bear the blear of disappointment in Sergei's eyes because I don't long for the same Russian life as him. I would rather fall through the ceiling or freeze to death than endure all of that.

The air out on the observation deck is prickly on my cheeks; heavy winter clouds in the night sky are green and black like a bruise, bloated with the reflection of city lights. The Moskva is solid ice below the cliffs, and weeks-old snow crowns the buildings in the distance, mottled and dirty. Filth and squalor. I tuck my knees under my chin and the centuries-old plaster under me creaks.

Nineteen sixty-four is dawning. We are throwing men and metal at the stars and placing nuclear missiles around the globe. Soon, we'll head to Berlin to witness the launch of the *Veter 1*, on its way to circle the moon, while we try to stop the American spies from stealing its secrets for themselves. And I will attempt one last time to run—toward what, I'll have to see.

I should be welcoming the new year, but looking out at

Moscow feels like a goodbye. I want to never again look at the skyline and see Stalin and Lenin looking back, standing atop the backs of the workers who made them gods.

Fireworks erupt over the Kremlin, illuminating its star-crowned towers with red and gold. In Novodevichy Monastery to my left, a solemn bell clangs. But the rest of the city, the city of workers and laborers, stays silent. For them, tomorrow is just another day.

Yulias of the world, unite. It's time to set you free.

CHAPTER 35

LARISSA GROANS FROM UNDER her hibernation nest of blankets on the cot. "Yeah, I've been to the vault. What about it?"

"Valya needs your help with something," I say.

She unravels her nest enough to stare at me for a few moments, blue eyes searching. Then she burrows back down. "It won't work."

I grit my teeth. "Is that just your guess, or a vision you had?"

"It's me trying to be left alone."

"Lara! This is serious." I swat at her thick swaddling. "What was it you told me? No point in looking at the past, might as well move forward? You've been looking in the past for weeks now."

The blankets quiver as she groans. "Next time I feel like giving you sage advice, I'll look ahead to see if you're going to use it against me."

"Just think about it," I tell her. "You know where I'll be."

Valentin's new jazz record trickles down the path to the vault—Miles Davis, the album sleeve says. The music is slow, but creeping, like at any moment it might jump out at you. It's a good sort of uncomfortable. I want to stay on edge.

"No Larissa?" Valentin asks. "It would've been nice to have her help. But I suppose it's one less person who could slip up."

"I'm not sure I can keep the secret myself." I settle next to him on the floor. Heat blooms across my arms so close to his, but I try to ignore it. There'll be plenty of time to run my fingers along his skin when we're free. Plenty of time to taste and hear my Valentin with no one to tell us what to do or to turn us against each other, against our fellow Russians for daring to aspire toward more . . .

"Valya, I need to ask you something." I trace a circle on the top of his hand. "A favor for me, once we're free."

He tilts his head to one side. "Of course. Anything."

"I think there are gaps in my memory." I wince and pull my hand back from him. Without meaning to, the crackly sounds of his scrubber ability is humming along his skin. "I don't know if it's something Rostov has done to me, or . . ."

Valya's eyes tighten behind his glasses. "You want me to try to restore whatever you're missing." He draws his shoulders inward, curling into the rising jazz melody. "Yul, I don't know if that's such a good idea. I wouldn't feel right tinkering with your brain—I mean, what if I did something wrong? I'd never forgive myself—"

"Please." I close my eyes. "I want to understand who I really am."

Again that deluge of emotion is threatening to drag me under, and I have to disconnect. There has to be some kind of release valve for all this emotion. Some way for me to get rid of it. I thought I'd done it, once. I don't want to drown in it like Anastasia did.

"You won't be able to change it, even if I can restore your memories," he says. "I don't know if it's worth the risk . . ."

Wood clatters at the other end of the vault hallway—someone moving back the panel to enter. I sit up straight, and Valya reaches for the volume knob on his record player.

Larissa slinks in, hair tangled around her shoulders, still in her pajamas. I relax; Valya leans back from the record player. "Feel better now that you're up and moving?" I ask.

She wipes her nose on her sleeve. "Turns out you lunatics are going to need my help after all." She sits down across from us, but her gaze is all over, drinking in the musty vault like it's a fresh spring day. "Yul, you were right, by the way. It's best to keep looking ahead."

Valentin looks at me with a smirk. "Funny, I was just telling her the same thing." He swaps to a nice loud Mussorgsky record, *Night on Bald Mountain*. "All right, Larissa. It's good to have you on our side."

The strings swirl around like wind whipping against a mountain's face; low horns announce a demon's arrival. Papa told me stories of Chernobog, the black god of ancient Russia who lived within the mountainside. Old gods like that were made to crush

such men as Rostov and Comrade Premier Khruschev. We could certainly use that power on our side.

"So. Have any of us ever been to East Germany?" Valya asks. Larissa and I shake our heads. "Me, neither. So we'll have to improvise."

He opens a yellowed, smelly book I recognize from the house library: *Capitalist Aggression in Post-War Germany*. It's old, probably from right after the Patriotic War, but there is a map of Berlin, complete with a demarcation line where now a concrete wall exists.

"We saw the maps of the actual launch site," he says, "but unfortunately, it's located about twenty kilometers from the wall, on a heavily guarded military installation. So I think our best chance will be when we are in Berlin proper." He circles a point on the map. "Most of the Party officials attending the launch will be staying at the Hotel Kepler, only a kilometer from the eastern side of the wall."

A new melody slinks around in my head, weaving between the demonic dances of Bald Mountain. I have heard it before, but I can't place the tune; it presses against the side of my skull.

"Rostov will put us there as well. He'll want us keeping tabs on the *nomenklatura*. If so, the CIA team is sure to be close by."

Larissa rubs her arms, like she's staving off a chill. "I really don't trust him, Yul. I know he didn't hurt you at Gorky Park, but you've seen what he can do to . . ." She trails off. "Others."

A way out. The words rise up from the noise inside my head. I can't explain the certainty I feel about our plans or even its source, but I know it's there. "This is different. I'm sure of it."

Larissa chews her lip without any emotion showing on her face, which makes me nervous. I wonder if she's seeing something now, if her tree of possibilities is charting out all the factors. But she doesn't say anything either way.

I gesture to the map. "Look—this checkpoint near the hotel might be our best chance. I don't know if the American soldiers working it are trained to repel psychic attacks, but I'm pretty sure our enlisted men aren't."

"It's promising, at least," Valya agrees. "You'll have to learn the guards' routes and look for paths that they may not know about. Feel out the scenery for us. And Lara, we'll need your help to choose wisely along the way."

"You'll be acting as our smoke screen for anyone who tries to stop us?" Larissa asks.

Valya winces. "I'll do my best, yes. I don't know, though, if I'm strong enough to stop Rostov. My biggest fear is if he brings the Hound . . ."

I look at him sideways. "That thing Rostov sent after you when you tried to escape?"

Valentin nods as the frantic devil's dance of string and cymbals crashes around us. "That was him. Another sick experiment of Rostov's. The poor creature's deaf, blind, mute. He gets around entirely on psychic ability—and more often than not, Rostov's explicit orders. Like a big, monstrous puppet."

I frown. "But what's the purpose? He's just exceptionally strong?"

Larissa shakes her head. "He's a tracker, for starters. You know how we can only use our powers at short distances? Not him. He can follow any psychic's signature across any distance."

"Then why hasn't Rostov brought him out before?" I ask.

"Because he also acts like an amplifier for any psychics around him. The time I encountered him, I nearly scrubbed myself." Valentin sighs. "Rostov wants us just powerful enough to be useful, but not powerful enough that we can overwhelm him."

Larissa snorts. "And he has to be careful about using him in crowded areas. There are some strange things that even Russians won't ignore."

"Rostov would rather use the Hound to track us than protect us. Ever had a belonging go missing from the house? That's Rostov, training the Hound on our psychic 'scent,' so to speak," Valya says.

The music reaches its peak. Dawn creeps around Bald Mountain as the church bells chime, too quiet now to cover up our conversation. Valya searches through his stack of records for the next concealing track.

Someone steps into the ring of candlelight behind Larissa, blocking out a row of candles.

"What is this?" Sergei asks, looming over us like Chernobog. "The Secret Psychic Record Club?"

"Something like that," Valya mutters. "Care to join us for some Johnny Cash?"

"Cash? Sounds like a money-grubbing capitalist swine." He smiles as if to show he's making a joke, but there's no humor in his darkened eyes. Valentin shoves his glasses up on his nose and keeps his head bowed, not answering him.

"Did you need something, Sergei?" Larissa asks. Her fingers tap against the floor, each strike sending a little shockwave of nervous psychic energy my way.

Sergei crosses his arms, still towering. "I was looking for Yulia. I, uh . . . wanted to show her something."

"I'm right here," I say, remaining seated. If he has something to say to me, he can do it here; I'm anxious to get back to our plans.

Sergei takes a step backward. His thoughts are iron clad with Tchaikovsky, but his eyes dart to Valya, and the space—the very minimal space—between our shoulders. "It can wait."

Sergei stalks out of the vault. I let out my breath, not realizing I'd been holding it; Larissa flops onto her elbows with a sigh. Finally, she is frowning. Not exactly the emotion I'd hoped she'd show.

"Only one thing is clear to me right now," she says. "Sergei is going to be a problem for our plans."

CHAPTER 36

BYELORUSSKY TRAIN TERMINAL is a castle in mint green, from the last days of the tsars when everything was slathered in pastel shades and tipped in gold. But the crowd flowing through the doors would disappoint those bustled and corseted dukes and countesses (if they weren't too busy throwing themselves in front of trains, like Tolstoy heroines). The glass and steel vestibule is massive, cathedral-like. Kruzenko and our flock of KaGeBeznik protectors guide us to a middle platform, where a substantial black iron train waits.

We are heading to Berlin to protect the secret *Veter 1* launch. Our mission will not be easy, Kruzenko warned us. We have no guarantee of what kind of threat we will face in Berlin: sabotage, assassination, theft of the rocket design or its components, maybe even kidnapping of *Veter 1* scientists. All this while evading the scrubber and his team—at least, that's what Kruzenko told us to do.

But that three-note melody in the soft hollows of my brain

says otherwise. *A way out.* Needles prick at my mind like some-one cross-stitching on my thoughts, but they are warm, hum-ming with the soothing tune.

Valya and Larissa aren't as pleased by the melody. Valya has stopped in the middle of the stream of travelers and grips his head like he's trying to keep a lid on a boiling pot. Larissa curls her arms around her wiry frame and whimpers. Only Major Kruzenko is smiling, smiling as blissfully as me. Why doesn't everyone else hear this beautiful melody?

"We have to get on the train." Valya speaks through clenched teeth, spittle spraying from his lips. "Yulia. Don't you hear that noise?"

"It smells like springtime, doesn't it?"

"Yulia." Valya pulls a dingy kerchief from his coat pocket and swabs at my nose. When he pulls back, the kerchief is smeared with blood.

"But I—" I wipe my nose on my sleeve, but my dark brown coat doesn't reveal anything. "But I feel just fine—"

Valya tugs on Major Kruzenko's jacket. "Come on, Comrade Major. He's nearby. We have to board now."

Kruzenko turns toward him with a slick red trail down her right nostril, curving like a scythe around her lips.

And then light blossoms on the horizon like a second sun. Dazzling, warm. I want to turn my face toward it like a flower and let it melt away the frost. Sticky warmth flows down my upper lip but I don't care, I just need to bask—

Valya wads up his kerchief and presses it against my nose. "You, too. Get inside."

We have a whole car to ourselves: Larissa, Masha, Kruzenko,

and I will share one compartment, and Valentin, Sergei, and Misha will share another with one of the guards; at the end of the car is the tiny closet with a hole directly over the rails, which qualifies as a toilet. We are lucky to have that luxury.

Rostov will be flown in with a Red Army convoy, joining us in Berlin. I am far more grateful for that.

Valentin pinches my nose and tilts my head back to stanch the blood flow before we part for our separate compartments. As he gives my forearm a gentle squeeze, I sense a terse little bundle of music slip under my skin. I mentally place it in my pocket for later decoding.

Once my nosebleed is stanched, Larissa and I head to the dining car. The train clatters along the iron road through Moscow's heart; the failing light shows endless smokestacks and snaggled wires overhead. We'll pick up speed as we leave the city, but for now, we're closed in a Moscow-sized aquarium. I reach out mentally around me as Larissa and I shuffle down the corridor. The glass panels make me feel empty, exposed.

"Why do you think the scrubber only affected you and Kruzenko?" Larissa asks under her breath as we pass a forlorn-looking man, staring out the window and smoking unfiltered cigarettes.

"I feel like I have this . . . connection to him. Maybe not a connection, but this certainty." I trace a finger around my temple. "I know he's dangerous, but I can't help but sense there's something more to it. I . . . I need to find out what."

Larissa presses her lips into a thin line. "How about you leave the prophesying to me? Besides, it doesn't explain Kruzenko."

"He must have had a reason for targeting her specifically.

Maybe he's encountered her before." I shake my head as I sink into an empty bench in the dining car.

My tea arrives with too much honey, wrapped in a metal *podstakannik* commemorating Yuri Gagarin's historic flight in space with a geometric, stylized swoosh of stars and meteors. Our dinner is an unidentifiable whole fish, eyeballs thankfully removed, and a bowl of boiled potatoes with mushrooms. Larissa flips through her book while she pushes the potatoes back and forth. I curl up on the bench and unravel the thought that Valya left for me.

You are right about needing to recover your missing memories. I fear they may be tied to the way the scrubber affects you. Stay in the dining car tonight until everyone is asleep. I'll help you as best I can.

Our teammates filter through the dining car, as well as heavy-faced old women and skeletal men with bear-trap jaws, but none of them glow with the scrubber's imprint. I try not to circle too close to their depressing, dull thoughts: fretting over dwindling rations or persistent coughs or promiscuous paramours in Murmansk. Misha and Masha enter in tandem and dine at the opposite end of the car, offering us nothing more than the occasional evil eye.

Larissa heads to sleep once the sky is too dark to mark the flurry of parallel naked birch trees whizzing by. I'm alone in the dining car with a group of loud, intoxicated Komsomol university students. Their thoughts are simple and clear. I wait for the screeching sound of the scrubber but it never comes.

Sergei and Valentin appear at the far end of the car. Sergei fiddles with his hair, trying not to scowl, while Valya wears his scowl like a medal. They give each other a look as they reach my booth, silently jockeying, then both slide onto the bench opposite me.

Valentin drums his fingers against the tabletop. *Sorry. We'll have to wait.* His thoughts never waver as he sends the message my way. He's calm in a way I can only dream of.

"We should reach Warsaw by morning," Valya says, as the train slows and the conductor calls out a station name somewhere in Belarus. "We'll arrive at East Berlin by afternoon. Doesn't leave much time to look around the city before dark."

I nod, keeping my gaze fixed out the windows, but I know what he means. He wants to scout our escape route.

"I just hope we're home before next week's game. Oh—Yulia, I didn't get to tell you!" Sergei pokes my leg under the table with his foot. "I'm on the third line for Spartak next year! Kruzenko's letting me play half the games."

I force a smile on my face and let Shostakovich fill the hollowness in my chest. As much as I want to be genuinely happy for him, I can't split that desire from the sadness at seeing him settle for this life, this gilded cell that the KGB would put us in, telling us it's a lavish Party apartment in Kutuzovsky. He deserves better; he deserves to be free. But he has to want it, and a lifetime of Party doctrine has clouded his thoughts more than any scrubber could.

"I can't wait to see you play," I tell him, the lie chafing.

The train clatters along the tracks, puncturing the silence that hangs over us. I try to think of something more to say— some way to get Sergei to leave, but everything sounds false and bitter in my head. I shift on the bench. Sergei looks between

Valentin and me, smile fading. Slowly, Sergei stands up, his Tchaikovsky music bursting with cannon fire. "Well, I, uh . . . guess I'd better sleep." He swings toward me, his eyes icy points. "You should, too, Yulia."

The dining car door slams behind him in a wave of winter air.

"He knows." I swallow hard. "About us."

"He *suspects*." Valentin slumps back on the bench with a sigh. "We'll have to be careful. Maybe it could work to our advantage. Distract him from what we're planning."

I shake my head, but I can't find words for the fear I feel rising in my throat. I can't worry about Sergei or our escape just now. I have to focus on why we're here. "I'm ready for what I asked you for."

Valentin studies me, gaze soft, but there's an intensity in his wrinkled brow that I feel, too. These are the last moments before something changes me on the outside as much as in.

I place my hands on the table, palms up, a sacrifice to whatever comes next. I need to know who I am. What's been taken from me. I don't care about the cost.

"You're sure about this," Valentin says, sounding like he already knows. He laces his fingers in mine. "Just relax your mind. Unclench the music around it and let yourself float . . ."

The train spins away from me. The world is dark, marred like a scummy pond. Three clear notes ripple the water as dark shapes dart below the surface. There's a submerged wooden cabin—our summer dacha in the forest, flooded, moss reaching up from its roof like groping fingers. The tower of Moscow State.

I skim above the water, letting the current carry me over these fragments of my past, staring up like drowned faces. The melody crescendos, but I'm not feeling that tenderness under my skin, that battered soreness that warns me not to proceed deeper into that patch of memory as surely as an electric fence.

You're still fighting it, Yulia. You have to let go.

A red and gold star juts from the water. I follow it below the surface; it's the top of a strange baton wielded by a statue of the Soviet Man, forever mid-stride. I've seen this statue before, though I couldn't say where. I catch on the baton and sink, following it down into the depths, toward the statue's base.

Better. Stay calm, Yulia. I'll do the best I can.

The statue is in the courtyard of a submerged compound: curved concrete and metal bomb-shelter doors. I glide toward the elaborate mural painted over the doorway, full of stern-faced Soviet scientists, measuring vials and flasks as a comet trail of double helixes, stethoscopes, chromosomes swirl behind them. I reach out to trace the Cyrillic letters chiseled into the door. *State Laboratory for Neurophysiological Chromosomal Research. Doesn't exactly roll off the tongue,* I think to Valentin.

The current shifts, tugging me down toward the open doors. No. Oh, no. As I'm sucked into the building, my ribs clamp shut and my heart pounds madly. I suck in saltwater.

Don't fight it! Valentin cries, as if it's as simple as that when I'm losing control.

I slam into a cramped child's desk, the kind we had in grade school, but this is no classroom. Wires slither out of my head and jam themselves into a blue electrical box studded with red lights. The room reeks of bleach and formaldehyde, a little too similar to the KGB interrogation room I remember from when Kruzenko first spoke to me.

We're getting closer, Yulia. But I'll have to work slowly. I don't want to hurt you—

The door opens with a flare of white light. I open my mouth to scream as the light pours over me like sandpaper on my skin. When the scream finally comes, it's raw as a wound, shredding apart—

The white light blinks out, and the pain sizzles out of me. *No. I'm sorry, Yul. I can't do this to you.*

Please. I watch the red lights do their strange dance up and down the control panel that I'm plugged into. *We're so close. I'm sure of it.* The fluorescents overhead sputter; the current starts to pull me away. *Valya, it's fading—please!*

I slam back into the chair with a clang; the whole room drains of water as the lights swing back into full staticky force. The door opens once more as a ghostly man-shaped blur steps inside. I lift my head toward him, but the wires attached to me limit my movement; I can only catch sight of him from the corner of my eye.

"My poor Yulia. This is so much worse than I feared." The man slaps a clipboard against his open palm. "Four little alleles, bits of your genetic code. If only you didn't carry the genes, this would not be necessary. I'm sorry it must be this way."

He drags a chair right up to me and cradles my face in his hands. I flinch away from his searing touch—then choke on a gasp. The fringe of black hair across his forehead, those steel-rimmed frames. I wet my lips; strain my vocal chords like the out-of-tune strings in the ballroom piano. "Papa?"

His blinding glow retreats in fits and starts. He slides a cigarette from behind his ear and lights it with a flick. "Your mother and I are at an impasse," he says, smoke oozing from his mouth and nose. "She thinks that we can train you ourselves. Teach you to keep your powers safe."

He taps the ash away with a trembling hand. "But I am not so convinced. Not because I find you weak, mind you—my darling girl, you are so much stronger than I could have hoped. Already you remind me of her, way back when . . ."

"When what?" I wheeze. "During the war?"

Papa nods. "Yes, it is not your weakness that I fear. It is the Party's strength." He takes a long drag on his cigarette. "They have methods, skills that our minds just aren't made to overcome. You know what I always say." He stretches one hand and leans forward, flattening his palm to my forehead. "An empty mind is a safe mind."

My eyes fly open, the laboratory, Papa, the current of my thoughts blazing away in an instant. I rip my hands out of Valentin's. "*Bozhe moi.*" I trip over the bench as I stumble out into the aisle.

"This stop, Biaroza, in the Soviet republic of Belarus," the conductor calls, as we slow into the station. I charge out of the dining car and pound down the steps straight into waist-high snow.

"Yulia, come back! Please!"

Valentin charges after me but I'm running straight for the thicket of birch trees, so bone-white and perfectly straight against the inky sky. Stars mix with snowflakes in the air. The only sound I can hear is the crunch of snow beneath and behind me, my ragged breaths, and the distant rumble of the stalled train. The trees swallow me whole.

In my thoughts, the three-note melody rings out tauntingly.

Hands close around my waist. Valentin tackles me into the snow. I stare straight up at the bared branches and dream of them coming to life, scooping me up, crushing me.

"Please, you can tell me. What's the matter, Yulia? Just let me know."

"The scrubber." I stare at my breath as it hovers before me. Words are too solid in this winter night. Snow is dripping through my sweater; my bare hands are going numb. "He's not American after all." I sink further into the white abyss. "He's my father," I say.

CHAPTER 37

"IT'S WHY I DON'T REMEMBER my powers ever showing up until after he'd left." I gulp down frosty air that worms through my lungs, both scorching and numbing. "He—he suppressed it, scrubbed out my memories of even having such an ability."

Valya lets me sob into his shoulder as he rubs my hands between his. We're both coatless, hatless, scarfless in the January night. "We can talk about it more, Yulia, but we have to go back. The guards are coming."

"Why? Why can't we flee now? I can't go to Berlin and face—I mean, how could he be so close to me and not even tell me—" I choke down a scream. "Look at all the people he's hurt!"

"Yul, look at *you*. At me." He helps me to my feet. "We're in no shape to run right now. We're in the middle of the Soviet Union in the dead of winter."

"Why wouldn't he say something to me? Why all of the

games?" I bite down on my raw bare hand, already throbbing from cold, to stop a sob. "Doesn't he care anymore?"

"He must have had a good reason." But Valentin's shoulders slump—he can't come up with a good reason, either. "He wants us to meet him in Berlin, we know that much. We have to at least learn why."

I shake my head, though I don't fight him off as he wraps his arms around me. "He should have told me," I whimper. I realize how pathetic I must sound, but I'm too numb—from the shock, from the cold—to care.

Two sets of boots crunch through the snow toward us—our guards. I look away, deeper into the forest, though I can't see far for the fog and snow. I ache to keep running but my legs sting from the cold.

"Fine." I shake snow from my skirt. "Let's go back."

"Comrades!" one of our guards calls. "I trust there is a good reason for this?"

Valya kisses my cheek and helps me back toward the train. "Sorry, comrade. The toilet was occupied."

I sleep like death and awaken well past noon to Larissa staring me down from her bunk. "Oh, good. You're alive."

"Good to know," I say, rubbing my head. I examine my fingers and toes—I have escaped General Winter's frostbite.

She cants her head to Kruzenko's bunk. "Her nose started bleeding again and she was talking nonsense. How do you feel?"

My eyes feel like I've been rubbing them with wool, and my joints ache, but I shrug. No nosebleed. "I'll survive."

Sergei is polishing off what appears to be his third round of breakfast when I enter the dining car. His gaze flicks toward mine. "Yulia," he says, hunching his shoulders forward as I slide into the booth across from him. "I . . . I'd brought my official Spartak team photo to show you." He manages a faint smile. "They used the photo from last year, when I first joined."

Sergei grins up at me in black and white, wearing a full set of hockey armor, skates, and jersey. He kneels before the goal net with the Spartak logo blazing across his puffed-up chest.

"Congratulations," I say. "I know how badly you wanted this."

"You'll come to my games. Promise? I'll get you box seats. I'm sure Kruzenko will allow it if I ask her."

He looks so happy in the photo; there's a light in his eyes that I've never seen, not even when he's at his most mischievous. "You said this is an older picture?"

"Unfortunately." He tilts his head. "I don't look tough enough in it, do I? I'm a lot more muscular now."

"And you've still got your tooth." I point to his grin—left front tooth and all. His front teeth buckle inward. I'd never noticed it before because it's less obvious with one of them gone. I look up at him with something dark pulsing through my thoughts. "Sergei . . . smile for me."

He pulls back his lips. "Like this?"

Sure enough, his remaining front tooth buckles in. "Your crooked front teeth. That's hereditary, isn't it?"

He shrugs his shoulders. "Isn't that your area of expertise?" he studies his grin in the photograph. "Maybe I should ask them to retake the picture. People take you more seriously if you've got some injuries, some scars . . ."

I study Sergei's stats printed alongside the photo. IVANOV, SERGEI ANTONOVICH. Ivanov is the default Russian name, the great anonymizer, like a Smith for English speakers—no surprise that the KGB would want him under a pseudonym. It's the patronymic that terrifies me, staring up at me. Antonovich. Son of Anton.

Sergei's talking, eyebrows drawn down. "Yulia, I've been meaning to talk to you about something. About you and . . . and Valentin—" but I can't listen. I stand up, stepping backward carefully. I wish I could unsee this. Realization is a shattered glass that you can't unshatter. All you can do is slice yourself on its edges.

"Yulia?" Sergei asks. "Are you listening to me?"

And his teeth—I've seen that genetic trait before. "Sorry, Sergei. Maybe another time."

I lock myself in the bathroom and watch the tracks whir past through the hole in the "toilet." Sergei's smile, those chiseled cheekbones and flop of blond hair. I've seen that face in fuzzy black and white. And then that tooth—

My fingertips trace the edge of the tiny mirror. Surely she used the restroom at some point in the night. Misha, Masha. Sergei, flexing in the mirror. Masha again. Valentin, refusing to meet his own gaze as he scrubs at his hands.

Kruzenko. She smoothes down her hair and checks her nose—no blood for now. Then she curls back her lip to pick her teeth.

I slump back against the wall and bite down on my fist to keep from crying out. Kruzenko's son. Son of Anton.

Major General Anton Rostov.

⭐ ⭐ ⭐

East Berlin is a concrete crypt. Everywhere I look, stark, flat buildings rise out of shell-shocked rubble and watch us with broken windows for eyes. The streets hold no cars. The old buildings—from before Stalin seized this land for his own—look safe from one side, but when we pass them, the rest is crumpled by artillery fire, the wreckage blocked off by barbed wire fences. The few people we pass fix their stares on their feet and hurry past us. Coal smoke and sulfur linger around every corner as we wade through half-melted black slush.

Valentin's arm presses against mine as we walk. *Are you doing all right?*

I'll live, I reply. Papa or no, we have to find our way out.

The streets turn from gray to darker gray as the sun evaporates. We trudge through the streets clutching our satchels, silent like the last survivors of a war. Finally, Kruzenko points ahead, to a squat Baroque building of grooved stone with its name spelled in lights, in elaborate German script: the Hotel Kepler.

"Remember, children, we must not discuss our purpose here. Stay on guard," Kruzenko says.

I look to Valya to point out the fire escape tucked behind the building's façade, but he's transfixed by something in the lobby windows. Bathed in the soft glow of a jewel-bare chandelier is a full grand piano, perfectly framed by the oversize window that looks out on what must, in better weather, serve as a café. Too much space everywhere; I only spot one alley curving behind the hotel. We cross around the wide traffic circle, with a cement plug where a war-shattered fountain must have been, and into the hotel's golden light.

Major Kruzenko handles our check-in and sends us to our rooms to change for the Party banquet. We can already hear laughter spilling down the lush carpeted hallway that leads to the ballroom. Dozens of the highest-ranking *nomenklatura*, scientists, and cosmonauts mingle, all anxious to see the *Veter 1* slingshot around the moon. Do they know the threat that faces the launch? That my father is circling us all like prey?

I only have to share my room with Larissa, and I couldn't be more grateful. There's barely space for us to walk past the beds. We'd never maneuver around Masha and her suite of luggage. "I wish we didn't have to play pretend around these people," Larissa says, as we unpack on our double beds. "It splits my concentration. I just want to do our job and get out."

"And by get out, you mean . . . our escape," I say. I glance at her from the corner of my eye as I try to shake the wrinkles from my satin dress.

She doesn't look my way. "Of course."

Lara manages to set our hair in gentle curls around the temples by leaving an iron to heat on the radiator. I choke down three glasses of murky tap water, and I almost feel human. Almost ready for the task ahead.

We ride back down the elevator arm in arm, our fake fur stoles slung across our shoulders. The doors glide open and gorgeous, rich music flows around us: the song Valentin's been playing so much lately. My heart edges up my throat, pounding anxiously, as I cross the marble foyer. It's as if time has stopped around me, leaving me with just the music, and Valentin hunched over the keys.

It's too beautiful. The notes are too crystalline. I'm afraid to move through them—I might knock them to the floor and they'll shatter.

"Hey! Yulia!" Sergei waves us over to the piano; I lurch back into myself. He's leaning over the piano, and from Valentin's steely expression, I'm guessing Sergei has been harassing him about one thing or another. *Bozhe moi*, I can't bear to look at Sergei now. I see his lineage in his nose, his ears, his chin. I wobble on my high heels as I carefully approach the boys.

Valentin glances up at me and the music falters. Two scarlet patches sprout on his cheeks as he stumbles to pick the tune back up.

"Damn. Looking lovely, ladies," Sergei says. "You especially, Yulia. Nothing personal, Lara, but Ivan was a good friend, and *some* of us understand the rules about things like that." He takes another swig of Champagnskoe. "Want to hear something pathetic? This stupid song Valya can't stop playing—he thinks it'll woo an ice princess like Yulia."

I stare slack-jawed at Sergei, like if I look hard enough, I can see some trace of that goofy, kind-hearted boy who showed me around the mansion months ago. But now all I see is Rostov and Kruzenko in his cruel smirk and clueless devotion to our work. His usual good cheer has burned away leaving this drunken, sloppy mess.

"Now would be a good time to stop talking," Valya growls.

"Valya says this song is called 'Yulia.' Coz it sounds like the thoughts in your head. What a borscht-for-brains. I mean, he's such a . . ." Sergei's words slur together as he leans, exaggeratedly, toward us. "Phony. Who says things like that? No one, not unless they want something from you."

"I told you to shut up." The music halts with a clatter. Valentin stands up, eyes burning like lit oil. His hands cock fists at the ends of his frayed suit sleeves.

"What? A failure like you doesn't belong with her. You must be working your scrubbing magic to get her to so much as look at you. I mean, even if she did slip on the ice and bang her head and somehow liked you—you'd just ran away and abandon her like poor Anastasia."

The piano bench screeches against the marble as Valya leaps up and seizes Sergei by the collar of his shirt. "This is nothing like Anastasia."

Larissa steps between me and the boys, like she can shield me from the truth. But it's too late. I stagger back from the piano like I've been punched. The—the girl who went crazy?" I ask.

Larissa squeezes her eyes shut and nods. "She and Valentin were planning an escape, then he went without her . . ."

Valya pulls away from Sergei. "Listen, Yul, it's not what you think—"

"Don't." I whirl away from him and totter toward the ballroom. My arms are electric with Anastasia's memories: her bed, her teddy bear, her razor blade finding release on the soft interior of her arms. In one brief stretch, a lift of hope, only for it to crash down catastrophically afterward. He'd abandoned her. Promised her a way out, then ran on his own.

Larissa scampers to keep up with me, but I shoot her a sneer. "You knew about this, and you didn't tell me!"

Larissa slaps me. I stop dead, trying to muster up anger at her, but my head is too full of fury for Valentin. I can sympathize with Anastasia and her head fogged with the thoughts of everyone around her. Every sweet word and glance from Valentin is cast in doubt now; they're all lining up to be sorted, to laugh at me for believing that he'd escape with me. I stare Larissa down for one moment—one moment is all I have strength for—then I slump forward, too exhausted to be angry anymore.

"First of all," Larissa says, "Anastasia is dead, and until we find a way to psychically resurrect people, there's no changing that. The past is past."

"Easy for you to say."

"Don't make me slap you again." Larissa smiles, placating, and guides me toward an alcove. "Second of all, Valentin didn't love her." Larissa's voice wavers. "She wanted him to, sure, but he didn't. Nothing like the way he feels for you—"

"What are you talking about?"

She snorts. "He may be a scrubber, but he's terrible at hiding his feelings when it comes to you." She shakes her head. "You tear his soul open, and it all comes spilling out."

Hope flutters in me, and I instantly hate myself for it. "That's not the point. It's what Sergei said—about Valentin leaving her behind when he ran away." I can barely force the words out of my mouth. "Is he using us to escape?"

"I don't know," Larissa whispers. Then tosses her head, golden curls swinging. "There's too much else cluttering my vision when I try to look at our escape. I think we have more immediate concerns."

I take a few sharp breaths and let them out. Righteous indignation burns through me, like strong alcohol, but it's all fumes now. I can't worry about what Valentin might do. I have to take care of Larissa and myself—we'll run with or without Valentin. I ring with emptiness, with aftermath. "Something about the banquet tonight?"

I reach for her hand, but she winces, pulling away from me. "No. It's better if you don't see." She swallows audibly. "Nothing specific, but glimpses of running, fighting . . . there's a fire, and . . ."

"Lara, please. If it'll help us, I want to see." We sink deeper into the alcove and onto a cushioned bench, shielded from the flow of Party officials by a potted plant. I prop my hand palm-up on my knee.

Larissa spreads her fingers across mine, skin tingling. Images jolt through me like electricity. All the possibilities run together like overlaid filmstrips, but one image burns through them all. Flames, twisting up the face of a great structure—is it metal, or wood? It keeps winking out of existence too quickly for me to tell, but then it's back, the angle changed, then gone again. Then it blooms in one great tuft of fire.

The images change. We're trapped inside a metallic room, no larger than a closet; sirens keen around us, lights flashing on a control panel. Something sinister thrums through the room's bones: a threat like a held breath. I brace myself for whatever is rushing toward us.

Larissa rips her hand from mine and screams. I jump up

from the bench, untangling myself from the images, and seize her shoulders, but she's too hot to touch. Her head's tossed back with one long, endless stream of terror pouring out of her.

Major Kruzenko charges toward us from the bar, Masha on her heels. "What? What? What?" she shrieks in staccato Russian. I stagger back, trying to shake off the electricity skittering across my skin.

Masha whirls on me. "What did you do to her?"

"Nothing!" I cry. "She was trying to look forward, is all."

"Lara. Dear child. You must calm yourself." Kruzenko glares over her shoulder at the medal-encrusted Red Army officers and their wives, regarding us suspiciously. "Apologies, comrades, this one has been suffering from a fever." She presses her face close to Larissa. "What did you see? Is it something about the CIA team?"

"Yeah," Larissa mumbles. "It must have been."

"Well, tell me, then! Quickly!" Major Kruzenko glances at me. "Get to the banquet, tell me what is said there. I have to take care of this."

But Larissa looks straight through me. Terror hardens in my stomach like a bad omen for our escape. I march toward the banquet hall, three notes in my head taunting me.

CHAPTER 38

THE BANQUET DRAGS ON AND ON, chronicling the many successes of the Soviet space program and praising the *Veter 1* scientists for designing a rocket with sufficient capacity to reach the moon. Tomorrow's launch will be conducted in secret, we are told, but if it succeeds in circling the moon, then the subsequent *Veter* launches throughout the year should give us a lunar landing by 1964's end.

"I must credit the *Veter 1* engineering team for this remarkable feat," declares Soviet Chairman Leonid Brezhnev, Premier Khruschev's second in command. He's a stocky black-haired bear of a man, curled over the microphone protectively as he growls into it. "You have put our men into space. You defend us with your missile designs." I've never heard someone sound so angry while giving a compliment. "The Americans are nowhere near our level of capability! Everything they create is a crude replica of our groundbreaking work! We remain unbeaten—a beacon for the workers of the world!"

Except the Americans have stolen the *Veter 1* plans. Except they are lurking in the streets of Berlin right now—to spy on the launch, to steal more information, and hopefully, to help us escape, though I'm still rattled from Larissa's vision. I crank up the Shostakovich in my head until it's suffocating me.

When he concludes, the audience applauds politely in our eerie Russian way: all clapping in unison, as if we're cheering on a dancer as she teeters on the edge of control, like in Stravinsky's *Rite of Spring*.

I toss and turn in the matchbox bed all night, trying not to think about Larissa's cryptic visions or Valentin's possible betrayal. I will escape with him if I can, without him if I must.

Finally, sometime past five in the morning, my growling stomach overtakes my need for sleep, though I'm not sure my nerves will allow me to keep anything down. I stumble through the still-darkened corridors toward the elevator. I need something to drown out this terror in my gut. I need a drink. Maybe I'll start smoking as well, unfiltered cigarettes like Papa, drawing death into me and blowing it back out. The elevator rushes to greet me, and I'm so relieved by its grinding gears that I don't hear the boots clicking on the wood behind me.

Major General Rostov slips into the elevator behind me, and as the door closes, he locks the grate in place and pulls the emergency stop knob.

"You are keeping something from me." His hand shoots straight to my throat and clamps down hard. "I do not enjoy being deceived."

Dear god who lies at the bottom of unmarked mass graves, dear Saint George and Saint Sergei, my mind is slipping away from me, Rostov is siphoning it away with each bit of pressure he applies.

One. Two. One. Two. A bullet shatters my sternum and nestles into my heart like a kitten nestles into your arms. A second enters my temple. I am a KaGeBeznik. I dared to challenge the status quo. I am a puppet on Rostov's strings, and I will pay for serving god and country, if god is Karl Marx.

"Very interesting." Rostov's voice is an icebreaker ship, plowing through the crust of my brain. "And I thought I'd covered my tracks so well."

One. Two. Bang-bang: a gun firing echoed by the double-thump of fallen bodies, ringing out over and over as he pulls the memory loose. It's bone fragments, shrapnel, casualties of war. Bang-bang. Something I'd rather forget.

"You managed to cling to this," he says, almost admiring. "Misha, Masha, Sergei—none of them could recall, even under extreme duress."

He dangles the memories before my face. The Chief of the First Directorate of the KGB is struck by the first bullet and falls forward over his desk. The blood spills onto the manila folder, which Rostov snatches away. The gunman—the poor soldier—then turns his pistol on himself, and his brain matter paints a lovely picture on the office wall. Rostov storms from the office—his office, now. He sees Misha slumped against the wall, and with a snap of his fingers, Misha now dances on his strings.

"How can you remember this? Why are you different, Yulia Andreevna?"

Rostov's hatred pours into me, scraping against the raw patches in my head where scrubbed-out memories remain. My own father's doing. I have to shove Rostov's hatred out before it consumes me, crushes me more fiercely than the hand on my throat. I have to reverse the flow. Focus, Yulia. White heat takes root in the dark soil that's choking me. It writhes past the worms and drinks up the moisture. And then it's draining away, away—

The elevator lurches. Rostov drops me to the ground with a yelp and stares at his bright red hand. "What are you?" he hisses. He bashes his fist against the button panel but we continue to move, up or down, I couldn't say.

Sharp hot blood runs down my nose.

The doors open; the grate opens. "Comrade Rostov!" I recognize the voice—it is not the usual voice of Valentin, but the suave, sexy psychopath he can become. "What a lovely surprise. I believe you're needed in your room."

Rostov staggers out of the elevator. I cannot tell if he is dazed or drunk. Perhaps I am one, or both. Static crackles all around, Rostov is on marionette wire, I am on wire, I do not know who commands whom. All I know is that I am on the floor, and then I am in Valentin's arms, propped against the elevator foyer of the boys' floor. Valentin pats my face, too gently to really wake me up. A door slams in the distance, Rostov pushed away.

"Yul. Yulia. Please, talk to me." Something warm sizzles against my cheek, and it occurs to me that it might be a tear. Valentin's? But his eyes seem so impenetrable. Nothing goes in or out. "What did he do to you? *Bozhe moi*, show me that you're okay."

"The murder," I mutter. "He pulled it out of me."

"What murder? Yulia, please, look into my eyes."

Adrenaline is still thumping in my veins as I look at him. He is not Valentin. He is that molten god of confidence and lust that I first met in Natalya Gruzova's building. But as the haze in my brain clears, I realize I don't care anymore. They are one and the same. I reach for his face to caress his cheek, to strip away his glasses, to taste his lips once more.

"Concentrate, Yul. I need to make sure you're all right." He brushes his fingers through my hair. "Let me check your thoughts."

"Relax. I'm fine." Damn his gorgeous, huge, dark, mournful eyes. Even though I'm furious with him, all I want is to kiss him until he smiles. "Rostov. Are we safe?"

"For the moment, but let's hurry." He helps me to the far end of the hall, a round room at the corner of the building that smells like dust and fancy cigarettes. I settle next to him on the couch, acutely aware of his warmth beside me.

"What was he after?" Valentin asks. "We can't run if he knows what we're planning."

"No. He doesn't know." I draw a deep breath and explain the murder I'd seen and how Rostov tried to make us forget, Valya's face darkening as I do.

"We have to leave. Now, if we can," he says.

I shrink back into the couch. "Valya . . . I want to run. But I'm scared."

He tilts his head, a sustained rest, waiting for me to go on.

"I'm afraid for my mother and brother. She's researching again, yes, but she's a prisoner still." I lean forward, and it's like I'm coming up for air. "They were going to send me to Moscow State, Valya. My dream. And Sergei thinks that I—"

"I don't give a damn what Sergei thinks," he snarls, and stands up to pace.

I clench my hands into fists. "But it scares me. You left Anastasia behind before. I'm offering you a way out. Is that what draws you to me? Am I just another puppet for you to use, like your scrubbing victims?"

Valentin cringes. "I wouldn't . . . I could never . . ." He circles behind the sofa, shadow falling across me. "I didn't ask to be this. I know I haven't always made the right choices with my powers, but . . . Please, Yulia. Hear my side of this."

I don't move, though I'm still shaking from frayed nerves and too little sleep.

"Anastasia was my friend," he says. His hand falls to my shoulder. "*Just* my friend. We'd come under the KGB's care around the same time. We'd both lost parents, and . . ." He exhales. "She wanted a romance when I needed a friend. But she was so volatile and wanted a lot of things that simply couldn't be."

I shiver as his other hand joins the first at my shoulders, massaging away months of paranoia and tension in my bones. "You tried to 'fix' her," I say. "Her jumbled thoughts. Just like I asked you to do for me."

"I knew it wouldn't work, deep down. I was too weak then, and too afraid of becoming a monster. Like Rostov. I don't want to use people this way—you have to believe me. But she begged me to, and I thought I could at least do *something*."

My head lolls with a weary nod.

He sighs. "So I tried. But Anya was already long gone by then—mentally. I waited to run, waited until I thought I might be strong enough to help her sort through whatever had her head so messed up. But every day in that place was like a noose tightening. And she slipped further and further away."

Exhaustion slumps me forward, saps me straight through. "I'm not sure I'm ready myself."

"You deserve freedom. You deserve . . . so much more than the KGB could give you. You're too powerful to keep caged." He sits back down beside me, pulls off his glasses, and rubs the sweat from his nose. "But I can tell you that I have faced similar choices. And when I stayed, I have regretted that decision ever since."

"What, you regret not trying to run from the mansion again?"

"No." His eyes cloud as early dawn sunlight filters into the hotel. "This is something else. When my father and I came to Moscow . . ."

I close my hand around his wrist as he stares forward with unfocused eyes. "Show me. If it's too painful—"

He shakes his head. "Everyone needs their secrets. Just as you didn't want me stepping into your dreams, I can't just show you these things."

"You are asking for a lot of trust," I say. The blood from my nose has dried; I can feel it crackling as I move my lips to speak.

"It has always been your choice."

I look out the window, at the weak orange hue of morning reflected on endless concrete hell. My last morning as a prisoner, if I choose it. My last morning of keeping my mother and brother safe. "Valentin."

He runs his finger along my arm. "Mm?"

"Did you really write that song for me?" His touch makes me

dizzy. It makes me believe, foolishly, that we can accomplish this mad plan.

"Of course," he says. "It's what you sound like."

"But my music barriers don't sound like that."

"I didn't mean your barriers," he says. "I meant you. *Yulia.*"

It's too personal, to let the sound of me be exposed. My essence shouldn't be out in the open for any passing hotel guest to hear. But what could they know? Only Valya knows me. Only Valya hears the silences that I can't hide.

I twist around and kiss him fiercely, desperately. I want to kiss him now in case I may never again. It tastes like a beginning, but I fear it's farewell.

"Yulia," he murmurs, pulling back. "Someone might see us." His voice doesn't indicate that this is a remotely terrible thing.

I seize him by the arm and slide down to the floor in front of the sofa with him. "Is that better?"

He wraps his arms around me and pulls me against him. His elbow was tailored for my palm; my nose was crafted for the hollow of his collarbone. He's searing hot, a coal just plucked from the fire. I want to keep that warmth for myself. I want Valentin's music in my veins.

"Let's run away," he whispers, soft as silk.

He kisses like the dawn. My hands stroke his stomach, his arms, and he sets me on fire; he claims my hair for his own as his lips explore my neck. The music dripping off him like fervent sweat mingles with my own and we are protected, sealed, lock forever in this symphony, in the sounds of Yulia and Valentin.

CHAPTER 39

WE ARRIVE AT the Krampnitz air base later in the morning. Its iced fields are glossy in the sun, and the brick and concrete buildings cluster around the airstrip like hunch-shouldered guards. The smell of jet fuel sears my nostrils as soon as Rostov rips open the van's door. "All personnel are on duty today, patrolling the perimeter and the observation rooms," Rostov explains as we climb from the van. "But if the scrubber is here, or any of the Americans, your duty is to find them at all costs."

I stop at the entrance to the main administrative building. The faded mosaic over the door depicts a black eagle, fringes of feathers dangling from its wings, clutching a swastika. I cringe. I'm not looking forward to whatever memories I stir up on my sweep.

Rostov and Valentin head off to question the guards and look for any of the tell-tale electrified thought patterns my father leaves in his wake. I trail down one thick plaster wall and back up the other side, fighting to keep my observations grounded in this decade, but nothing leaps out at me. Uniformed officers and men zipped up in flight suits running back and forth, heeled secretaries shuttling stacks of folders, the crackle and beep of radar, Morse code, *Sputnik* satellites screeching from the vacuum of space.

A tense moment in the control room: a woman's voice screaming through the speakers, begging and pleading and crying out for mercy. I pause and tilt my head. When did we try to send a woman into space? It must have been another secret launch, much like the one we're about to witness. Victories get slathered across the front page of *Pravda* and bragged about across the globe. Failures are erased, blipped from existence, a speck on the radar one moment and gone the next.

"Find something?" Pavel asks, appearing behind me. I lurch nearly out of myself, then clamp my fists. Of course he's here. I've had too little sleep and there are too many thoughts racing around in my head.

"It's nothing," I tell him, and storm down another corridor.

I take a wrong turn into the locker room, where Misha is chatting up a group of flight techs as they help the cosmonauts strap into their elaborate suits. A pale blue thermal costume, then a bright orange padded enclosure. The techs scrub at their faces, attaching wires and nodes and strange caps, doing their best to work while answering Misha's ramblings with pointed one-word replies.

One of the techs glances up at me as he snaps on the cosmonaut's bulky glove. Familiarity itches at me: something in that quick flutter of eyes, up and then back down. Papa? No. This man isn't a radioactive wave scouring through me. I can see his features just fine. No rolling tide of faces and shapes.

"Come on," Pavel says, nudging me in the back. "Lots more to examine."

Someone yelps on the other side of the row of lockers beside us. The gasps spread like a contagion, followed by thundering footsteps. "Fire!" someone shrieks. The techs hop up and pry fire extinguishers from the wall before darting over as well, Misha hot on their heels.

My heart pounds. The fire Larissa had seen. It has to be Papa's doing. I squash my hand against the locker, digging too deep, desperate to find his trail—

"Help them!" the familiar-looking tech shouts at Pavel, and shoves him in the direction of the panic. Then he seizes me by the wrist.

Another layer of fog sloughs off inside my mind as a three-note melody rings out. He's Papa's teammate—the man in the fedora who worked with Natalya Gruzova. "Where's my father?" I whisper.

"Not now." Another quick glance in the direction of the fire. I can smell it now—charred paper and rubbish. "Mozart Café, three blocks south of the hotel. Three o'clock this afternoon. Don't be late. We can't afford to wait around."

He strides back to the cosmonauts and kneels down to buckle their boots.

After a few seconds of hissing fire extinguishers, the noise dies down and Pavel charges back toward me. "Probably some idiot throwing his cigarette in the trash," he says. "Come on. Lots more to check."

The American's words simmer inside me as we finish our sweep, though I keep Shostakovich at his normal intensity around my thoughts. I'll have to wait until we're back at the hotel to tell Valentin. Everyone's on high alert today. I only hope Masha and Sergei weren't looking in remotely when the man passed his message to me.

We turn up nothing; Rostov orders us to stand guard in the observation deck, a balcony over the main control room where Comrade Premier Nikita Khruschev and Yuri Gagarin will watch, along with a handful of Party officials. Larissa catches my arm outside the observation room and pulls me away with widened eyes.

"What is it?" I ask. I lower my voice. "Your vision with the fire—"

She laughs, brassy and bright. I think it's the first I've heard her laugh since Ivan's accident. It melts away some of my fear. "No, nothing bad has happened. But did you see Comrade Gagarin in there?" She giggles again. "Oh, Yul, he is a sight for sore eyes."

I dig up a weak smile for her—more because I'm relieved to see her happy again. Unconcerned. But I need to ask her about her visions, find out what she sees about us meeting the CIA man. If Masha or Sergei overheard.

By late morning, we shuffle into the back of the observation room, with stadium seating and a massive plated glass window covered by metal slats that can lock shut like blinds. I join Larissa against the back wall. On the airstrip, the *Veter 1* rocket assembly lies flat on the ground, encased in metal scaffolding and hydraulic lifts ready to pull it upright once the cosmonauts are on board. They stride across the field now, carrying their kits beside them like suitcases, escorted by the medical techs. Is the American among them? I swallow hard, wondering if he went to all this trouble just to bring this message to me, or if his real purpose here is yet to come.

The cosmonauts are sealed into their capsule. At this distance, the circular window on the capsule is only a speck; the whole conical capsule is nothing compared to the swooping cylinders attached to it, ready to fling the men into space. Then the hydraulics slowly lift the capsule end, bringing the entire rocket upright.

Larissa snorts next to me. "If Ivan were here," she says, "he'd be making a dirty joke right now."

I glance back out the window, then cover my mouth. "That's terrible." I stifle a laugh. "Now I can't unsee it."

Valentin slinks up to us and flattens against the wall next to me. "What's so funny, ladies?" he asks. Larissa and I look at each other and giggle again. Valentin smirks and shakes his head. "Well, it's sure nice to see you both in good spirits."

Masha twists around from the seat in front of us. "Real mature, girls." Her chilly gray eyes take me in. "Not that I'd expect better from someone who lurks in men's locker rooms."

Stomach acid burns at my throat. *Bozhe moi.* She saw, she must have seen. I toss her a condescending grin and keep Shostakovich level, but I'm burning up inside. Valentin snakes his hand into mine—does he know I'm panicking? I clench his hand with all I can, trying to drain this terror away.

Suddenly, the sounds of chair seats flapping upward ripples across the observation deck. The military officers are standing, ripping off their hats and tucking them under one arm as they strike a salute. We straighten and salute, twisting toward the

back door. Comrade Premier Nikita Khruschev enters, surrounded by several scowling men in his orbit, a blob of flesh and
tweed, concealed by his entourage. So this is our fearless leader.
The man who condemns Stalin with one hand while the other
condemns thousands more to die. Mama said he's better than
Stalin; more progressive. Papa said that even Hitler fit that description.

He approaches a microphone at the front of the railing that
peers down into the control room. The microphone shrieks as
he leans in. "I trust that today will be a great day for Soviet scientists. For the workers of the world!" He pounds both fists
against the railing. "You may begin!"

The operations room beneath us buzzes with men shouting
back and forth in clipped Russian syllables: technical terms like
"parallax" and compacted acronyms I couldn't possibly untangle, calling these terms back and forth in a musical round. Orange lights glow beneath the cylindrical rockets under the
capsule; the airstrip tarmac shimmers from the sudden heat. The
rocket itself quivers on its launch pad like a dog straining at its
leash, shedding chunks of ice and paint. The metal scaffolding
around it folds open like a flower.

"Five."

The Party officials and military officers around us lean forward, just a fraction in their seat. The air goes still with collec-
tive held breaths. I lean forward, fear and excitement buzzing
under my skin.

"Four."

Valentin's hand tightens around mine. *We're meeting my
father this afternoon,* I tell him, concealing the thought in our

songs. *Café Mozart, by the hotel.* My pulse patters fiercely in my ears as the rocket's rumble reaches us.

"Three."

Three notes, waltzing around in my head in three/four time. Papa's sad smile as he glanced over his shoulder before vanishing from our lives. How will it feel to see him again? Will he melt away my fears and doubts, or try to scrub them away like a monster?

"Two."

The technicians lined up on the tarmac fold their hands behind their backs. One man glances backward, just for a moment—the American. He's too far away to see clearly, but I'm sure he's smiling.

"One."

Larissa gurgles beside me, strangling off a scream. Her whole body radiates terror. That inevitability whipping toward us like a tundra wind. I am petrified, unable to look away.

"Null."

Fire billows from the thrusters. The rocket lurches upward. The applause is already starting as the rocket clatters up its track.

Then the second gout of flame bursts out of the capsule window.

Metal screams against metal, audible through the quadruple-plated window, as the rocket tips over, fire blazing from both ends, hungering to meet in the middle. The cheers melt into screams. Fireman charge onto the tarmac, bundled into bubbly bomb suits, but they're too late. The flames grow fatter on the fresh winter air, the whole rocket shaking with explosive potential—

The metal slats clatter shut, submerging us in darkness, though the blossoming explosion is seared into my eyes. I blink it away madly, staggering toward the door, but it's blocked by the guards. The overhead lights flicker on to reveal the room in chaos.

Cold sweat runs down my back. Either the rocket was flawed from the beginning, or my father and his friends have just killed our cosmonauts. I search that snapshot in my mind of the American on the tarmac, smiling back at me. *Bozhe moi,* what have they done?

"Stand back!"

"Premier! Quickly, this way!"

Khruschev's guards all but carry him out the door, then seal it back up, leaving us in the panicked dark. His second-in-command Brezhnev raises his hands. "I will ask you all to please calm down. There has been a slight technical problem, but I assure you—"

"Sabotage," Rostov growls. I didn't even notice him approach me. "The bastards got through somehow. And Khruschev is too much of a coward to confront them."

But the plodding brass of the national anthem swallows up his words. Everyone snaps to attention and crosses their hearts—everyone but Rostov.

> *An unbreakable Union of free republics,*
> *Long live the will of the free people,*
> *The united, the mighty, the Soviet Union!*

Rostov is a generator about to fry. His hat crumples in his fist.

The great Lenin has lit our path,
Stalin taught us faithfulness,
To labor! To greatness and beyond!

The air around us sizzles with Rostov's rage. He was looking for Papa—a scrubber, like him. But he didn't see the real saboteur, just like Sergei said—because he wasn't looking for him.

Workers of the world, unite:
Flag of the Soviets, flag of the people,
Lead us from victory to victory!

Rostov clamps down on my arm. *Yulia.* My own name becomes a traitor in my mind, slithering around me, circling. *I have a special mission just for you.*

Something snaps in me—like a rubber band stretched to breaking point. I slump into him as pops of color flood my vision. Bang-bang. I can't break free.

Valentin turns toward us, his mouth a round O of panic. All color flees from Larissa's face. "Yulia, wait!" But I can't. I can do nothing but obey.

Rostov shoves past the guards—rather, the guards fly back from him, on jerky mechanized legs. A dizziness like deep hunger keeps me off balance. I am dimly aware of the building around us, then winter air like a slap. I scan the airstrip for the American, but he's long gone; the air reeks of metal and smoke. Rostov shoves me into a military truck and we rumble along the road. Sirens whirl in front of us in hypnotic syncopation all the way back to the hotel.

One foot after the next. I am Rostov's marionette. Back into the swelter of Hotel Kepler. The radiator blasts me like a prison cell slamming shut. Sweat rolls down my spine, between my shoulder blades. My puppet master steers me into the elevator. The face I see reflected in the brass trimming is not my own; it is the loose skin of a girl with all her insides scooped out.

"Come, Chernina," Rostov says, as the elevator gates latch shut. "We must set Premier Khruschev straight."

CHAPTER 40

PREMIER NIKITA KHRUSCHEV, the First Secretary General of the Communist Party and the leader of the Union of Soviet Socialist Republics, is slick with sweat from his bald dome to his sagging gut. His shirt is half-unbuttoned, and wiry chest hair spills from it like white worms. "Don't issue anything yet," he yells into a telephone. "I'm not pointing a finger at the Americans until we decide if we want this to be public at all."

"Comrade Premier," Rostov says. "A word, please."

Khruschev slams down the phone and whirls toward us. "General Rostov." The tumbler of vodka slides out of his hand; from his shining red Rudolph nose, I'm guessing he had a few on the truck ride back here. "Of the Committee for State Security, yes? KGB? I'm sorry, but as you can imagine, I have some rather pressing matters to deal with right now. I was not expecting you."

Neither were his guards, when Rostov reduced them to knotted, convulsing lumps in front of his hotel room door.

"You have been allowed to desecrate our founding principles for long enough, comrade." Rostov snatches the vodka from his hands. "We have abandoned the teachings of Marx and Engels. The guideposts of Lenin and Stalin."

"Stalin was a monster. A murderer. I've said it before and I'll say it again," Khruschev says. "What's your point?"

"At least he saw a blatant attack for what it was. The Americans were responsible for what happened today. They *must* be punished!"

Khuschev leaps from his chair, but he barely reaches Rostov's sternum. "Punished? And where is your proof?" He sighs. "I have tried letting your kind of Party man steer the nation before. But what did it get us? We humiliated ourselves in Cuba. We have killed our best and bravest cosmonauts today, *we* have, in our haste, and—Yeargh!"

His rant dissolves into anguished screams as waves of pain radiate from Rostov. Were he not forcing me upright, I'd be doubled over from the piercing whine. The sick-sticky smell of death flutters its fingers under my nose.

"This humiliation cannot go unanswered. *We* must not appear weak," Rostov says. Khruschev has a mental shield—it must be standard training from the KGB now—but it's weakening by the moment. Khruschev marches back to the telephone, eyes dead, lips slack. He picks up the receiver.

"Yulia," Rostov says. "Read the documents inside the Premier's briefcase."

As if I have a choice. My hands slam against the double-locked satchel. The Premier only carries one set of keys; the other must be back in Moscow. Rostov mashes my fingertips into the soft leather until memories of the daily work of filling this satchel leap out. Each morning, armed guards deliver a fresh set of papers. Strange, unrelated words, printed in equidistant spacing across each page. Codes.

My throat spasms as if trying to seal itself shut. Nuclear launch codes. Rostov means to make Khruschev recite them, input them at a distant missile launch site, and start a new world war.

"*Read them*," Rostov hisses, his voice grating my mind as if it were cheese. This morning's codes stream before my eyes. Rostov bores into my brain. A dial tone fills the air between Khruschev and us. Mechanically, he punches in a phone number.

"I'm listening," a voices says on the other end of the line.

Dacha. Tributary. Concerto.

"Dacha. Tributary. Concerto," Khruschev recites into the telephone, his voice deflated.

Alsatian. Thorax. Liquefied.

Row after row, Rostov funnels the code from me, working down the page from the memory, then pours it out of Khruschev's mouth. The last ventriloquist act the world shall know, before we are bathed in white sunrise. The silos are opening with each row he recites; the missiles are warming up, ready to trot onstage for the grand finale as the last line draws near. My brain blisters under Rostov's touch. I must fight back. I cannot fight back.

Bang-bang. Here lies Yulia, who thought she could escape. You can't outrun a mushroom cloud.

What was it that I tried so hard to forget? The deeper Rostov digs, the more wounds he rips open; the more long-buried pains are brought to the fore. I cannot hold them inside, hoarding them greedily, collapsing under the weight of the world's emotions. I have to set them free.

And then, like an explosion in my chest and in my head, the memory reappears. Bang-bang.

No, that doesn't quite do justice to the detonated emotions surging out of me, memories and pain and gunfire and Papa and hatred and Rostov's despicable smile. I fling myself at him, palms raised, and clamp onto his throat.

BANG.

His awful attack at the KGB headquarters, staged to look like a murder-suicide. It floods back out of me and into him, sharp as gasoline, and I am the match. I do not merely drink up emotions and memories. I push them away.

BANG.

Rostov's control retracts from me. Khruschev slumps to the floor as Rostov loses that thread, too. I jam the pain under his skin. For every time he scrubbed our memories, every time he used our powers against our will. Every indignity I've suffered, whether from my parents trying to protect me or the KGB trying to exploit me. My fingertips are rage. My palms are vengeance. It all comes gushing out of me, overwhelming Rostov's steel-wool thoughts with my own.

Blood trickles from Rostov's nose as he collapses onto the Premier's bed, head turned toward me, his breathing steady but shallow. I feel empty and purposeless, like the first day of summer after school ends, but I am free.

No—I am *almost* free.

I am trapped in a hotel room with two unconscious men, one

the leader of the unfree world and the other its near-destroyer. "Allo? Allo?" cries the man at the other end of the telephone, waiting for the rest of the code that would lob destruction across the world. I slam the receiver back onto the cradle.

Think, Yulia, think. Each thought is a colossal effort. The window. I lunge for the window. Please, don't be sealed shut—

Valya's face looms before mine on the other side of the windowpane, crouched on the fire escape. He motions me away from the window, and as soon as I'm out of the blast radius, he slams his foot through the glass. "Are you all right?" He peers around the bizarre scene.

"I will be. How did you find us?"

Larissa's head appears next to his on the fire escape. "Please. It's like you were setting off psychic fireworks in here." She jabs her thumb toward Valentin. "He, ah, *convinced* Kruzenko to bring us back to the hotel after you left with Rostov."

I approach the window, arms open, and Valya snags me in an embrace. He rocks me back and forth, and I almost let myself cry. I feel like I could dissolve into him, what little of me remains. But we have to run. Valya kisses my forehead, then helps me climb out.

"You came back for me," I say. The words sound stupid hanging in the air between us, but they mean so much.

"I always will."

We soar down the fire escape. "Where's everyone else?" I ask. "What about the guards?"

"I had Kruzenko give them some work to occupy them," Valentin says.

Larissa nods. "We're not sure how long the effect will last, though. I'm predicting it'll break at some point between here and the next block."

"Hopefully by then, we'll be at Café Mozart," I say. And then we'll escape to the great, vast, unknown life on the other side of the concrete wall. We're free. We're almost free.

Our tufts of breath come rapidly as we continue down the street. The factories and sparse shops face us like headstones— flat gray, pocked here and there with premature decay and the occasional Democratic Republic of Germany flag that hangs listlessly over the door. The boulevard is more crowded than yesterday evening. Perhaps it's the magical afternoon hour when all the factories close and everyone rushes home to barricade themselves against the East German secret police—whatever the case, they are the perfect cover for our escape. They're shouting, exclaiming. It's beautiful noise. Thoughts shoot around us, frantic, animated, terrified—

We reach the end of the block, ablaze with wonderful orange light. I weave through the crowd toward Café Mozart, another Baroque relic in the sea of modern cement buildings. Cherubs pucker their lips over the doorframe, and wrought-iron patio furniture lies in wait for warmer weather. It's perfect—just what I'd expect from Papa as a Western gateway to our new life. I'm so transfixed that it's a moment before I finally realize what's happening.

Café Mozart is on fire.

CHAPTER 41

I CHARGE FOR THE FRONT DOOR, but a gout of flame sputters in my path. Valentin and Larissa seize me by either arm. "Yulia, stop! It's too late!"

"I have to get inside." I wrestle against them, reaching for the doors. Never mind the glass panes already smashed out, or the wide display cases inside wreathed in fire. "I have to read the walls—find out where they've gone."

"Give it up, Yul! We're too late!" Larissa cries. Smoke spews around us as they drag me backward through the congealed snowdrifts on the sidewalk. "They're already gone."

I shove off of Larissa, but Valentin manages to tackle me to the sidewalk. Black snow slides down the neck of my sweater. Everything is happening as if underwater. People are pointing and shouting, their thoughts bristling all around us, but it's so slow. Valya and Larissa are screaming at me wordlessly. Why can't they understand? It's our last chance—we can't let it get incinerated. I just need a scrap of paper, a fork, anything that was in the café when this all took place.

A plaster column crashes through the front door in a cloud of ember and ash. I prop myself on my elbows, watching fresh flames swallow up the entryway. My throat is tight, and not just from the smoke. Foolish Yulia. Daring to think she could escape. Didn't she learn her lesson in Natalya Gruzova's palatial apartment?

I press my hands against the sidewalk, pushing myself to my feet, when three notes surge through me. I glance down and spot the crushed butt of an unfiltered cigarette.

"We have to go *now*." Larissa tugs at my arm. The crowd is concealing us, but it won't last.

"I need one second." I scoop up the cigarette butt.

Papa is standing on the sidewalk corner, checking his pocket watch as he smokes. Half an hour to go, but never too soon to start a sweep. He watches the ration line across the street; he listens to the tailor next door pedaling her sewing machine. He isn't nearly so fuzzy as he usually is. He must be keeping a low psychic profile.

A car screeches up to the curb and the other man jumps out. "Change of plans." He's speaking German, though his accent is all rounded corners and blunted *r*s.

"What's the matter?" Papa takes another drag on the cigarette.

"Rostov left the base right after Khruschev—had your girl with him. I came as soon as I could. I don't know if she'll make it—"

"Then it's too dangerous." Papa reaches into his front coat pocket and pulls out a half-drank bottle of vodka. "I'll have to trust the thoughts I put in her head."

The man hands him a scrap of fabric, which Papa stuffs into the bottle's neck. He holds his cigarette to the rag until it sparks, then catches, leaping up the rag.

"Get ready to run," Papa says.

And he pitches the flaming bottle straight into the café's window.

"Yulia." Larissa shakes me back into the present. "If we circle back to the hotel now, we can go straight to Kruzenko, tell her what Rostov's done. She'll protect us. It's not too late. The secret police aren't here yet—the Stasi—"

The fire is too hot on my face. I look at her pleading eyes, at Valya's dour expression. But I can't give up now. Papa is counting on me.

"The Americans know this place is compromised but they haven't given up on us." I straighten my shoulders. "We have to run."

We push out of the crowd just as a fire truck whines in the distance. I run my fingers along the building wall, seeking that three-note melody. "They turned down here." I beckon Valya and Larissa around the corner, past the flaming café. The cold air is thick with smoke; the fire's smell mingles with factory waste as we plunge deep into the industrial district along the Berlin Wall's edge. There are no cars parked along the street to hide behind. No thick drifts of snow. Smoke scrapes through our lungs with a rusty spoon. But the melody in my head is bewitching, calming. I know we're on the right path.

"The Stasi will be coming soon," Larissa warns. "If not for us, then for the fire."

Valentin glances at me, his face hardened. "Yulia—your nose is bleeding again."

I reach up to dab it, but stumble forward as a chunk of rubble catches my foot. "Damn it." Then pebbles spray across my face. "Okay, what the hell—"

"It's Masha," Larissa says. "I guess she isn't completely terrible at telekinesis anymore . . ."

"Watch out!"

Valya shoves me to the wall right before a chunk of concrete goes whizzing past where I just stood. "We have to shake her off."

"Up here." Larissa charges past us along the wall of the massive factory. "Valya, distract her."

"Masha?" Valya shouts, stepping out into the street. A crooked piece of piping crashes into his knee. "Masha, you really should know better by now. You're nothing to Rostov—just a means to an end!"

I'm so much more. Her words rattle through my skin as she pushes her thoughts through the alleyway. *Imagine how I'll be rewarded for catching you traitors.*

I follow Larissa into a ridge in the concrete factory wall. She points to a basement window peeking above the street surface. "Think we can fit in there?" she asks.

I jam my boot through the window with all my force, snapping the metal bar apart as the glass pane shatters. "We'll try." I glance over my shoulder. Did I see shadows flickering through the abandoned scaffolding across the street?

"Khruschev will have Rostov killed for what he tried to pull,"

Valentin shouts. "He'll see our whole program as a threat. Don't you know what happens to threats?"

Never. I'll never be useless like you!

"Your loss," Valya says. Light flares through the alley in a supersonic screech. I grit my teeth, my nails digging into the concrete wall.

"What did you do?" Larissa asks as Valya jogs up to us.

He grins devilishly. "The psychic equivalent of jamming my thumbs in her eyes."

I make a mental note to kiss him later for that, and tug my sweater sleeves down over my hands. I dive through the broken window feet-first and slam into cold concrete. The landing reverberates through my bones. Hot, tangy blood dribbles down my chin. The basement is dark, with only vague shapes of discarded machinery looming out of the blackness like ancient rubble. It reeks of mold and motor oil. In the distance, I hear the rumbling factory floor.

"Is it safe?" Larissa asks from the street.

"Come on down." I step away from the window; the streetlight illuminates a fresh cut along my calf from the broken window. "Watch the glass." I step forward into the darkness, kicking aside a pile of rubber tubing. There have to be stairs somewhere, some path Masha can't track . . .

I see you.

Sergei's voice. I stop cold. The only sounds now are my short, panicked gasps of breath.

"Sergei?" I whisper. Dirt skitters underfoot as I turn in a circle. "Please don't lead them to us . . ."

Metal thumps overhead in an irregular beat. My ears ring with painful silence. I creep toward the far end of the basement with only the faintest blue glow from outside to guide me. The sound of my breath chases me in circles.

Footsteps rush toward me. "Yul?" Larissa's voice. "We're over here."

I press against a metal door, reach for its lever and give it a yank. A thread of Papa's melody warms my hand against the metal and pours out of me in a contented sigh. "This is the way."

CHAPTER 42

THE PISTONS AND ARMS HAMMER away in the main factory at the top of the stairs. Like in Moscow, the machines are manned by women, their eyes hollow like jewels lost from their setting as they feed cotton strips into the machines. We move like wisps along the back wall until we find an exit door on the far side of the factory and slip through.

"Wait." Valya holds us at the alley's mouth, and we take cover behind a trash bin. Dozens of boots crunch through the snow, growing louder and louder. They move through the swirl of a fresh snowfall: two columns of soldiers down the main street. I wonder if they're taking orders—mentally or otherwise—from Rostov.

A scarlet drop flecks the bank of snow beneath me. My nose smells like metal and warmth.

Larissa stares at me with icy eyes. "Rostov is getting closer. He's starting to see the right path to us."

"Just give me a moment." I peel back one more layer on

Papa's memories. *Come on, Papa.* Three notes envelop me. *Show me the way home.*

I shove off the bin and step out of the alley. Valya grabs me by the shoulder to tug me back, but I'm locked onto my target: a demolished building halfway down the block, with one western wall still standing, though it's scarred from mortar shells. It looks like a sternum with all the ribs snapped off where the floors have collapsed. "There. There's a way out in there."

Larissa and Valya exchange looks. "Looks like a death trap to me," Valya says.

Larissa winces and falls backward. "Rostov. He's getting inside my head through Masha, and I—"

"I'll handle it," Valya says. A static roar engulfs him, but then he yelps, and the roar dissipates. His jaw tightens as he looks between Larissa and me. "He's too strong. It's like he's . . . amplified himself somehow."

A vein dances on Larissa's forehead; her eyes are bloodshot. She's grinding the heels of her hands into her temples like she's trying to squeeze Rostov out. "Yul, I have to stay here. Keep him focused on me so you can escape."

"No." My chest constricts. "We're almost there, I promise. Come on, we can—we can carry you if it hurts—"

"You don't get it!" she screams. "If I go with you, those possibilities that I see, the branching choices you make—they'll be that much clearer. And Rostov will be right there in my head, watching them being made. If I stay behind, at least I can give you a head start."

I clamp my hand on her wrist. "Please, Lara, you haven't come all this way not to leave with us!"

But she shakes me off. "I can see my future, right?" She smiles. "I can play their games and be just fine. It's the ones like you and Valya—the ones who won't play by the rules—who fare the worst. I'll be all right. I swear." Tears quiver in her eyes. "Besides, I owe you. For helping them catch you . . . I think I can buy you a few minutes more."

"You always were the stubborn one," Valentin says, offering her a rueful smile. "Ivan loved that about you." He tugs on my shoulder. "We have to go."

I force myself to step back from her. "Are you sure this will work?" I ask, trying to keep my voice from wavering.

"Rostov wants to see the possibilities of the future." Larissa manages a half-smile. "I think I'll let him see *just* what I see."

Larissa slinks to a sitting position in the alley and closes her eyes. Her music stops; her mind opens wide. Even at a distance, the images spiraling off of her make me dizzy—hundreds and hundreds of scenarios, all overlapping, some strong and others weak. A sentence being spoken over and over with each word tweaked. People jumping in front of cars, getting crushed—and then the same people stepping back onto the sidewalk at the last moment.

"It's working," Valentin says, though his mouth is grimly set. "Let's go while we can."

"Be careful, Larissa," I whisper. I want to hug her, but I don't dare break her concentration—her icy blue eyes are squeezed shut, tears eking through her lashes. She looks so young, yet so accepting of her heavy burden. I only wish I could show such strength. I twist away, shaking my head, and dash across the street with Valentin.

The doorway to the wrecked building is intact, save for an actual door—a stacked stone archway leads into nothingness. We step through the arch and onto a waterfall of rubble. Peeking through the debris is a black-and-white checkerboard floor, scorched and scarred.

"Where now?" Valya slides down a shattered stone heap and onto the checkered floor. It sags dangerously to one side.

I'm afraid of what memories this miserable ruin might hold, but Papa's melody is gone. Valya watches me expectantly, keeping his head low. His music is all knotted up, and I have no interest in untangling it to hear how little he's trusting me right now.

I sink down onto the floor beside him. The stone creaks underfoot. I crouch down and drag my hands through the dust and snow along the tiled floor—

Sirens whirring overhead. She wears two fur coats and a heap of pearls and gems around her neck. The first mortar shatters the ballroom, stripping the hanging red banners to ribbons.

Now or never. The leather suitcase straps cut into her satin-gloved hands. Clattering tanks in the distance draw nearer. Her heels ping across the checkered floor as she counts the tile—one white, one black up; one white, one black, one white across. She drops to her hands and knees, brassy blond hair falling across her face, and digs at the tile's edge.

The black chasm beneath the tile yawns at her with musty stench.

I jerk back into the present. "There's a passageway. Under the floor. She used it to escape the Allies when they captured Berlin—" I shake my head. "Never mind. Just look for an opening."

To his credit, he doesn't call me crazy, and drops to his hands and knees to search. "Over there." He points to a chunk of debris where the snow has frozen over its edge, spilling onto the stone floor. "It could just be dirty snow, but it might be a hole."

"Only one way to find out." I kick the ice squarely with the heel of my boot.

The ice squeaks together as it compacts. I smash it a few more times; rocks shower down on me from the remnants of the upper levels. One last kick—and my leg goes clear through into a pit. I sink into the hole up to my thigh.

"No!" Valya locks both hands onto my arm. "Pull with me, Yul—"

But he slips and crashes against me. The last of the ice frozen over the hole gives way. I tumble down, practically doing the splits as my other leg comes through the hole, and Valya crashes on top of me on a bed of jagged stone.

There is blood on my lips and an eerie song in my head and my hands are cold and raw and I'm not certain I can feel my left ankle.

"Are you all right?" Valya tries to push off of me, but manages to crumple me up more in the process.

"My left foot—" I try to wiggle it inside my boot. Pain splits up my leg like ice shattering. I stifle a whine.

"Can you walk?" Valya holds out his arm for support as I pull myself onto my right foot. I take a tentative step down the rubble pile, but as soon as I put weight on my left foot, it gives way under me. I crash to the ground.

"I can walk." I force myself to stand again, keeping my left knee bent to minimize the weight on it. "We'll just have to go a little slower."

Valya nods, the streetlights from overhead glinting off his glasses. "The question is, where?"

I hobble to the left and, bracing myself, prop against the wall with my palm.

She's down here with hundreds of other wives, and some of their husbands, in soiled, shabby uniforms. They speak in terse bouts of German that ricochet off the tunnel walls like gunfire. Overhead, the streets rumble with rolling tanks and mortar shells, as pebbles spray from the ceiling. They huddle close and march forward.

"This way." Even in the dark, I see the layout of the tunnels from the memory. The wall becomes my crutch, supporting me as I hop into the black abyss, Papa's song growing heavier in my head.

Memories leap out at me as my hand skates along the stone. An argument among the officers' wives. The shelling, far too close. The men want to change out of their uniforms in case the Allies capture them—if I understand their German, they mean to surrender if the tunnel is found and beg that they were only following orders, that as soon as they could they fled the Nazi ranks.

They're filthy fascists, scampering under their own city like cockroaches. But I see myself in them, too. Justifying the pain I've caused others—the lives of wildlings, of scientists like Gruzova that my father has destroyed to reach me. I feel the salty bite of tears on my wind-burned cheeks, but I tell myself it's only from the pain in my leg.

My hand pounds the wall again, sinking back in time. The next shell sounds like a thunderclap instead of a distant drum. Shards of rock gout through the air, frozen in place as the lights suddenly wink out. Everyone stops. The women cling close to their husbands, those with husbands left to cling to. A little girl cries in the background. The collapsed rocks shift and flow toward them, and daylight appears. The helmeted heads of Allied soldiers emerge, their rifles raised.

"There's a break in the tunnel ahead." I hop along the wall faster, bobbing up and down on my good foot, bad, good, bad. The light of street lamps trickles through the darkness. I'm putting more and more weight on my foot. Tendons strain and pop but I can bear the pain. We are almost free. The light is clearly coming through the collapsed part of the tunnel from the memory—we can climb out of it onto the street level. A few more yards. My papa is waiting for me.

A shadow crosses the light. A curve of jaw, a bald dome. Just like Valentin's memory from when he escaped. He stops moving beside me.

With a crack of his knuckles, the Hound straightens up within the tunnel, blocking out the light from beyond.

CHAPTER 43

YULIA ANDREEVNA CHERNINA. Rostov's sandpaper voice scrapes through my head, as cruelly as if he were standing right before us, as the Hound looks me up and down. *I am beginning to think the Chernins are more trouble than they are worth.*

"I'm sure Premier Khruschev feels the same about you. When's the execution, comrade?" I take a step backward, but my bad foot tweaks, and I nearly collapse against Valya at the sharp pain.

Rostov chuckles through our minds; it makes the Hound smile in his own ghastly rictus. His face is partially illuminated from the street beyond him: the dim glow of freedom. The light glints off his crooked teeth and my stomach churns to see my suspicions confirmed. I sigh. Well, I'll use what I must.

Your mother has been most cooperative, Rostov says. *She has revived the program; she'll help us replace all the wildlings your father wiped. And as you've already witnessed, Khruschev won't be a threat to me much longer. His refusal to confront the Western fear mongers is a shameful mark on our history, one soon to be erased by wiser men. But you, and Comrade Sorokhin—you don't want your own role in our new order?* The Hound steps forward. *A chance to shape it into whatever you want the Soviet Union to be.*

"We'll take our chances elsewhere," I say.

That is not for you to decide. He pauses. I know the expression he must be making now, wherever he is: the skin puckering around his eyes as his mouth narrows to a pencil stroke. *Proceed.*

The Hound lunges for me and snatches me by the throat in one swift arc. I'm soaring upward to greet the sky. I am a *Sputnik* satellite. I can look down on my country and my world and laugh at how pitifully small we all are.

My head strikes uneven stone as I come crashing back down to earth.

"You've tried to control us—make us your own. But we're not like your Hound here, blindly following orders!" Valentin throws himself against the Hound's arm and sinks his teeth in, somewhere high above me. The Hound whips his arm around, flinging Valya away.

Valentin Borisovich Sorokhin. I see that one failed escape was not enough to teach you your place. It's a pity. You had such promise as a scrubber. You could go much farther than even your father did once I'm in charge.

Valya howls. The sound is agonizing enough to shred my heart. I can't use my legs; I crawl forward on my elbows toward the sound and reach out for him—

"No! Don't touch me!"

The waves of psychic noise pour from Valya like a jackhammer. Rostov is killing him from the inside out. Turning him into a lovely corpse, formaldehyde and cyanide, like Lenin or Saint Sergei. The cacophony pushes me away from him; it is a physical force, a wave shoving me back into the grip of the Hound.

What monster would do this? The Hound rings hollow as he reaches for me again. He must have once suffered whatever Rostov's doing to Valentin. His vision and hearing, his thoughts and dreams, emptied out and stuffed back in to fulfill Rostov's every wish.

Papa's melody trickles through my nose with blood. *I'm sorry, Papa.* The Hound snatches me back up; I'm too battered to fight back. *I got so close.*

The last movement of Papa's melody breaks inside of me. Papa on the Ferris wheel; Papa leaning over and pressing the melody into me. A message inside the words: "Your power is so great, my Yulia, but you only use it in one direction," he said. "You let others push their memories and ideas onto you. One day, you must learn to push back."

The Hound hoists me over his shoulder with a feral growl. Our skin makes contact—I open myself completely for that one second, letting all his rage flood into me.

Then I count. Two, one, null.

And throw both my hands against his bald head.

The Hound's rage pours back out of me—how his own father treats him, how he's turned him into a pawn. Envy—the chafe of rough burlap as his brother is rewarded, eating fine meals and playing hockey for cheering crowds. It's Rostov's doing. His own father, turning him into a blind, ignorant beast. Let the Hound amplify *that*.

Valentin's screams have stopped. I twist around to see why but my fingers slip—and I can't risk letting go.

You don't know anything, Rostov snarls. *How could you possibly guess—*

"You aren't the only one who knows a little about genetics."

My hands are slick with sweat; I dig my nails into his flesh to keep my grip. I have to push, even as the Hound's thoughts come rushing in. Memories. Emotion. Conflict. Sergei was the only child Rostov and Kruzenko meant to have. The hound was born with multiple complications, and they only made him worse with their genetic meddling—trying to create the perfect psychic spy.

But he was far from perfect. Locked away in a lab, his own brother and mother terrified to look at him, and his father slowly making a puppet of him. Burning his eyes, bursting his eardrums, until he was reduced to nothing but an extension of his father, a psychic doppelganger and homing pigeon.

My touch draws these memories in; my touch pushes them away. I am no longer the memories' pawn. They are my tool. My weapon and my gift.

The Hound wheezes and whimpers. He reaches back and pries one of my hands loose. The memories are fading. My back smashes against jagged rocks, though I can barely feel it through the tingling void under my skin. Too numb with shock, too empty to fight on. I reach out with my fingers because they're the only things I can move. Valentin, my primitive mind reminds me. I have to find Valentin.

His skin is cold; my fingertips cling to it out of sheer desperation. His music is gone. His memories and terrors and dreams are a film on his surface, and I catch sight of them without even meaning to.

His father with a glass of vodka in one hand and a Makarov pistol in the other. Valentin swimming through the Black Sea under a melting sun, then he's sucked under by a wave, torn from his mother's grip. This must be what he didn't want to share with me. Everyone deserves their secrets—but the pain they're causing him right now is just the weapon I need.

Valentin's anger mingles with what little emotion I can still muster up. It's like fire on oil. The Hound reaches down to throw me again. I latch my nails into the skin of his forearm. I don't need to understand Valya's memories to use them. The Hound buckles backward, wailing at my fresh onslaught.

Music floods the air around us, pouring from Valentin's motionless body. Bright, bouncing, in perfect harmony:

And when you touch me I feel happy inside,
and when we touch there is this love I can't hide,
I can't hide . . .

But I need more. Rostov is howling his wordless rage in my head, but he's still in control of the Hound.

You'll have to knock him out to break his link with Rostov.

I look up. *Sergei?*

The pile of rocks behind you.

I nod, just barely, and snag the largest chunk I can.

One crack isn't enough. The Hound bucks wildly, swinging

me on his shoulder. I strike him again, again. Rostov's acid thoughts scour at the periphery of my mind as the Hound claws frantically at me. One last chance—I bash him in the temple, just above his ears, his ears that jut out like his mother's. He totters back and forth as Rostov's screaming fades.

He falls to the ground like an avalanche, pinning me under his unconscious weight.

"Valentin?" An iron band constricts my chest as I scan for him in the darkness. I worm my way out of the Hound's grasp, each movement shooting pain through muscles I didn't know I had, but my legs are still trapped. "Valya, are you okay?"

He'll live, Sergei says.

I swallow hard. *But what about you?*

In the distance, I hear the whine of unoiled brakes.

I know how to handle Rostov. Don't worry about me.

I pry my good leg free, but my shattered ankle—I have to slide it out one agonizing centimeter at a time. *Why help me? I thought you said running away was foolish. That I should be a real Russian woman and live the life I'm dealt.*

I was wrong. You make a terrible Russian. I can almost see his boyish smirk. My foot finally pops free; I swing myself onto my good leg. *And if you're crazy enough to run from Rostov twice— toward the American scrubber, no less—well, then you deserve what you get.*

"Thank you," I whisper.

You can thank me by never getting me caught in one of your schemes again. I don't want to hurt you, Yulia, but I will not always be able to avoid it. And he is gone.

Valya groans as I approach him, and the iron band eases up

on my chest. I rush toward him, swallowing down a yelp of pain, and kneel at his side.

"Yul . . ."

"Come on. We have to go." I swipe at my eyes. Blood trickles from his nose and ears; his glasses are askew. "Please, Valya, come with me . . ."

His eyes open and his hand gropes before him. I lace my fingers in his. If I can force rage upon Rostov and the Hound, surely I can infuse Valya with peace. The strength we need. I close my eyes and show him my very favorite memory.

And I'll tell you something I think you'll understand . . . I wanna hold your hand.

CHAPTER 44

THE HOLE IN THE TUNNEL opens onto a field that ends against the hulking wall. Stubborn, fierce little weeds peek through the layers of ice and slush. We're fifty meters from the checkpoint, lit up like Red Square. Only fifty meters separate us from West Berlin. Guards perch in a tower above the wall; their spotlight sweeps across the field and pins us. The razor wire coiled around the tower looks alive, like a great python. I hold Valya firm.

"It'll be all right," Valya says, wincing into the harsh glare. "We can do this."

One precarious step after the next. A massive sign announces "You are now leaving the Russian sector" in Russian, German, English, and French. The East German and Russian soldiers at the gate watch our lopsided approach.

"Declare yourselves." The first guard walks toward us as we exit the field, his AK at the ready.

"We have the Americans' permission to cross," Valya says.

"You do not yet have mine. Your papers, please."

I glance toward the guard box in the middle lane of the road. The man inside reaches for his radio. "Valya, look out—"

Valya throws out his hand and the guards on the roadside, the man in the box, even the men in the tower all snap into a salute. The guard in front of us doubles over, clutching his head.

"I have your papers right here."

A light like the sun crests on the other side of the red-and-white-striped gate. Slowly, the glow dims into Papa, striding forward with a thick sheathe of documents raised. He is brightness and warmth, and just looking at him, I feel my heart sing. He turns toward me: his scruffy black hair and his lopsided grin as he puffs on an unfiltered cigarette.

"Of course, comrade. My mistake." The guard falls back. As Valya and I limp past him, I hold him tight, keeping the song between us alive.

We step across the border into West Berlin.

"You look like death," Papa says. He pulls me into his arms. He smells clean, even under a film of cigarette smoke. He's my Papa, just as I remember him, but stripped down, polished, disinfected. I don't care. He feels like home.

"Rostov tried to take control of Khruschev and launch missiles," I say. "You have to warn your American friends. He might be planning a coup."

Papa releases me and holds me at arm's length. "You're sure of this?" He motions to a gaunt man in a fedora, who watches us from a safe distance. "Call Langley, Fort Meade. Find out what they know." He sounds so confident in his English, like he's been speaking it his whole life. He turns back to Valya and me, and slips into Russian. "As for you two . . . Let's get you some medical attention."

Two attendants rush forward to help Valya, while Papa braces me against his side. An ambulance waits for us down the rubble-free street—slick white metal, brand new and glistening. Papa's smile is the same as ever, so boyish. It reminds me a little of Sergei, but I shake that thought away. He helps me onto a stretcher in the back of an ambulance, next to Valya, where a nurse is attaching him to an IV. Our hands fall over the stretchers' sides and tangle up. I don't ever want to let go.

"Rostov," Valya mumbles. "They have to stop Rostov." His eyes flutter shut, and he drifts off to medicated sleep.

A blue-suited man with full, healthy cheeks and a skinny black tie leans to Papa's ear, though he keeps his eye on me while he does so. He's the other team member—the one at Krampnitz who told me where to go. I offer him a feeble smile. He grins back at me, with a little too much sympathy. Papa nods and dismisses him with a flick of his fingers. The ambulance door latches shut.

"Our intel sources confirmed that the Party's called an emergency meeting. They mean to ask Khruschev to step down."

"Is that good or bad?" I ask.

"Less destabilizing than if he was assassinated. And certainly better than nuclear war. But depending who they put in charge . . ." Papa shakes his head. "Nothing we can do about it tonight. You're free now—that's the important part."

"And Mama," I say. Why didn't he ask about her? The Papa I remember rushed to give her a kiss the moment he got home, before he so much as acknowledged Zhenya and me. I take a deep breath. "She's restarted the program."

Papa turns away from me so I can't see his face. Compared to when he was working as a scrubber, his mind is calm, but I sense the turmoil shifting within him.

"We'll deal with that later." Papa sits back down and braces himself against the ambulance wall as we take a sharp corner. I reach for Papa's knee. I love him, I will always love him. But I have to know. I want to understand.

"What did you do to them?" I whisper. "The other wildlings. And—and me."

Papa laughs, though his eyes are hardened. "Erasing their knowledge of their powers, as best I can. I was only trying to help you, little dove. But I wasn't as strong then. It only held for a short time. Now, it should last much longer. Perhaps not forever, but we'll be rid of Rostov soon."

"We will?" I ask.

Papa smoothes my blood-slicked hair. "Shh. Later. Rest now, while you can. We're headed for the States."

I sigh, as if the last weight has finally lifted from me—or maybe it's the shot from whatever the nurse is now giving me. "You really can get us in?"

"Of course I can. I work for the CIA now. And if you wish it, you will too." Papa grins his sunbeam grin. "My brave Yulia." It's as if he never left my side. "Your powers and your life are yours now. You can use them however you like."

AUTHOR'S NOTE

The need for secrecy is woven through so much of Russia's history. Russians even invented the espionage concept of *maskirovka*, an elaborate masquerade in which nothing is ever what it seems. I loved the idea of injecting yet another layer of secrecy and paranoia into that history through mindreading. While the events of *SEKRET* are fictionalized, the circumstances are very real. Stalin's ideological purges killed millions of Russians, and sentenced many more to hard labor in the Siberian gulags, a fate documented in Aleksandr Solzhenitsyn's *One Day in the Life of Ivan Denisovich*. Despite Khruschev's attempts to back down from Stalin's rhetoric, the pall of forced compliance remained, amplified by fear of Western infiltration as Russia sought to win the Cold War.

SEKRET takes place in the 1960s, but much of that era was influenced by Russia's and America's actions in the 1940s during World War II, also known as the Great Patriotic War for Russians. Though Josef Stalin, the Soviet Premier at the time, allied with Hitler, Hitler betrayed the Russian people by invading in the winter of 1941 and blockading the port city of Leningrad (now called Saint Petersburg). Over a million Leningraders died of starvation and exposure until the Red Army was able to smuggle food and supplies into the city over the frozen riverbed. Helen Dunmore's *The Siege*, while fictionalized, chronicles their extreme quest for survival.

Once the Allied forces routed the Nazis and retook Berlin, the United States and Russia divided the country of Germany between themselves, in effect sparking the Cold War. The years 1963–1964 were a major turning point in the Cold War. After America and the USSR came within minutes of igniting a nuclear war during the Cuban Missile Crisis, they adopted a more conciliatory tone on the surface, but waged a vicious espionage campaign against one another in secret. East and West Germany, and East and West Berlin, became a testing ground for the greater conflict and hosted countless spy struggles like those in *SEKRET*. Tunnels, cafés, dark alleyways, and abandoned factories witnessed an untold history of power shifts and lost lives— David Stafford's *Spies Beneath Berlin* attempts to reconstruct some of it.

When Nikita Khruschev came to power, he tried to shed the doctrine of fear and cult of personality that characterized his predecessor, Josef Stalin, but his temper often got the better of him. Peter Carlson's *K Blows Top* characterizes his mercurial approach to foreign policy and statecraft. For a snapshot of middle-era Soviet life, John Gunther's *Inside Russia Today* from 1956 (unearthed for me at an estate sale by my intrepid bestie Alison) can't be beat.

In hindsight, we think of America as "winning" the space race, thanks to Apollo 11's successful lunar landing in 1969. But in the early 1960s, the Soviets were still leading the race, which had come to symbolize a proxy war between the East and West.

They launched the first satellite, the *Sputnik-1*, in 1957, which gave Russia the ability to transmit signals across the entire world; it was months before America was able to launch its own. The Soviets also launched the first lunar probe and sent the first man into orbit. While the *Veter* space program is a fictitious creation, many Soviet space programs were shrouded in secrecy, and we may never learn about every launch, both successful and failed. However, Jamie Doran and Piers Bizony's *Starman*, a biography of Yuri Gagarin, offered me an excellent glimpse of the Soviet program and its triumphs and tragedies.

Both the CIA and the KGB experimented with psychic abilities. The CIA's most infamous program, MK ULTRA, involved dosing subjects with LSD for a variety of applications, including an attempt to awaken psychic potential. Stalin consulted with an alleged psychic during World War II, and rumors of Soviet extrasensory perception (ESP) programs prompted further remote viewing research from the CIA in the Stargate program of the 1970s. As far as I know, however, none of these projects produced lasting results.